CRIME IN THE BIG EASY

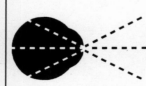

This Large Print Book carries the
Seal of Approval of N.A.V.H.

CRIME IN THE BIG EASY

DEBORAH LYNNE

THORNDIKE PRESS

A part of Gale, Cengage Learning

GALE
CENGAGE Learning·

Farmington Hills, Mich • San Francisco • New York • Waterville, Maine
Meriden, Conn • Mason, Ohio • Chicago

LIBRARY OF CONGRESS CATALOGING-IN-PUBLICATION DATA

Lynne, Deborah, 1953–
   Crime in the Big Easy / by Deborah Lynne. — Large print edition.
     pages cm. — (The bayou secrets romance ; #1) (Thorndike Press large print clean reads)
   ISBN 978-1-4104-8092-7 — ISBN 1-4104-8092-5
   1. Large type books. I. Title.
PS3612.Y5517C75 2015
813'.6—dc23   2015012516

Published in 2015 by arrangement with Barbour Publishing, Inc.

Printed in Mexico
1 2 3 4 5 6 7 19 18 17 16 15

ACKNOWLEDGMENTS

I'd like to thank the city of New Orleans — more specifically, the French Quarter, for the perfect backdrop of my story. And to think I was born there . . . The Big Easy. There's more than Mardi Gras to enjoy in New Orleans. The streets are alive with the sounds of laughter, music, and the voices of many clusters of people walking the sidewalks, enjoying the ambiance of the city.

Again I'd like to thank my friends Emy, Marie, Marty, and Charlotte, who read, reread, and then read again my novels to help me fine-tune each book. I also thank my readers who buy my books. I love my job, and I'm glad so many people still love to read fiction.

Last, but not least, I thank Ramona Tucker, my wonderful publisher and editor. She guides me in the right direction, tightening my novel even more. I am blessed to call her my friend as well.

CHAPTER 1

"I don't care what you tell him, Captain. Ask the chief if he wants this case solved with the real murderer behind bars." The lieutenant shifted his feet slightly as he looked anxiously around the phone at the redheaded woman sitting calmly in the chair facing the front of his desk.

Reporters. Ugh. He didn't care for them. Sure, they had a job to do, but too many times reporters got in the way of him doing his job — catching a killer.

Questions flashed, one right after the other, through his mind. He tried to pay attention to his captain's bellowing, but that woman disrupted his thoughts.

What does she want? Can she hear everything I'm saying? Does she know what we're talking about?

Sure, she appeared not to be listening or paying attention to his phone call, but down deep he knew better. She was a reporter.

They had their ways of getting what they wanted. Deadlines — that was all they worried about. Not the victims. Not the families. And certainly not the next casualty! That was how they got their stories, filled their papers or their magazines.

Who let her back here anyway? I'll give him a piece of my mind after I throw this woman out of here. I have enough to deal with around this place without adding unnecessary and unwanted interviews to my schedule.

His gaze stabbed in her direction but as quickly slid back to the phone in his hand. Lieutenant John Bradley didn't like discussing his latest case with the captain while that woman — that reporter — sat and listened to his every word, but right now he had no choice.

When she first arrived, he tried politely to send her on her way. It didn't work. As soon as he opened the door to his office, she rushed over to the empty chair by his desk and sat down. When the phone rang, he hinted for her to leave so he could take the call. He hoped she'd step out of his office.

But no. Instead, she smiled sweetly as she said, "No problem, Detective Bradley. I'll wait." Flipping a mass of red curls behind her shoulder, she crossed one leg over the other as she glanced around his office, as if she were interested in where he worked. She didn't fool him, not one iota.

John grumbled to himself, knowing she was hanging on his every word.

John should have thrown her out but didn't need the bad press. He resisted the urge, not knowing his boss would get into such a deep discussion of the two killings that had happened on the edge of the French Quarter while she sat across from him. His team was investigating both of the cases, and he was the lead detective on them. The New Orleans Police Department as a whole didn't need any more negative stories scripted in the paper or flashed across the news broadcasts. And he, for one, didn't want to add any more negative publicity to what they were already getting.

"John, do you hear me?" The captain's words silenced John's present thoughts of the reporter and brought his attention back to the matter at hand. "I'm pushing you, Lieutenant, because the chief is pushing me, because the commissioner is pushing him. Do I make myself clear? Get after it!" He barked his words loudly in John's ear. "Find something to link those two girls' deaths so you can find the killer. I'm sure they're connected." The captain's words grew stronger with each breath. The man wanted answers from his lead homicide detective, and he wanted them now.

Unfortunately, John didn't have the answers he needed. He wished he did. John only had more questions — but not for his captain, so the detective remained silent. If that reporter wasn't sitting there watching his every move, he'd tell his captain to back off. Insist the captain give John and his men some room to work. But seeing those green eyes locked on him, he didn't dare say a word she could take and print in her paper.

"We need a suspect, a name to give the commissioner. You got that, Bradley? Get me a suspect!"

John's knuckles whitened as he squeezed the receiver, pulling it from his ear. He felt daggers flying from his eyes as he glared at the phone.

Frustration will get you nowhere, man. Stay cool. Those words filtered through his mind as he tried to restrain his tongue. Oh, how he tried. For one second, then two. He even held it for three. His lungs filled with air as he held back his angry retort. Finally he could hold his words back no more, but at least he had enough sense to keep it from the intruder. Returning the phone to his ear, he turned his chair almost completely around, exposing his back to the reporter.

Then in words spoken firmly but almost in a whisper he said, "Then hang it on some wino on Bourbon Street if it makes you feel better, Captain. But me, I want to get the real sicko behind bars and put him away for life. So get off my back, please, and let me do my job."

At least he controlled his impulse of slamming the phone down on the captain like he wanted. That was showing some restraint on his part, wasn't it? Sometimes this job got the best of him, but he knew he was a detective for a reason — to protect the innocent, to save people from becoming a victim, and to serve the public. When evil won out on the streets, his job was to find the guilty and put them away.

John regretted losing his cool with his superior as fast as it had happened. Instead of saying any more, he clenched his teeth together and waited for his captain's response.

In his ear came the sound of a long slow breath being drawn, and then a quick release of air followed. Suddenly, in sharp, choppy words the captain said, "I'm disappointed, Bradley. Apparently you're not listening to me."

John shook his head as he rose, and his pent-up breath released slowly, all the while keeping his back to the reporter. *Oh, I'm listening all right. I can't help but hear you.* He stretched the phone cord taut, resisting the urge to yank it out at the base. Deep within he knew he had to be straight with the captain, but he also needed some space to do his job, some privacy. That woman made it impossible for him to talk freely, so he returned to biting his tongue, almost drawing blood.

"I said find a connection. Get a lead. Something!"

John had to tell him something and make sure the reporter didn't hear a word. Swallowing hard and taking control, he spoke in a very low voice. "Sir, in the beginning the only connection we made, besides the obvious fact that both were women found strangled in the early morning hours in the same general area of the Quarter, was that they were both single. That's it. That does not connect the killings; it just gives them one more thing in common. The MO *appears* to be the same — so far — but we haven't ruled out copycat killers either. The papers gave too many details on the first one not to think a copycat was possible. And even though the fibers were a match on the rope, it is a typical material of a common rope found at any of your local hardware

14

stores and chain stores. We must be able to do our job and do it thoroughly, even if it takes a little time." *There. I stayed calm, kept my voice low. Hopefully Captain Stewart will get the message and back off.*

"Time is something you may not have." The captain spat his words and followed it with a grunt of frustration. "So right now you have no one? No leads? No speculations?"

John sighed. "Of course we have speculations." But that wasn't enough. They needed evidence. They needed proof that backed up their speculations — not that he would share his theories now. John didn't want Miss Jaymes hearing what the department thought until they had the support to back up their speculation. The last thing he needed to see splashed across the front page of the *Morning Tribune* was COP SUSPECTED IN KILLINGS. The police could conjecture all they wanted, but they needed proof, the truth, and evidence to back up their theory.

"Spill it."

So the captain does know me. He paused for only a moment before responding. "Captain, I can only say this once, so please listen closely. There is a reporter sitting in my office, and I don't care to have my theory plastered across the headlines in the morning paper." John made sure his back was still to the reporter just in case she could read lips. He could never be too careful. In a hushed whisper he said, "We had thought of the possibility of someone dressing as a police officer, maybe even using a patrol car in order to pull these women over in the early morning hours. Why else would a woman, alone, stop at that ungodly hour in such a secluded area?"

"That sounds promising. Have you checked out your theory?" Hope rang out in the captain's voice.

"We're running it down now, sir," John said, still speaking very low. "Again, we have to be sure of all the facts before we start making claims. It takes time. So far every patrol car has been accounted for, so it's still speculation." Taking a moment to hold onto his composure, silence filled the airwaves for a moment or two, and then John said, "And although we haven't found anything connecting the victims, we're still looking for a possible connection there, too."

"John, you know what I'm telling you. I'm telling you to work harder and let's close these cases before the killer strikes again. You got it?"

Pulling the receiver away from his ear for the second time, he glared at it. *Oh, yeah. I got it.* Of course he got it. He got it the first time the captain said it. John wanted his cases solved as much as the commissioner, the mayor, and the governor, if not more, and for the right reasons. John wasn't up for reelection. He wanted the Quarter safe again. He didn't want to see another woman killed. John felt strongly that a madman wandered the streets of New Orleans looking for the opportunity to do it again. He had to find him quickly, and he vowed to do just that.

"That's my goal, sir." Pivoting his head slightly, he scowled at the reporter for a second, then turned back toward the wall.

If looks could kill, his certainly would do the job. Taylor watched the dark-haired detective in deep conversation with his superior. *Glad that look is for his captain and not me.* The reporter watched those expressive blue eyes dart her way and then as quickly avert in another direction in the room. He truly wished she wasn't there. Taylor smiled to herself. What better timing to be sitting in front of his desk than when he was talking this case over with his captain?

She wished she was privy to the whole conversation, but she only managed to catch

17

snatches of the discussion. Unfortunately, the man kept lowering his voice, speaking softer and softer with every comment made. Taylor felt certain the exchange was about the killings. That was just what she wanted to hear him talk about, but to her, not his captain. As she strained to listen, trying to catch every word, she pretended to look around the lieutenant's office, trying not to appear interested in his dialogue.

Did she fool him? She doubted it. Unfortunately, the low hum of his computer as well as the rattle of the air conditioner worked as a great sound buffer, keeping his words from reaching her ears.

The detective's office wasn't as fancy as the lobby of the police station she'd entered from the Quarter less than half an hour ago. Taylor never would have known it was a police station when she first stepped inside the building had it not been for the cops in uniform. A couple officers stood behind the big long counter that divided the room and two more sipped coffee, discussing something of interest. Behind the two chained-off areas, one to the right and the other to the left, sat desks scattered in a fairly neat order, and behind most of them sat policemen and women. Some talked on their phones, holding deep conversations, while others typed into their computers. People off the street sat in chairs next to some of the desks. They were either reporting a crime or asking for help. A steady murmur of voices filled that room.

In her mind, she compared the differences between the outer room and the detective's office as she locked her ears on him, listening for any clue to the two deaths on the edge of the Quarter.

The police station's lobby had high ceilings edged with triple crown molding and intricate corners covered with elaborate carvings of small statuettes. Five crystal-looking chandeliers adorned the great room, keeping it well lit if she remembered correctly. As a reporter, she was trained to observe and remember things. Pristine white covered the walls while a sea of soft blue carpet covered the floors. Not the typical police station, but in New Orleans, especially in the French Quarter, not too many things were typical.

Detective Bradley's office, however, except for the high ceiling, was a normal cluttered detective's workplace. Papers covered his desk, each in small stacks neatly scattered on the surface. *Oops.* Maybe it wasn't so normal after all — too neat. Her eyes re-scanned the room. Several file folders stuffed with more papers were piled in one orderly stack on the corner of the desk, and an almost-empty styrofoam cup of coffee perched within arm's reach to the right side of the papers in the file folder he had open — his right side, her left. Dark gray file cabinets lined the short length of the back wall in the small office, making the room seem even smaller.

A strange neatness in this clutter made his office highly unusual in her opinion — at least by comparison to the cop shops she normally had the pleasure of viewing. Those offices always sat in disarray.

Definitely different.

Slowly Detective John Bradley pulled the phone back to his ear as he swiveled slightly back around, almost facing frontwards. In a restrained voice he replied, "Yes, sir. I understand. Yes. Yes. No, sir."

His words were still of no help. The reporter sat in the straight-backed chair across from his desk, her ears straining. She struggled hard to hear every detail of the one-sided conversation. Unfortunately it wasn't much.

Taylor knew what he was discussing — the two murders on the edge of the Quarter — and whom he was discussing them with. That subject matter was precisely why she was there. What she did hear him say, she already knew. She'd give anything to have heard what he said when he lowered his voice after he turned his back on her. Those words would have given her more insight as to what had been discovered so far. But since she was not allowed to hear the conversation in its entirety, she wished the detective would get off the phone and give her his undivided attention.

The detective's voice returned to normal as he said, "We're checking all our leads. As soon as we have something conclusive, you'll be the first to know." Swiveling the rest of the way facing his desk, he slammed down the phone.

She heard that. The captain would be the first to know anything new. Of course. Now, however, she wanted the detective to tell her what leads they were following and what they were suspecting . . . anything she could share with her readers.

Releasing a long pent-up breath, he lifted his deep blue gaze and locked it with hers. "Miss Jaymes, what is it you want? As you can see, I'm a busy man." His jaw jerked as he stared down at the papers in front of him.

Agitation radiated from the detective. The tone he used while talking to his captain gave her the distinct impression she wasn't going to get much from this man, but she had to try. That was her job.

"Like I was saying before your phone call, Detective Bradley, I'm Taylor Jaymes, a reporter with the *Morning Tribune.* I'm doing a follow-up piece on the two victims that were found strangled in the past two weeks. Have the police determined if they were connected or not? From your conversation, what little I overheard, I gather you can't tell me that yet, but maybe you could tell me something else. You do realize it has almost been another week since the last killing? If it is a serial killer, there may be another murder in the next night or two. Now would you care to comment? Is there something you'd like to share with the public?" Taylor held her pen poised, ready to take action. She would have used her recorder to get it precise, but this lieutenant didn't allow recordings in his office. Only when he was giving his press releases could reporters record him.

The detective's inquisitive blue eyes moved slowly over Taylor's face. She felt a slight tingle as he scanned her head to toe. His dark brows drew together as a frown fashioned on his shapely lips. Taylor was torn between admiring his striking looks and figuring out what he was thinking about

22

her as he checked her out thoroughly.

She didn't have to wonder long about that questioning look. His gaze pinned her as he leaned back in his chair. Softly, he said, "You're the reporter who almost died about five months ago when tracking that string of burglaries in the jewelry shops on and around Canal Street, aren't you?"

Taylor felt her face light up as she moved her hand gently to her chest. She loved it when someone recognized her work or her name. Of course, she would have much preferred he remembered the great string of articles she wrote instead of how she got too close and almost lost her life getting the story. "Well, a good reporter goes where the story leads and doesn't worry about the pain she must suffer to get it."

That unforgettable sound of the gunshot flashed a memory of what followed, a sharp burning pain in the right shoulder as warm blood saturated her shirt and oozed down her arm. Maybe she didn't almost die — the wound wasn't that serious even though it hurt like the dickens — but had the cops not shown up when they did, the next bullet would have hit a more vital organ. Who knows what would have happened to her and her story?

"Humph," he muttered. The frown deepened. The detective shook his head and rose. He strolled around his desk over to the door. Taylor followed him with her eyes but not with her feet. She wasn't ready to leave. Not yet. She needed a statement from him.

Detective John Bradley grabbed the knob, turned it, and said as he opened the door slightly, "Miss Jaymes, I'll tell you what I told the captain. We have no more information at this time." He glared hard as he spoke in a firm, concise voice. "When we have more information we can release to the press, you'll get it along with everyone else." Opening the door the rest of the way, he stepped back, giving her room to exit. "I'm sorry. Maybe next time."

Under his breath, she could have sworn she heard him mumble, "I hope there is no next time." If she were tenderhearted like most women, she would have taken his comment personally. But after ten years of chasing stories, her heart was made of leather. It was business, not personal.

Taylor rose, closing her pad. Pinching the strap of her handbag, she placed it over her shoulder as she made ready to leave. "Detective Bradley, I do wish you would trust me. I won't print anything you don't want the public to know. I'm just trying to do my job. I think there is more to these murders than you want to share. I think the public has a right to know. The people need to be warned before someone else becomes the next victim."

He said nothing in response, but she saw that muscle in his jawline jerk. Then she saw him talk without saying a word. His clear blue eyes narrowed, staring straight down into hers as she moved closer to him. She felt a catch in her chest. Was it the way he looked at her? Or was it her, reacting to his looks? It didn't matter. Taylor knew what he was saying. He wouldn't tell her a thing, even if he had something to say.

She stepped into the doorway. As she was about to leave, she cocked her head toward the dark-haired detective. "If you change your mind and decide you would like to tell me more, here is my card." Taylor reached into the pocket of her light linen blazer and pulled out a business card. On the back of the card she jotted down her cell number. "You can reach me anytime. On the front is my direct line at the paper and on the back I wrote my cell." In a softer tone she added as she pressed the card into his hand, "I really would work with you on this case, printing only what you want told, if you would guarantee me the final details first.

Sort of an exclusive, giving me the jump on the other papers."

No verbal response came as he closed his hand around her card, so she shrugged and continued to walk out the door.

After taking a few steps down the hall, Taylor stopped. She spun on her heel, her sparkling red curls flying around with momentum and cascading down her left shoulder, past her elbow. She lifted her gaze and said with a Southern drawl, "You know I can make the cops look great, if you'd give me the chance. And right now y'all can use all the good press you can get. You haven't had much lately." She flashed a devious smile to the grim-faced detective and hoped that did the trick.

He ran his long fingers through his wavy black hair. For a moment, hope stirred her heart. He was going to give her what she came for. *Yes!*

Dropping his hand by his side, a tight smile stretched his lips. John Bradley sighed, shook his head, and then lowered his hard blue eyes on her again. "Cops aren't supposed to look good, Miss Jaymes. They're supposed to look mean and tough. Good day!" He dismissed her by turning his back on her and walking toward his desk.

"I'll be back." Taylor threw her words at

the back of his head then strode down the hall. The sad thing was, she wasn't even sure he'd heard her last remark. At the end of the hall she took the elevator down and then reentered the lobby. As she stepped into the air-conditioned room, cooler than the detective's office, she recalled his last statement: *"Cops aren't supposed to look good."*

Simmering over his words, she lifted an eyebrow. "Too bad, Detective Bradley, 'cause you sure looked good to me," she whispered to herself. Taylor remembered the wave of his coal-black hair, the clarity of his sky-blue eyes, the fit of his jeans, and the few dark curling hairs where his shirt connected two buttons down from the collar. She could feel her lopsided smile widening into a full-fledged grin.

Glancing around the lobby, she saw the two uniformed police officers behind the counter staring at her. Each probably wanted to know what she was grinning about. Both knew she had been with Detective Bradley, and most likely, both knew his reputation and opinion of reporters. The two men probably figured he wasn't too happy to see her. They may have even expected her to come running out in tears.

Too bad.

Her grin deepened even more. She'd get

27

her story. Taylor wouldn't give up without a fight, and she fought to win.

CHAPTER 2

The heat of a scorching New Orleans summer day slapped Taylor in the face and engulfed her whole being as she stepped out of the police station. Drawing in a deep breath, she paused and then blew it out again. It was the latter part of June, and summer had already jumped in with a bang. This year would be a scorcher, if today's heat were any indication. The Big Easy had its own type of heat. Not only did the humidity rise unbearably, mingling with the heat, but also the wetness jammed into every inch of your clothes as the damp material clung to your body. Down in the Quarter a breeze usually helped you through the negative side of the weather.

In New Orleans, the high temperatures of the day also affected the scents in the air. And those smells weren't always pleasant. Today was no exception.

Taylor lived on Royal Street near the

corner of St. Peter, only a few blocks from the police station, so she had left her car in the small parking spot hidden within the building of her duplex for tenants only and walked to the station earlier that morning. Many of the streets in the French Quarter had no parking, making the Quarter a wonderful area for walkers to enjoy the galleries, eateries, and jazz venues that filled the city. The music was heard mostly during the nighttime.

Heading toward her apartment for her car, she experienced most of the smells that the French Quarter offered, even this early in the morning on this hot summer day.

When she passed a pile of trash bags stacked one on top of another at the curb near a place of business, the stench of dirty garbage slithered through the air, piercing her nose. Two brisk steps later, the fresh aroma of hot baked bread teased her senses, making her wish she had grabbed a bite to eat before leaving this morning. Less than a block down the street, another fragrance wafted through the air as the corner tavern's alcohol added its aromas into the atmosphere. Mixed with all those heady scents was a light hint of orange — something the Quarter's cleaning crews used to sanitize the streets every morning. What a blessing!

Taylor loved living in the French Quarter. Her mother and father failed to approve her choice of living quarters after raising their daughter in the Historical Garden District. They felt she could have chosen better, but as an artist in her own right, practicing the art of writing, the art of journalism, Taylor knew she had selected perfectly the place she called home. Mom and Dad checked on her fairly regularly. She sensed they wished she were more like her sister, Tina. The "good daughter" married and settled down right around the corner from their parents' home. And, of course, she gave them grandchildren. The Jaymeses were still waiting on Taylor to find the man who would change the shape of her life forever.

That wasn't going to happen as far as Taylor was concerned. She had plans and dreams of her own that she would not give up for any man.

"Oh well, we can't all be perfect," Taylor murmured as she ducked into the hidden parking area and headed toward her car.

Pulling out the key, she pressed the button to unlock the red Mustang and climbed inside. After cranking it up, she immediately put on the air conditioner. No one in their right mind would buy a car in the South without an air conditioner in proper working order, or they would suffocate. She only put the top down in the spring and fall or on hot summer days when she took time to visit the Mississippi, Alabama, or Florida beaches. She then dressed for fun in the sun with her bikini top and a pair of cutoffs over the bottom of her swimsuit. On those few days, she didn't mind her hair whipping around in the wind, tangling more than normal. Today, the top stayed up.

Taylor drove straight to the paper. The employees of the *Morning Tribune* seemed to be bustling in fast motion. Had something new happened? Maybe. She wondered what it might be for a moment. No, she decided it was the normal hustle and bustle to get the paper ready for its next release.

Taylor sighed. She missed the smell of printer's ink that used to fill her nostrils as a young teenager when she tagged along to work with her father. Simple computers and printers had replaced the major machinery that used gallons of wet printer's ink when grinding out a daily paper — "the good old days," as some still referred to them.

Taylor had always wanted to be a news-paper reporter like her father and his father before him. It was a family tradition. She hoped one day her name, when heard, would be immediately connected with the

Pulitzer Prize for investigative reporting. She received several local and state awards for some of her stories, but her goal would not be complete until she received the longed-for Pulitzer.

And she hoped that when she received that prize, offers from newspapers across the country would come flooding in. In her dream, she received offers from the *Los Angeles Daily Journal,* the *Houston Chronicle,* the *Chicago Tribune,* and the *New York Post.* If any of those papers offered, she'd be off in a flash. She loved her job and the thrill that came along with it, but those papers could help her achieve a name beyond anything she had ever dreamed.

With fast-paced steps and nods to her fellow employees, Taylor made her way through the newspaper building and to the editor's office. Passing the empty desk of his secretary, she scooted on by to his office. There was no one to announce her or to stop her from going in. She smiled.

After three quick raps on the door, Taylor turned the knob and let herself into Mr. Cox's office. It always smelled of a combination of pipe tobacco, printer's ink — thanks to a newspaper-scented candle — and leather. He, too, loved the old days and had expressed missing that smell of printer's ink.

When Taylor had found that perfectly scented candle, she couldn't resist it. She had bought it for him, not trying to score extra points. No, Taylor didn't think that way. She had done it because she knew he'd love and appreciate it, which he did. On some days, one smell was more predominant than others. Today it would have to be the leather, she decided. "Morning, Chief."

A heavyset, balding man looked up at the intrusion into his peace and quiet. "Morning, Taylor," he barked in his usual tone. Everyone knew not to take exception to his gruff voice, unless of course they had done something wrong or not done anything at all. "What are you up to on this hot and sticky June morning?"

With a grin as broad as Texas, she replied, "Finding my next story." Lowering the pitch of her voice, she leaned slightly toward his desk. "The world is full of corrupt and greedy people. Ain't that grand?" Rising to her full height of five feet, one inch, she wiggled her brows, laughed, and then added in her regular voice, "Makes for good copy, don't you think?" She truly didn't like the corruption or the greed. In fact, what she loved about her job was revealing it. Shedding light on the fraudulent goings-on in the city and exposing them. Her job was to help make the city a better place to live in while she earned that Pulitzer Prize she dreamed of having one day.

Allen Cox shook his head as a smile spread across his face. He slowly rubbed his chubby hands together. "You're in an unusually good mood today, Taylor. You must feel a story coming on. You always act stranger than normal, if that's possible for you." He chuckled as his thick brows rose and fell and motioned her to sit as he tilted back in his executive chair. "Speak up. You have my full attention."

Taylor sat and crossed her legs at the ankles. With her back rigid and shoulders straight, she felt the excitement rise within her. "I stopped at the police station this morning before coming to work, hoping Detective Bradley would be able to connect the two killings outside the Quarter by now . . . if they are connected, that is."

"Hmmph. So your senses are telling you the two murders may be connected? Did he confirm or deny? Did you get anything from him? That's the three-million-dollar question, you know." His brows rose and fell.

Chuckling at her boss's wit, she thought how lucky she was to work for such a robust man who thrived on telling the truth to all. She loved his bizarre sense of humor, too.

He knew the police didn't usually confide in a reporter. Strictly the facts, after the fact — that was all they shared and on their terms, but Allen Cox loved his reporters to push, trying to get a little more than the other paper every time. The *Tribune* was always filled with facts, and he frowned on reporters who tried to slip in their own point of view on stories. After readers read the facts reported, it was left up to them to decide if the news was good or bad and how it affected their own lives. "So true. It's like pulling teeth getting anything from Detective Bradley. He's worse than most, I do believe."

The chief nodded.

"Chief, most detectives don't share much, but Detective Bradley is tighter-lipped than most. I didn't get far, but I did get to overhear the detective being reamed out by Captain Stewart. Well, he didn't tell me that was who he was talking to, nor did I actually hear the captain raising Cain, but from what I heard on Detective Bradley's end, it sounded like that to me. They are really pushing him to find the killers and close both of those cases in the Quarter quickly." She recalled the detective's expression. "I guess the commissioner is giving the chief of police a hard time. Election time is right around the corner, so the governor is probably pushing the mayor's buttons, who is probably pushing the commissioner's buttons, and it trickles on down to the detective in charge of the case. I think they call that the domino theory." She shook her head in aggravation. "You know politics . . . or, should I say, politicians." Not all, she knew, but in general this seemed to be the truth.

Mr. Cox tipped back further in his chair after he lit his pipe. Taking a puff, he eyed Taylor. "What are you sensing about this story?"

Clasping her hands in her lap, she leaned forward. "I think there's more to the story than what they're telling us, sir. Only I'm not sure if the police are keeping it from us, or if they don't know it yet. They want us to believe both killings were two separate incidents, maybe even copycat killings, but I think we have a serial killer on the loose. The way the detective talked to Captain Stewart, I think he believes the same thing. He just can't prove it yet. Plus, he didn't want to say too much with me in the room. The call came after I got there, and he hadn't managed to throw me out yet." A slight groan slipped out. She knew how much the man had wanted her out of earshot. She almost felt sorry for him but didn't dare give him privacy for the phone call . . . not that it helped her get anything she didn't already know.

Taylor swiveled toward the big window that overlooked the city. Gazing out at the clear sky, she recalled Detective Bradley's grim face. A chill swept through her body. "If it is a serial killer, that's bad news. It means another woman will be showing up dead in a day or two if they can't put a stop to the killer now. The detective knows that, too. I'm sure of it. His eyes spoke volumes, although his lips never said a word to me."

Mr. Cox nodded again. "You're probably right."

"I could tell something was bothering the detective about the murders, but he wasn't even able to tell his captain what he was thinking. Maybe it was a gut feeling and he doesn't share those with his captain. I don't know . . . but I felt something stirring the air in his office, and it wasn't the air conditioner." Taylor had a gut instinct of her own.

From the time she was small, her dad used to tease her about how great a reporter she would be because she had such good instincts. He taught her to follow her feelings. He said that was what made the difference between a great reporter and an ordinary reporter, not that he remembered today what he had preached to her as a small girl. It was like her dad had lost the vision, the burning desire that swirled in a reporter's veins when they caught their next story. She sighed.

"It sounds like you're on to something there."

Glancing back at her boss, Taylor knew she had to convince him to let her drop everything except this story. She wanted to spend every waking minute on it. This could be her Pulitzer. Taylor took a deep breath. *Here goes.*

"Chief, I finished the article on the bank embezzler and the human interest piece on the teenage boy who saved the little girl from that crazed pit bull. I need —" She looked sweetly at her boss with a smile that melted most men, leaving them putty in her hands. Unfortunately her boss wasn't like most men, and neither was that detective today. "I need my piece on the follow up of the two murders to be brief — no background remarks and no mention the police are looking for a possible link in the two killings. Not that he told me he was, but I know that he is. I'll give just enough facts to inform the readers of the updates on the police's search for the killers, but nothing to encourage them to connect the two. We don't want to give this killer any spotlight, encouraging him to go on." She bit her bottom lip.

Besides, she thought, if Detective Bradley read her report trying to downplay the murders' similarites, maybe he'd think twice and share info with her.

"There is a connection, you know, and I'm going to find it . . . if you'll give me time to really dig into this story." She was practically pleading her case through her eyes.

Mr. Cox rose to his feet and stepped around the desk. "I have always found your instincts to be correct, Taylor, but I have to think on this one for a moment." Standing over her, he looked down as he appeared to think harder.

She held her breath in that moment of silence.

Finally, he leaned slightly against his desk. "If the police can't connect them, what makes you think you'll be able to? Do you really think you'll get more than they could?"

Taylor nodded confidently. "Yes, most definitely. I'm going to dig and dig until I find something to connect those killings. Besides, I know there is a link. I know it here," she said as she pressed her hand to her stomach. "It's my gut. Remember, Dad always said I had good instincts."

"Hold on, Taylor." He shoved his hand out like a stop sign, and then shook it quickly back and forth. "Don't try to get your way by pulling your dad into it." He smiled as he spoke, though. He and Taylor's dad had been reporters together back in the day, and she'd been known to use that connection before to get her way with Mr. Cox. It worked most of the time. What could she say?

Holding both her hands up in front of her, she shrugged. "I'm not. It's just that the police haven't found the connection yet, and I know it's there. I'm going to go over my notes and my pictures from the two crime scenes. Follow the two girls' steps in the weeks prior to their murder. And do more digging. I'll find the connection. Besides, sometimes people tell reporters things they would never tell a policeman. Something will turn up. It has to, if they are connected . . . like my gut is telling me. I also plan on becoming Detective Bradley's shadow. I'll get my story," she voiced strongly.

Mr. Cox crossed his arms over his chest. "That's the spirit. With determination like that, how can you lose? And how can I refuse? Okay. I trust your instincts. You can keep your story brief."

"Chief, while you're feeling confident, I need to ask one more favor. When I said I needed more time, what I'm asking is, can you let me stay on this story exclusively, at least for the next week? That'll give me time to really follow those timelines and shadow the detective. I have to stay on it, sir. I know there is something there, something different about those killings. I just have to find it or be there when the police find it."

Taylor leaned back in the chair, dropping her hands to her sides. Mentally, she crossed her fingers, hoping to obtain the go-ahead.

Her boss raised his brows. "You think I didn't catch your unspoken request the first time? I got it. I'm giving you a week to look into it and try to find the connection. One week. That's all. If you don't come up with something good and concrete, we'll stop the intense investigation and just report what they tell us like everybody else. One week," he repeated. "Then you're back working whatever story you find or we throw at you."

Taylor jumped to her feet. "You won't regret it, Chief. I'll get the story." She pumped his hand enthusiastically and dashed out of his office, waving to Char-

42

lotte, his secretary, who was back at her desk.

At her own desk, Taylor went through her notes. Rereading the facts on the two murders, she came to the same conclusion as the detective. The two victims, Trudy Walker and Stephanie Gauthreaux, didn't seem to have anything in common other than their gender and that they were both single, with no apparent significant other.

The police had checked with friends and family to try and find someone with a motive for killing them. Unfortunately, both girls proved to be very well liked. There was no one to suspect in relation to either girl. *Could it be random?* She doubted it.

The girls each lived alone but had friends and family members Taylor could talk to again. She had to come up with some newer questions, or maybe after a few days to think about it, their friends and family would have new answers to some of the same old questions. That was a thought and a hope.

"I'll start there," she told herself as she printed a copy of the victims' background info she had in her computer file. "Neighbors and friends might be able to give me more information now — now that the major shock had worn off. Maybe I'll even catch a neighbor home who wasn't there before." She'd find new info. She must.

Taylor decided she would spend the rest of the day trying to find out more personal information about each girl and figure the timelines for the week prior to each of their deaths. Tomorrow she would follow the detective.

After straightening her desk, she grabbed her purse and headed out of the building.

Her first stop was the public library. She found an open table with a computer in the reference department and pulled up the New Orleans and Metairie telephone directories for the past five years. Although the reports she had made listed a few friends and family members, Taylor decided to check for neighbors who lived near each girl for a while. Using the cross directories would make her search more simple. Maybe she could come up with someone there, someone new that neither she nor the police had questioned.

Taylor went back year by year, checking to see who lived in the same neighborhoods as the girls for the past five years. *Great!* They each had a few, so now to find the neighbors who knew them more personally. If they lived by one another long enough, someone was bound to know something.

In less than an hour, Taylor found three

neighbors of Trudy's and four neighbors of Stephanie's who might be able to shed some light on the victims' personal lives. She had jotted down the names and addresses, along with the phone numbers, and then quickly closed her small notebook and stuffed it in her back pocket.

Next came the leg work of going to each of the homes, hopefully catching the residents there and talking to them, and even more importantly, getting them to talk to her.

Trudy, the hairdresser, had lived off the Huey P. Long Bridge in a large brick complex of apartments. Everyone's front door opened up to the same courtyard. Her neighbors were all at home and very helpful. Taylor found Trudy had worked at Mr. Jack's in the Quarter for several years and seemed to love her work creating new and wild hairdos for people. She appeared to be a likeable person. Other than not having a special man in her life, she lived a very active one. Taylor wrote as fast as the girl's neighbors spoke, making notes to review later.

Stephanie's neighbors were not as helpful, as they didn't really know her. She had lived in Metairie, a suburb of New Orleans, at the Chateau Villa. The apartments were considered very nice. The cost for rental was about three times more than the cost of Trudy's. Neighbors basically kept to themselves in this high-rise establishment. The few who knew Stephanie only knew she was an accountant at the bank on Clearlake. Other than that, they knew nothing about her.

Although both were single females, they had little in common according to the neighbors. The ladies' jobs were very different. Trudy styled hair while Stephanie managed money for clients and the bank. The bleached blond with the orange spikes lived in the lower part of town, while the red-head lived in an apartment in the high-rent district. The hairdresser came from a large family, and her education ended at the completion of the twelfth grade. The accountant, however, was an only child with a college degree in accounting.

Thinking back to her talk with the neighbors, Taylor decided Trudy's neighbors found her friendly and enjoyed having her as a neighbor. In fact, the third neighbor Taylor interviewed, Sarah Adams, seemed to know her better than the other two.

Taylor remembered Sarah had peeked through the crack in the door before she opened it. "May I help you?" Sarah asked in a timid voice.

Holding up her identification, she said, "I'm Taylor Jaymes with the *Morning Tribune*. I'd like to ask you a few questions about Trudy Walker."

As the door opened wider, a sad expression crossed the woman's face. Standing behind the screen door, Sarah said, "Such a tragic thing to happen to a sweet young girl. Come on in and we can talk," she said as she pushed the screen door open. "Would you care for a cup of coffee?"

"Thank you, but I'll pass. I appreciate the offer, though. Did you know Miss Walker very well?"

"Yes."

The woman appeared to be in her midforties by Taylor's estimation.

"In fact, sometimes she came over and had coffee with me on Saturday mornings and we talked about her week. For being such a friendly girl, she lived a pretty lonely life. I have a teenage daughter who liked to go over to her apartment some evenings to talk. My daughter probably asked Trudy for some advice, trying to get a younger person's point of view, if you know what I mean. Sherry, that's my daughter, misses her a lot." Pointing to a chair at the kitchen table, she motioned for Taylor to have a seat.

"Are you sure you don't want any coffee? How about a soda or water?"

Taylor shook her head no as she asked, "You said she lived a lonely life? So Miss Walker didn't go out much? Other reports state she dated a lot. Do you think Sherry would be willing to talk to me? And, of course, you could sit in on the conversation if you'd like. Maybe she could clear up my conflict here, since she was friendly with Miss Walker."

"I'm sure my daughter would be glad to help, but you misunderstand about Trudy's dating. She went out every weekend and sometimes during the week. Trudy dated a lot, but she always said the men she dated weren't worth the trouble. She was looking for Mr. Right, the kind she would want to settle down with and raise a family. You know what I mean?"

Taylor didn't think a man like that existed. No man could make her want to settle down and raise a family. That would involve the two C's that she avoided as much as possible — cooking and cleaning. Those were the two things Taylor hated most. Besides which, she had great plans with her career and couldn't see going any other direction. To follow her dream, she had to stay single. A man would never let her cover the stories she covered. They would be too protective of her.

Instead of giving a reply, she said, "So she dated a lot of men, but you're saying no one special, right?"

Mrs. Adams nodded. "Yes. No one special in a very long time, but it didn't stop her from looking. She was such a sweet girl. I'm sorry I don't know anything to help you, but I sure hope the police find out who killed her. That person deserves to suffer. I know her family is grieving."

After thanking her for her time and leaving a business card so Sherry could ring her later, Taylor left. One thing was for sure, Trudy had no difficulty opening up to her neighbors about her main problem . . . loneliness. She dated a lot of men, but none had been the kind of man to get serious over. So Trudy was lonely and looking for love.

Stephanie, on the other hand, wouldn't open up to her neighbors. No one knew much about her, although a couple of the neighbors had admitted to seeing one man visit her apartment frequently. They appeared to be romantically involved. Unfortunately, since the neighbors never spoke one-on-one with her, no one knew his name. Taylor got a fairly good description of the man, which might come in handy down the road. She wondered if the police had talked to the man yet. Surely he came forward when his girlfriend was murdered — unless he had something to hide.

She would ask the detective if they knew of Stephanie's boyfriend, and hopefully he would supply a name to her. Fat chance, but she would ask.

That night, while eating a chicken sandwich she had thrown together herself — her form of cooking — Taylor scanned her notes thoroughly once again. The line of work she chose left little time to slave over a hot stove in the evening, especially when she never knew if she would have to dash out on a moment's notice. Because of this, she was well known at the Court Tavern around the corner from her apartment, as well as Dante's Pizza and Pasta, which she also frequented regularly. New Orleans, especially the French Quarter, didn't lack in exceptionally good food for a person's taste buds, so why even bother to cook fancy meals? She could get those at one of the restaurants near her . . . takeout, of course. In the meantime, these smaller taverns made cleaning up after meals such a breeze.

By the time she had gone over her notes several times, even though she still hadn't talked to the victims' family members, coworkers, or close friends yet, Taylor felt she knew more about the victims than she did her own sister. Well, maybe that was stretching it a bit. Taylor did know Tina better, but she felt she was getting to know these girls more and more with each interview, which should bring an added touch to her story. Humanize it.

Standing, Taylor stretched, arching her back as she twisted slightly left, then right. A yawn escaped. Covering her mouth with her right hand, she glanced at the watch on her left arm.

"Midnight!" she screeched as she threw her hands into the air. Earlier she had planned to make an early night of it so she could beat the lieutenant to the station in the morning. Tomorrow she planned to become his shadow . . . well, today now.

Taylor heard her mother's voice ringing in her ears: *If only you were more disciplined, like your sister.* Ignoring the voice in her head, she set her alarm for five, hoping she would wake up with the first beep that sounded in the air. "No hitting the snooze," she grumbled to herself.

In no time, she showered, changed, and jumped in bed, snuggling under her covers.

Taylor barely remembered putting her head on the pillow when darkness descended.

CHAPTER 3

An annoying ring persisted. "Shut up!" Taylor growled at what she thought was her alarm clock. She'd promised herself she wouldn't snooze, but seven more minutes . . . what would it hurt? Her hand shot out, trying to stop the noise. She pressed the snooze button, but the ringing continued. She must have pressed the wrong button. With eyes closed, her fingers danced across the nightstand, trying to find that magic button to bring silence into the air. Taylor found the button on top of her clock again and pressed it harder this time.

On the next ring she cracked open an eye and looked toward the window. *It's not even daylight yet.* Why is that stupid thing ringing? And as she started thinking her alarm was going crazy, the third ring started. Suddenly it dawned on her that the alarm clock beeped. It didn't ring.

Instantly she shot up in bed, reached past

the alarm, and snatched up her phone. Through blurry eyes, she squinted at the clock. *Four in the morning?* Early morning phone calls meant only one thing — trouble with a capital T.

"Hello," she said, then listened anxiously for a response.

"Morning, Taylor. Sorry to wake you so early." A feminine voice came across the line. "But I thought you'd want to know this. It might be connected with the stories you're working on."

Taylor flipped on her bedside lamp as she recognized the voice of the girl who worked the nightshift at the city desk. "Hey, Babs. What's up?" She grabbed the slender silver pen and black notebook that she always kept next to her bed for emergencies such as this. The good reporter was always prepared. Her father had taught her well.

"You know the two murder cases you're following? There has been another killing, and it sounds similar to those two . . . also done in the Quarter. The police are on their way now to where the body was found. Are you ready for the address? It's only two blocks from where they found the last body."

"Sure, go ahead." Taylor jotted down the information. "Thanks. I'll talk to you later."

She slammed down the phone and threw

back the covers. Jumping out of bed, she pulled off the T-shirt she slept in and then dug through her dresser drawer trying to find clean undergarments.

"I've got to catch up on my washing," she mumbled as she grabbed yesterday's jeans and tugged them up over her hips. On top of the dirty-clothes hamper she grabbed her bra and slipped back into it. At least she found a clean V-neck T-shirt with a shiny finish hanging in her closet. It was one of those that fit her curves snugly. Not her first choice — in fact, it was her last choice — but at the moment she had no choice. Slapping on some baby powder, she slathered deodorant under her arms before pulling the shirt over her head.

"Later today I will do my washing," she vowed, knowing it might come to be and yet it might not, depending on her time. Work always dictated her day-to-day life. Maybe she did need to become more disciplined. No. She was disciplined where it counted . . . with her work.

T-shirts and jeans proved to be Taylor's usual form of dress. On special occasions she slipped a blazer on over her T-shirt, dressing up her jeans slightly like she'd done for her visit yesterday to see the detective. And for even fancier occasions, which she tried to avoid as much as possible, her closet held a couple of skirts with matching blazers and even a fancy dress or two. Those were gifts from her mom and Tina. Both always tried to make a lady out of Taylor. What was that old saying? "You can't get milk from a turnip?" She tried to tell her sister that, but Taylor never wasted her time on her mom. Taylor knew better. Her mother would never stop trying to make a lady out of her.

After pulling a brush through her hair and sliding her toothbrush across her teeth a few times, she was about to race out of the apartment when she remembered her vow. "I may not have time later, but I can take half a second now." Hurriedly she grabbed a laundry bag, stuffed a good bit of her dirty clothes in it, filling the sack to full capacity. "I'll treat myself today and drop these off at The Washing Well . . . after I check out the crime scene, of course."

The Washing Well offered a full-service laundry that washed and folded the customer's clothes at a price. Sure, there were washing machines and dryers the customer could use, but when Taylor was busy, she didn't mind paying the extra fee. At the moment, she was past busy and gave in to the side of her that not only hated cooking, but cleaning as well. This was another reason she couldn't be like her sister, married to a man, having his children, and maintaining his home properly. Not Taylor's thing. As far as she was concerned, she was already married — to her career. That was enough for her.

She knotted the bag closed and threw it over her shoulder.

Taylor swiftly ripped the note out of the tablet and stuffed it in her jean pocket. Glancing at her reflection in the bedroom mirror, she frowned. "You don't look much like a reporter," she criticized, shaking her unruly curls. Blowing off her thoughts, she dropped the bag to the floor and grabbed a cap off of her dresser. She dragged her fingers through her hair, slapped the base-ball cap on her head, and then clipped the back of it around a self-made ponytail. A mass of thick locks spilled out of the back of the cap as she situated it just right on her head. That was the best she could do at present to control her long red curls. Taylor grabbed the bag of clothes again, her purse, her camera, and darted out the door.

Jumping in her car, she started the motor and slipped out onto the street. It was practically empty. Taylor knew right where she was going; it was around the corner from the Quarter, actually on the edge. This body was found on Iberville, only two blocks from Canal Street and no more than a block from the Interstate. The other two bodies had been found within a five-block radius of this one. It was still dark enough for headlights as Taylor whipped her Mustang through the streets of the French Quarter. From approximately ten at night until about two or three in the morning the Quarter stayed busy, but this was the right time to slip out quickly.

Taylor was thankful for that. She should be there within a few minutes, she told herself as she turned on her radio.

CHAPTER 4

"Have they dusted for prints inside the car yet?" John asked.

"Yes, sir," said a young policeman.

"Good. Then turn off that radio!"

The police swarmed the area, along with the crew from CSI and the detectives helping him on this case. John had called them right after he got the call. Each looked for anything they could find to give them a clue as to what happened while making sure they didn't disturb any potential evidence.

"Sir," the same young policeman who was first on the scene said to Detective Bradley, "we didn't find any signs of a struggle . . . just like the last two times. It looks like the girl wasn't aware of any danger. Her purse was open, and one of her hands still clutched it like she had been digging into it." Shaking his head, he said, "I don't understand how a girl alone could be that unaware of how dangerous it is on the streets."

"I agree with you." *Was she looking for her license?* John wondered. *Had she been pulled over by a fake policeman? Is our speculation reality?* The woman digging through her purse gave more credibility to his thoughts. He didn't say that out loud, but it was fact.

The uniformed officer cast his eyes back toward the vehicle.

John wished they had already captured this man before another life had been taken. "Okay, Nelson, we'll get the crime lab to go through the contents of her purse back at the station when they check the car more thoroughly. Make another sweep of the grounds. See if you can find any kind of strong cord or rope." The killer had never left a clue before, but there was always a first time. Would they get lucky? He doubted it, but they had to look.

"Why isn't this area taped off yet?" John shouted for whoever would listen and act accordingly. "You know it won't be long before the news media gets wind of this. They'll be destroying evidence before we can even find it."

Headlights hit John square in the face as he was talking. "Speak of the devil —" He didn't need to finish his statement. Everyone knew they were about to be covered with TV cameras and news reporters.

John glanced at his watch. *This reporter made good time. He must be listening to his scanner all night waiting for a story. They're getting too fast for me.* He stared for another moment into the bright lights.

CHAPTER 5

It took less than ten minutes for Taylor to reach the scene of the crime. The police were already there. Her headlights flashed on the dark-haired detective. *Detective Bradley.*

Shutting off her engine, Taylor doused her lights. She pulled her digital camera out of its small case. By always keeping the setting for flash as needed, she managed to get shots worthy of the newspaper. Taylor admitted their photographer took better pictures, but sometimes he wasn't at the scene fast enough. She'd learned a long time ago to always be prepared.

The orange and pink glow forming in the dark sky cast a soft haze over the scene. Within the next hour, the morning sun would peek out over the horizon, illuminating the full horror of the crime scene.

As Taylor walked up to the yellow sedan, she clicked off some shots of the vehicle from each angle before approaching the driver's window. At two prior murder scenes she'd managed several viewpoints, but no angle as close as she was about to take this morning for the third scene. Usually the yellow tape kept her back.

Holding her camera just right, seeing the woman's head leaning back against her headrest, her skin tinged a shade of gray-blue, Taylor held down the button for a picture. Normally the victim's body was covered by the time she got on the scene. She must have made really good time this morning.

For her next shot, she focused on the victim's hand clutching her bag. As she held down the button again, waiting for the flash, a hand caught her arm in a viselike grip and yanked downward. "What do you think you're doing? You know you can't take pictures of the victim."

Tugging her arm out of the grip, she dropped her hands to her side and swiveled toward the voice. "Well, Detective Bradley, how nice to see you, too," she said in a tone dripping with sugary sarcasm.

"I should've known it would be you." Throwing his hands up in disgust, he grumbled, "How did you get here so quickly? Did you put a bug in my car or something?"

Taylor chose to ignore his words. The fact that she planned to follow him starting today made his question a little too close to the truth for comfort — not that she would ever plant a bug in the detective's car.

Locking her gaze on him in an attempt to distract him, she spoke as her hand with the camera eased up slowly, hoping to get the right angle again — this time without him stopping her. "I'm only doing my job, Detective Bradley. I told you I'd be glad to work with you, but you haven't agreed. So, in the meantime, I have to stay on top of things for myself." Lifting her camera a little higher, she made it even with the window of the victim's car and stole a glance as she directed the viewfinder toward the hand in the purse again. Not looking, she held the button down, keeping her arm stiff in case the detective got wise and grabbed her arm again.

The flash went off. The detective pivoted toward the camera, then glared back at Taylor. "I better not see that victim in your paper, or you will find yourself brought up on charges. Do I make myself clear?"

"No problem there."

"Well, back up and don't touch anything. Wait until they cover the body before you take any more pictures. I mean it! Or I'll take your camera. You shouldn't be so close. You could be destroying vital evidence. Besides, you know the rules." Detective Bradley stomped away.

Taylor slid closer to the driver's side. She knew better than to try and get another shot for the paper. He wasn't kidding about taking her camera. He would. His reputation preceded him. But he couldn't stop her from gathering some pictures in her mind while she had the opportunity, even though she couldn't shoot any more shots at this close an angle.

Scanning the woman's badly bruised face and slowly working her gaze downward, Taylor saw the ligature markings on the victim's neck.

"Get a grip," she told herself. Slowly she released the breath she'd been holding. Taylor had no idea what had gotten into her. She'd been to plenty of crime scenes. For over ten years she'd been chasing stories and had seen unbelievable things, more than most people. Sometimes blood would be splattered here and there, and more than one body would be lying around.

Why was this one different? Why was it getting to her? Then she remembered — usually the bodies were covered and she

65

only saw the victims in pictures afterward from the coroner's office or old shots from family albums. This time the image had a face, and she'd seen it close up. She'd even beaten the medical examiner there. Maybe this was the break she needed.

As she eased back slightly from the car, another thought sent chills down her spine. This woman, like the other two, was close to her own age.

Too close . . . too personal.

The detective had lost interest in her and was talking to one of the men who were from the crime scene investigative unit. Thankful for the solitude, Taylor surveyed the area. The crime scene sat at the side of a main road, a business area in fact. These kinds of businesses were run nine to five, not like the French Quarter establishments that were open almost all day and all night long; therefore, there was probably no witness to the crime . . . again.

Too bad it hadn't been raining so at least mud tracks could have formed in the dirty areas, giving the police an idea of what make of vehicle to look for. There wasn't even enough dust collected on the roadside to leave markings from the tires of the murderer's car, at least not that she saw. The police probably patrolled this area more now because of the prior murders. One of the cops had probably spotted the car on the side of the road with no one else around, making it look suspicious. Surely there was no eyewitness, because, like the two before, the crime took place in the wee hours of the morning, and very few people were out roaming the business district at that time of the night . . . or morning, you might say.

The coroner arrived as she was scanning the area. When her search turned up nothing, she started questioning two of the police officers who were putting up the tape.

"Johnson!" Bradley called to one of the officers.

"Yes, Lieutenant?"

Detective Bradley took two long strides and closed the distance. "You and Brown take the evidence you gathered back to the lab and start on your report. Tell Smitty to finish putting up the tape. More reporters are pulling in. Move it, and I'll handle the press."

Johnson and Brown didn't argue. They knew better, Taylor decided. Both walked away without another word.

"Miss Jaymes, any questions you have, ask me. Leave my men alone. Now get behind the tape." The detective turned his back on her and headed toward the coroner.

"Lieutenant Bradley, I'd like to get a statement from you," Taylor called to him as he started to leave. She knew he was giving her the brush-off, but this was her job. Like it or not, she needed to get the story. He could work with her or against her. It didn't matter to her.

Well, she thought as she watched him stop in his tracks and turn her way, *I'd rather he work with me.*

CHAPTER 6

At the sound of her voice, John stopped and slowly pivoted, focusing his hard glare upon her. He frowned. "When I'm finished collecting all the facts, I'll be glad to answer your questions. Do you think you could carry yourself over to your car and wait there?" John figured he had enough problems without having to deal with a nosy reporter. She might look good, but that didn't get the mystery solved.

Dismissing her from his thoughts, John stepped toward the coroner. "Morning, Bob. Got anything?"

About that time another car and a van pulled up.

Just what I need — more reporters and television cameras. Great!

"John, it looks like she's been dead for about two to three hours. That would place her death between two and three this morning. That's not the official word yet, but that's what it looks like from the liver temp. I'll let you know for sure on my official report later today." The coroner pushed his wire-rimmed glasses back up on his nose, and his fingertips brushed the edge of his stringy gray hair that fell forward over his brows. Closing his black bag, he rose to his feet. "The markings on her throat look like they were made with the same rope that killed the other two girls. When the fibers are tested, if they are the same synthetic fibers as before, we'll know for sure. It looks like you won't be guessing anymore. You'll know you have a serial killer on your hands."

John blew out a gush of air. "That's what I thought." His hands brushed the rough shadow of whiskers that he'd had no time to remove this morning.

"Looks like you're dealing with a real sick person, probably a sociopath. The killer apparently gets pleasure out of killing young, innocent women. And, sad to say, he's showing no signs of remorse. All three women have been in their late twenties to early thirties." Scratching his head, Bob added, "I just don't understand how he gets to them so easily. None show any sign of a struggle. It's like they think of the killer as a friend."

"We're thinking it might be someone

dressed up like a cop. You know, nowadays you can get a uniform from any costume shop in town. And if someone saw a red or blue light flashing, they might think it was a cop and pull over. If the killer walked up dressed as a policeman, most people would probably try to cooperate." John glanced at the stretcher where the body now lay covered up. "All I know is, I need to solve this case soon before he tries to claim his next victim." *And before the FBI comes in and claims it as their case. Not that I wouldn't welcome help, but these are my victims and my streets I need to protect.*

The older man slapped John on the shoulder. "Good luck, son. You'll need it. I'll have my report on your desk before noon." On those words, Bob left. His assistant had already loaded the body on the wagon.

John watched as the tow truck hooked up to the victim's car. The investigating crew had all departed, leaving two uniformed officers to keep the news media behind the yellow tape now in place. He wanted to get out of there himself.

But as he headed toward his car, he saw that brassy redhead perched on the hood of her car. Closing his eyes, he grumbled under his breath. A couple of reporters with their camera crew were behind the yellow line filming . . . probably for the morning news broadcast. As he moved closer, some flashes went off as snaps were taken of him.

I'll make one quick statement and that should satisfy them until later today. Speaking loudly, he said, "As soon as we get results back from the coroner's office and our lab, I'll be ready to make a statement. Probably won't have anything until around one this afternoon. See you at the station." Before he could walk away, hands shot up in the air and questions showered him from everyone — except Taylor Jaymes. She stayed patiently on her car, not moving a muscle.

"Was the victim killed like the others?"

"Do we have a serial killer?"

"Did you find any evidence this time?"

"Have you gotten yourself a suspect yet?"

As all these questions bombarded him and he watched the quiet reporter sitting on the hood of her car, John held up both his hands. "No answers now. All I can tell you is we have a dead body. Not much to report yet, so you might want to wait on getting anything out, but that's up to you."

While he talked, he saw her in the background, still not moving. It was like she wasn't worried. She must have an inside source to not be at the front of the crowd demanding answers. Maybe she thought their talk yesterday gave her exclusive rights, and he was her inside source.

Well, he would put a stop to that way of thinking. Swiftly he walked past the other reporters and stopped in front of her car. "Look, Miss Jaymes, I'm tired and I need a cup of coffee. Why don't you follow me back to the station, and we can talk in the cafeteria while I drink my first cup?"

Why did I say that?

John realized he had wanted to control the situation. What was he doing? He had meant to set her straight right then and there. Be done with her and send her on her way. Maybe he thought he'd have better odds setting her straight back at the station. That had to be it. The detective had read her articles before and knew she got into her stories. Her reporting style seemed to always get her right in the middle of the investigation she reported. He needed to stop her right up front. John didn't need or want this woman in the middle of his crime scenes. He had a job to do, and she was merely a nuisance slowing him down.

Taylor slid off her car and dusted off her backside. "Great. I'm hungry myself."

After the dust was removed from her pants, she looked up at him. He could see she was studying him, but it took him a second or two longer to tear his gaze away from her. Gritting his teeth, he began to stride away.

"Lieutenant," she called, stopping him in his tracks.

His blood heated up as he faced her one more time. "Follow me in your car," he barked but low enough so the other reporters wouldn't catch wind of his meeting with her. Then they would all want one. John turned again and headed to his car.

As he passed the other reporters, he didn't even give them a glance. *They all need to wait. They want a story. I want a killer stopped.* His needs overrode theirs.

Why had he given that one reporter special permission to talk to him earlier than the rest? It had to be because he believed she had inside sources.

It couldn't be anything else, he thought as he started the car's motor and backed away from the crime scene. As he passed the area slowly, he saw the lights and cameras focused on his policemen keeping guard. John wasn't worried. They wouldn't open their mouths. He needed to get back to the station and put all the facts together on this one, combine them with the other ones and start finding connections. There had to be some, other than the obvious.

Heading back to the station, he glanced in his rearview mirror and saw the reporter's red Mustang.

Help me, Lord.

CHAPTER 7

Taylor turned the key. The engine of her Mustang sprang to life. She smiled to herself. The detective seemed angry, and she wasn't exactly sure why. Maybe it was the way she caught him looking at her, or was that her imagination? His eyes said one thing one moment, and then in the next, they gleamed the opposite. Total confusion.

"He didn't have to bite my head off no matter what he was thinking," she said aloud. "I didn't make him look at me."

Taylor started to complain about the detective's temper when she heard her favorite song come to life on the radio. It distracted her immediately. Instead of fussing, she cranked up the volume and started tapping her steering wheel to the beat while she sang at the top of her lungs, "Well, I got friends in low places . . ."

By the time she turned into the police parking lot behind the lieutenant and found a parking spot near him, she was in a better mood. The murder and the detective's foul temper had slid to the back of her mind. The DJ was talking about being on the lookout for the Moneyman as she killed her engine. "I should be so lucky," she said aloud as the thought of winning a quick hundred bucks made her smile grow. Who couldn't use an extra bit of cash?

She was humming as she stepped out of the car. Detective John Bradley was heading toward her. Locking the car door, she met him halfway. "One can't be too safe," she said, quirking her brow. "What better place to rob me than in the parking lot of the Eighth District New Orleans Police Department with police all around?" She flashed him a grin.

John watched as she laughed. That reporter sure was young. How could a woman as young and as innocent as she appeared to be, be in her line of business? A crime reporter had to be tough and daring. If reporters weren't careful, they wound up hard-hearted and cold . . . or dead and cold.

As his eyes studied Taylor from behind his dark shades, he walked up the steps close behind her to the front door. The scent of her perfume aroused his senses. Emotions stirred in his chest. Shaking his head, he wondered where that came from. First off, she was too young. Second off, since Jennifer's death, he hadn't even looked at another woman. He had even sworn off women altogether — especially women in a dangerous line of work. Maybe the fragrance reminded him of Jennifer.

John decided, after everyone tried to set him up with their wives' best friends or whomever, he was destined to be alone. That was when he swore off women forever. For six months after Jennifer's death, he spent a lot of time soul searching. He couldn't understand why God would take Jennifer's life, yet let him live, but then God showed him there was still plenty of work left for him to do. It was hard to accept at first, but finally John started pouring his heart out into his work and kept busy. If that was his call, then so be it. He removed his gaze from the fiery redhead and murmured, "Nope, not me."

"What?" Taylor asked over her shoulder.

That was when he realized he'd spoken his thoughts aloud. He hadn't planned to, so he chose to ignore her question.

Stopping short, she turned slightly and said, "I didn't understand what you said."

He practically ran her down when she

stopped so quickly. Instantly, he scooped his hand under her elbow, turned her back around, and kept them walking toward the door. "It was nothing," he said. Once inside, he pivoted her toward the elevator.

Pressing the Up button, he said, "It's on the second floor." The double doors opened, and they stepped inside. He reached out and pressed number two. Out of the corner of his eye, he saw her staring, and it didn't matter. That subject was not open for debate. He hadn't meant to speak aloud; she didn't need to know what he had been thinking.

When they sat down to drink coffee, he would talk to her about what was going on . . . to a limit. For now, he had to make sure she stayed focused on the matter at hand. He needed her to understand she wasn't getting special treatment or inside information. None of it. She would get her information along with all of the other re- porters.

Taylor watched but didn't say a word. She wondered what was going through the detective's mind. He had to break this case. The killer needed to be caught. He was the man to do it, too, she thought. Sighing to herself, she hoped he would find out she could be of use to him. Especially since, at the present, he had nothing to go on.

Once in the cafeteria line, she grabbed a tray. Her stomach growled. *Feed me. Feed me.* Grabbing a plate of beignets, she then filled her mug with hot chocolate. Glancing at the detective's empty tray, she asked, "Don't you eat?" Not giving him a chance to answer, she admired the white pastries on her plate. "This looks good. I can't believe the police cafeteria serves beignets. Mmm."

"I'm getting a cup of coffee and some toast." As he fixed his cup of coffee, a petite, yet full-busted, blond-haired woman brought him toast.

"Hey, John, I put strawberry jelly on your toast this morning. Sweets for the sweet." The waitress smiled at him. "I remembered Jennifer saying a long time ago that you loved strawberries." She flashed her lashes in his direction. Then she spotted Taylor, and her smile transformed into a tight-lipped frown.

Taylor wasn't bothered at all. She looked back at the woman without revealing her thoughts: *You're nuts! Who in their right mind would think the detective was sweet. I doubt if he has a sweet bone in his body.* Finally, the woman stormed away. Taylor's lips turned up slightly. *So much for her.*

At the table, the detective took the trays and set them aside. Pulling out his notepad, he started looking over his notes as he sipped on his coffee. She presumed it was his findings from this morning. Taylor wasn't waiting for him to share. *He probably won't, but who knows?*

At the moment, those powder-puff sensations were drawing her full attention. She figured the detective would tell her whatever he brought her here to say soon enough. Picking up a beignet, she licked her lips in anticipation.

While her eyes were focused on a doughnut, John studied her behind the guise of looking at his notes. He knew every word he'd written. Didn't need to read it again to discover they still didn't have much. Maybe he could use the help of the press. Maybe. He knew his team didn't seem to be getting anywhere. But how could she help him? After her last story, he knew she had some inside sources on the streets. Maybe she could get some information that could help point the police in the right direction. Evidence was what he needed.

He watched her enjoy her pastry. As she took her next bite, he eased his notepad down. "You know those things aren't good for you. You should be eating a grapefruit or something. Not all that sugar."

Taylor chewed a few more times and then swallowed. She sipped her hot chocolate before locking her gaze on him. "So you think your coffee and toast is better for the body?"

John glanced down at his toast smeared with strawberry jam. "No. You're right. Mine is no better, but I usually eat a healthy lunch and dinner. Can you say the same?" Looking at her slim, trim figure, he doubted she ate any more than her unhealthy breakfast. One meal a day and it wasn't healthy.

Her green eyes glared at her half-eaten plate of beignets, and her fingers drummed on the table. She appeared to be trying to think of some smart answer to give him. He snickered. That would be her style.

Then she blurted, "A chicken sandwich with some chips. That was supper last night. For lunch yesterday, umm, let me think." She closed her eyes. They popped back open as she said, "Oh yeah. I remember. I had a good juicy cheeseburger and a basket of fries. I ate at the place on Canal by Macy's." Her eyes widened. "And I had a salad with it. Salads are nourishing."

He wanted to laugh. She seemed so proud

of her eating habits. Instead he shook his head in disbelief. "Do you eat like that all the time?" When she nodded, he huffed. "How do you keep your figure? It's so unhealthy the way you eat. I have to say, you don't have to worry about a bullet taking you down early in life like I said yesterday. You're killing yourself now. Your veins are clogging up even as we speak."

She lifted an eyebrow. "So you think I have a good figure?"

Out of everything he just told her, that was all she grasped? John wanted to throw his hands up in the air and walk away. Instead, he sighed. Her voice had sounded teasing, almost flirty, and John didn't like it. He'd been serious. Also the little get-together they were having was business, not personal. Flirting was personal. She seemed to take everything lightly. This wasn't where he wanted to go, nor needed to go. He frowned and fell silent. John wanted her to know he was annoyed. He turned his attention to his coffee and toast. That shut her up.

Good. Now her attention seemed to be back on her food. Worked for him. After he finished his coffee, he picked his notes back up. This time he shared some of them with her as she jotted notes. He kept his tone strictly business. He finished with, "After checking every forensic lead, if we get anything concrete, we'll let you reporters know. I'm sharing these notes with you to let you know we are working every possible lead. We want the killer found. So far he's eluded us and managed to keep from leaving any clues, but these type killers do mess up. We just hope it's sooner rather than later."

"I can't believe you gave all of this to me. Thanks."

"That should do it." John slipped his notepad into his breast pocket. "If forensics uncovers anything new that I can tell you, I'll phone the paper. What I gave you will be basically the same statement I'll give the rest of the press later this morning, minus a few details. I don't want to give this maniac too much publicity. Sometimes they thrive on hearing about themselves or reading about what they have done. It spurs them on to do more. Right now, he's killing one woman a week. I don't want to make it two."

"So now you believe it's a serial killer?"

"Same man did all three, we feel sure. After the tests today, we'll know. So don't forget to call before you finish your piece for the paper."

"I'd like to ask you a question about the

second girl who was killed, Stephanie Gau-threaux. Do you know who her boyfriend was? His name and address? And have you talked to him yet?"

That caught John slightly off guard. He glanced over his notes before he responded. He wanted to be sure. "We didn't know she had anyone special in her life. Where did you get that piece of information?"

"From her neighbors."

They all told us they didn't know anything about their neighbor. Everyone claimed to keep to themselves. Maybe this reporter could be some help to us after all. "We didn't know about him. But it's something to check into. Thanks for the info."

Taylor closed her notebook. "What makes people do things like what this guy has been doing?"

She's a reporter, and she's asking me that? But her question seemed genuine, so he answered. "It could be a number of things. Usually it can be traced back to something in the killer's past that hurt him or her emotionally or physically. They repress it, and then something happens to make them snap." He rubbed his face and raked his fingers through his hair. "And other times, there is no simple explanation at all."

Taylor rose, picked up her purse, and

dropped a five on the table. "Thanks for your time and the information. Please think over my offer to work with you on this." She waited for a moment by the table without saying a word. Probably hoping for a response.

John rose and, starting at the top of her head, slowly looked his way down the length of her body. How could any woman as pretty as her want to put herself in constant danger chasing crime stories? It made no sense whatsoever. He admitted to himself only moments ago that she might be a help in this investigation, but down deep he knew he didn't want to bring anyone in on it. Especially her. She could get herself killed. He would handle this on his own . . . well, with the help of New Orleans' finest.

John shrugged as his eyes connected to hers. "Don't count on it."

He left her standing by the table.

CHAPTER 8

On the drive to the paper, Taylor scanned the city she loved so much. New Orleans, a city that truly never slept, was filled with beauty. Not so much a superficial beauty, but one that took years to achieve. The flavor of history kept it alive — the plantations of old restored to their original beauty, along with the riverboats and streetcars that ran up and down St. Charles and Canal. What a sight! The spirit of the city never died.

New Orleans stepped into the twenty-first century just like every other city in America, only without losing the history that was evident everywhere you looked. The mix was magical. In the later twentieth century, New Orleans added places like the Superdome, Aquarium of the Americas, and the Convention Center. What would they do in this century? While grand hotels were sprinkled throughout the city, the streets in the Quarter flowed with old Dixieland jazz, along with rhythm and blues. Now even country music spilled out along the streets of the grandest city Taylor knew.

The *Tribune* was located in the business district of the city; however, the spark of New Orleans was still evident on Poydras and Commerce. It didn't take Taylor long to get to the paper. Quickly she headed upstairs, via the elevator, to her workstation.

Snatching her digital camera out of her purse, she tossed her bag under her desk and sat in her swivel chair. As she touched the mouse, her computer hummed as it came to life. Instantly, a bright light lit her screen. Flipping open the bottom compartment on her camera, she extracted her memory card and inserted it into her computer. When a square screen popped up, she clicked on DOWNLOAD PICTURES. In no time, her shots were displayed in a smaller version.

Sliding the mouse to the left, Taylor directed the pointer over the first shot she had taken. Before clicking on it, she noticed a stack of messages next to her phone and tried to ignore them. But her eyes darted back to the stack, torn between looking at the pictures and seeing who had left messages for her.

I better check out those messages before I get too deeply engrossed in my pictures.

As much as she wanted to take a closer look at the pictures, she knew she needed to see what had come in after she left yesterday. Maybe someone called ready to give a statement . . . maybe a statement related to the latest killing. Glancing through the notes, she saw most were from her family — her sister once and her mother twice. "I'll have to call you both later," she said as she put the messages aside.

The last one, however, was from someone who didn't leave his name but said he would call back. "That's strange," she murmured. "Oh well, whoever you are, mister, I don't have time for you now. My love life will have to wait." Laughter bubbled from within. Her love life? That was a joke. Who had time?

She casually put that note aside with the others. But as she started to turn her attention back to the pictures at hand, she snapped the pink slip of paper back up and scanned the message one more time. "Unless, of course, you're a source wanting to give me an anonymous tip. That I'll take now," she whispered as she studied the note. "Call me. Now!"

Smiling to herself, she knew she could use all the help she could get. It wasn't like the detective was going to give her anything. Opening her bottom desk drawer, she pulled out the prints she had copied from the other crime scenes and laid them out in between her computer and her keyboard. She noticed again how isolated the areas were where both cars were found, just like this morning. There were no places of business open in those areas. In fact, the first one sat right outside the hustle and bustle of the French Quarter, a rundown and dirty area. No businesses, no houses — nothing in the background except old, empty warehouses. The second scene was close to the third one. It at least had businesses behind the car, just none that had opened yet.

Looking at the emptiness surrounding them, along with the pink skies of early morning dawn, sent chills running down Taylor's back. What possessed those women to stop for someone in those areas? Did they not realize their lives were in danger? They had to.

Although the pictures portrayed horrible scenes, excitement coursed through her veins. As she added glossy photo paper in her printer, clicked the appropriate places on the computer screen, and then hit EN-

TER, she waited for her new photos to print. Oh, how she hoped this would be the case that brought her closer to her dream. If she could get noted for this story and it got picked up across the wire, one of the bigger papers, maybe even *The Miami Herald,* would want to make her an offer to work for them. This would get her closer to her goal, winning the Pulitzer. The more crime she helped solve and the better stories she wrote, the more notice she got. Eventually she should get an offer from somewhere, a more noted paper with a prestigious name.

But could she leave the city she loved so much? Maybe she wouldn't have to. To get involved in the work she longed for and the stories she only dreamed of, she had to move up in her field. But did she truly have to move across the country?

Of course she did. She wanted her name known all over — national notoriety. Certainly, she would move wherever her work took her. As much as she hated the thought of leaving New Orleans, the city she loved, she loved her work more. She would move. Make no mistake about it. Her work was her life.

As the pictures printed, she started typing the article for the evening edition of the paper, telling New Orleans about Trisha

McIntyre, a young female found early this morning, strangled to death. She wanted to tell the women of New Orleans to take heed, not to do anything as foolish as stopping for some strange reason in the middle of nowhere. Tell them to use their heads. They never knew who could be lurking in the darkness. But she didn't. She also didn't mention the fact that there could be a connection to the three murders in the past two weeks. Taylor didn't want to give the pervert any limelight for what he or she had done; besides which, the police hadn't confirmed it yet.

In less than thirty minutes, Taylor had the new prints laid out with the others. As she studied them, she thought about the facts known to her. All three victims were strangled at the same early morning hour, in the same general area, and all were young single women. Well, two were — she didn't know about the new one yet.

Stephanie, the first victim, was involved with a man but not married. And as far as Taylor knew, no one had interviewed him yet. Why was he staying out of this? Why hadn't he contacted the police?

The second victim, Trudy, was single and not involved with anyone. Taylor didn't know the facts on the third victim yet, but if it was the same MO, she was probably single, too.

"Did they know one another?" Taylor asked herself aloud. "Maybe they knew each other at an earlier time in their lives."

She scanned the pictures. "There's got to be another connection." She squinted closer. Something kept drawing her to the rear shot of the latest victim's car. Finally, she pulled out her magnifying glass and studied every inch of the rear end.

"Oh my gosh!" she whispered when she found what had caught her attention. All the air in her lungs left, and she shuddered. It was the bumper sticker. Why? Because it was just like the one on the bumper of Taylor's car. The sticker revealed the girl's love for country music and the station she preferred listening to . . . just as Taylor's car bumper did. Icy fingers danced across her shoulders as she realized the latest victim had a connection to her. Grief for Trisha McIntyre's young life lost swept through Taylor.

New Orleans was noted for jazz, not country, even though a few stations had started featuring country artists. Country music had grown over the past decade, so it, too, was moving into the city a little at a time.

Her eyes glanced at the other cars, wondering if either revealed anything about their owners. Since no pictures focused closely on the rear of the cars, she had to use her magnifying glass again.

"Wow! I don't believe it! Stephanie, too?"

Astonished, she pulled the picture of the second victim's car closer to her. Studying it carefully, she leaned in toward the round object in her hand magnifying the bumper of the victim.

Her stomach knotted at her discovery, and she slammed down the magnifying glass. Part of her was excited at the thought she might have made the connection between the three women, but the other part made her nauseous. Now she, too, was connected to them. Admittedly she wasn't as young as they were, but close, and she was a single woman who loved country music. Could that be the key? It had to be.

With shaking fingers, she lifted her phone and punched out the number of the police department. "Lieutenant Bradley, please."

In seconds, she heard his gruff voice. "Bradley here. Can I help you?"

"Detective Bradley," Taylor said in a soft voice.

"Speak up. I can't hear you," he growled into her ear.

Taylor felt weak. Knowing this connection was one thing, but verbalizing it was another. Speaking it out loud would make it real. Swallowing a hard lump in her throat, she said, "Lieutenant Bradley, it's me, Taylor Jaymes. I found something you should see. I-I-I think I may have found the connection between the three victims." She stuttered as part of her fought trying not to even speak this truth into existence.

He didn't respond immediately. Taylor wasn't even sure he was still there. *Speak up, Detective. Did you hear me?* She wanted to scream at him, but fear rattled her nerves, and she seldom felt fear. "Can you meet me somewhere, or can I come to you?" She held her breath waiting for his response. Before it came, she added, "It's important."

A heavy sigh touched her ears. "I don't have time to meet you, Miss Jaymes. I have a meeting to go to. I doubt you found the connection we're looking for, but I appreciate your exuberance."

Hardheaded men! "You have to see this. I'm telling you it's important. It's the key you've been looking for. I know it. I feel it." Her voice rose with each sentence she spoke. How could he not want to know the connection? It was his job!

Silence filled the line. Then, "If you've

found a connection that points to the victims' deaths, I'd like to see it." His voice was hesitant. "You can come to the station, but you have to come right now. I'm expected in a meeting with my boss and the commissioner in half an hour. Be here within fifteen minutes."

"It'll take me longer than that just to drive to the station. Be late for your meeting. It's what you're looking for. I know it. A few minutes late won't hurt. I promise it'll be worth it."

"I'm sure it's important, but I doubt my captain will see it that way." His voice sounded like he didn't believe her anyway.

"He'll be glad you kept him waiting." He probably thought her call was just another excuse to try and convince him to let her work with him on this case. "I'll be there as fast as possible. I'm running out the door now." *But if I get a speeding ticket, you can fix it for me,* she thought but didn't say. "Wait for me." Her fear dissipated, and excitement coursed through her veins. "It's the answer you've been looking for."

"You sound pretty sure of your findings, Miss Jaymes. I can't imagine what you could have uncovered that the police department couldn't find." A fraction of a second later, he said, "But hurry on over, and I'll take a look. I really do have a meeting with my captain and the commissioner."

"I'm on my way!" Jumping to her feet, she slammed down the phone and stuffed the pictures in her purse.

In record time, she was out the door, speeding to the station. She didn't take time to enjoy the city she loved, nor did she crank up the radio and sing along. Instead, her mind stayed focused on the connection between the girls. They all loved country music so much that they stuck a bumper sticker on the back of their car to tell the world. Within the original fifteen-minute limit, she made it to the station, shoved her gear stick into NEUTRAL, and set the parking brake.

This time the detective didn't keep her waiting. The policeman at the counter said, "Go right on in. The detective is expecting you."

She walked straight to the elevator and hit the button for his floor. As the doors started opening, she slipped out and scurried down the hall to his door. Knocking twice, she entered, not waiting for him to answer.

Without saying a word, she walked to his desk and pulled out the three photos. Sticking her hand back in her purse, she pulled out the magnifying glass and said, "Look at their bumpers."

She watched as the detective studied the prints closely. Finally he said, "I don't see how we overlooked this. We've searched prints inside and out and other items found in the cars, trying to find a connection. I guess no one got around to looking at the bumpers, for clues." He ran his fingers through his dark hair again.

Taylor noticed he did that when he was thinking. She wished she could do that to him.

Whoa. Where did that come from? Her mind was supposed to be on this case, not on some guy. "So do you think this could be the connection?"

"It's possible. It's definitely a lead." He glanced at his watch. "I really have to go to this meeting, but I'd like to talk to you a bit more when I get out, say around three or four?"

She was disappointed. She wanted to talk now . . . not later. Taylor thought he would call off his meeting and start following up on the lead she'd thrown into his lap. *Well, fine. I'll follow up on it by myself.* She sighed softly, then said, "I can't meet you until six tonight. In fact, I'm really busy, so let's just meet over dinner."

His brow furrowed, but he said nothing.

"Don't get any funny ideas," Taylor snapped. "I said let's meet at dinner because that will be all the time I can spare you. I have a busy life, too, you know."

Swiftly, she thought of what she wanted to eat tonight. Other than the pastry treats she had that morning, she hadn't eaten all day. Without giving him a chance to come up with another idea, she blurted, "Okay. Meet me at Dante's Pizza and Pasta. It's on St. Peter — not far from here."

"Don't you ever eat anything besides junk?"

She rolled her eyes. *What a dumb time to think about eating healthy. Besides, who has time to be choosey?* "Just be there. We'll discuss my eating habits another time." Taylor stood. Reaching for the pictures, she said, "I'll take those, thank you. Didn't have time to make you copies. Have a good meeting." With those words, she turned and left his office.

So put that in your pipe and smoke it, she thought. In no time she made it outside and headed to her car. Before she started following up on the lead she'd found, Taylor decided now was the time to drop off her clothes to be cleaned. Around the corner from her house was The Washing Well. It only took a couple of minutes to park in the unloading zone, drop her clothes off, and then get back on the road. What a way to do housework. "The only way," she murmured.

Even though she'd led the detective to believe she had a busy life, other than taking the next few hours locating the country bars in the area and doing a background check on the third victim, she had nothing else to do. In fact, had she not found the connection, she'd already have been through finding the background info.

Using her cell phone, she located the bars in a twenty-mile radius of where the bodies were left. She found three in the Quarter and two outside the Quarter. After leaving the detective this evening, she'd copy pictures of the three victims and go visit the bars. See if anyone recognized them as regulars . . . or even better, remembered seeing them the nights they were killed.

Next, she found the latest victim's address in the white pages on her cell. Taylor drove by Miss McIntyre's home, scoping out the neighborhood. If she had been a cop, she'd intrude on the neighbors now, asking questions, but tomorrow would be soon enough. Give them a chance to feel their grief.

A short article would be in the evening edition about Trisha McIntyre's untimely death. Taylor decided this would give the neighbors a chance to read about Trisha's death in the paper, and maybe by tomorrow they would be willing to talk about the young girl's life.

Taylor took time to run back by the paper and make duplicates of the three pictures so the detective could have his own copies. She'd give them to him when they met for dinner.

After finishing everything she had to do, she picked up her clothes, already clean and folded, and then headed home. It cost her more this way, but what she made up for in time was worth every penny. She didn't have time for mundane things.

When Taylor dressed for dinner, for some strange reason she didn't dress in her normal fashion, jeans and a pullover shirt, although her favorites were all nice and clean. Without even thinking about it, she pulled out her emerald-green short skirt and blazer and paired a paisley print silk blouse with it. Sliding into a pair of dressy, yet comfortable, black shoes with a heel, she took a few extra minutes in front of the mirror touching up her makeup and hair.

By 5:45, Taylor had already slipped out of her apartment and walked down the street to Dante's. She wanted to be sure to get them a table on the far end so their chances of being overheard would be slim. Their subject matter didn't need to be shared with anyone. Of course, in New Orleans, especially the Quarter, people didn't take time to listen to other people's conversations; they were too busy having fun.

After sitting for a while at the table, she glanced at her watch. It read 6:15. Anger started to boil within her, and her stomach roiled. She was hungry. Those beignets hadn't sustained her except for an hour that morning. Time had kept her from grabbing lunch. And by the time she had a moment, it was too close to meeting Detective John Bradley for dinner. She didn't care one bit for this guy keeping her waiting. What if he decided not to come at all? Maybe now that he had the new lead, he really didn't need to talk to her. Maybe he wasn't going to show up at all. Maybe by asking her to meet him later, it was his way of keeping her from following up on her own lead.

She wanted to be angry at her new thought, but instead, she found herself more disappointed that she had dressed up for nothing.

By 6:30, Antonio, Dante's son, called to Taylor, "Are you going to eat tonight?" She was a regular of this establishment, as well as a few others around the Quarter. "Or would you at least care for a beer while you wait?"

The old Taylor surfaced — the one before she apparently went gaga over the detective. "Forget him. I'll order now. If he shows up, he'll have to eat what I pick out. I'll take a large special with everything but anchovies." If he showed up at all, she would share it with him; if not, the leftovers would be breakfast in the morning.

Shortly after she ordered, a tall, good-looking man in a blue suit walked into the eatery. When she realized it was John, her spirits lifted. Taylor waved above the crowd to get his attention.

Yes, he made it.

CHAPTER 9

John spotted Taylor and headed for the
table. "Sorry I'm late. That meeting lasted
longer than I expected. The governor joined
us."

The whole time John had been in the
meeting, his mind toyed, or more like worried, over what Taylor would do with her
discovery. Taylor could have rushed back to
the paper and written up an article, flashing
what could be the connection to the public
across the front page of the evening edition
of the *Tribune.* For her, that would have
meant getting a front-page scoop, and
wasn't that what reporters lived for? He
could see the headline now: CONNECTION
BETWEEN DEATHS FOUND BY REPORTER,
followed by the subheading, "Serial killer
loose in New Orleans . . . beware."

Those thoughts drove him crazy. It was all
he could do to stay focused on the governor's words. John couldn't wait to get out

of there and meet with Taylor so they could discuss what she'd found that connected the three deaths.

After all that worrying and fretting during the meeting, he surprised himself by taking time to swing by his place to shower and get a quick shave. Then he changed before dashing over to Dante's Pizza to meet with Taylor. That baffled him, but it also gave him the opportunity to glance at the cover of the evening edition. He found she'd kept her word and hadn't printed anything about what she had found — yet.

"You look tired but fresh, if that makes any sense." A crease formed between her brows. "It must have been a rough meeting. I can't believe the governor crashed it. You must really be in the hot seat now . . . at least until you crack this case. Lucky for you, I found a connection. Hopefully it will help you." Her innocent eyes rested on him as she spoke.

His gaze darted around the room before he leaned toward her and in a hushed tone said, "I did tell them that a connection may have been found, and I needed to go follow up on it. That was when they got all fired up and kept insisting I tell them what it was or give them a name of who we suspected. I don't know if the meeting was more like a roller coaster or a spinning top. We went up and down, back and forth, but mostly kept talking in circles."

She shook her head in what seemed like pity for the poor guy. And that poor guy was him. John wasn't used to being thought of that way.

With a tight-lipped smile he said, "I finally told them, when we find a suspect or two who we can link to these crimes, they would be the first to know. Until then, what we had was a theory with plenty of speculation. Thanks to you, we may have more. I didn't say that, though. Instead I said this lead may be the starting place to look for the facts we need, and they finally let me go."

Eying his dinner partner — the fiery, red-haired woman, with deep green eyes accentuated by her emerald-green suit — he wasn't sure if the green set off the fire in her hair, or if it was the flames blazing from her hair that ignited a combustible reaction in her fancy suit and his mind. He glanced away. What had gotten into him? John hadn't responded like this to a woman in years. His work had been his life and it still was. But as his gaze returned to her, he had to admit that he liked the way her eyes sparkled. In fact, he wished this dinner was for pleasure and not business.

Clearing his throat, he fumbled with the napkin on the table. "Dinner. Why don't we order — before we start talking business, that is? I think I skipped lunch today and I'm starving."

A shimmer of red splashed across her cheeks. "Oh no. What did you do?" As a police detective, he knew the look of guilt if he ever saw it.

She lifted her shoulders slightly. "Sorry. I've already ordered dinner." Holding her hands up as if to stop an onslaught of whatever the detective may have for her, she cocked a brow. "You weren't here, and I was hungry." In the silence that followed her admission, she bit her bottom lip.

"God help us. You ordered for me, too?"

She nodded.

"I know it's Dante's Pizza, but I was hoping they had other Italian dishes, like baked chicken brushed with olive oil and seasoned with rosemary, oregano, and thyme, cooked slowly, falling off the bone it's so tender, and a salad on the side. Umm. Now that I would enjoy."

With a crooked grin, she shook her head.

"I can only imagine the junk I'm about to put in my body. When I was a rookie, I lived on greasy junk food, but I promised myself when I moved up the ranks, I would eat only healthy food from then on. So break it to me gently."

He winced as he smiled on the inside. He knew already pizza was the main dish here with a few Italian sandwiches available also. Truly he was picking at her and her eating habits, which also amazed him. Joking around was another thing John rarely did, if ever. What had come over him? "No, seriously, what did you order?" he asked and then waited for the worst.

Lifting her hand in the air, she signaled the man behind the counter. "Antonio's coming. You can order yourself something to drink."

"I'll have a Coke," he told the waiter. *So she knows him well.*

"Taylor, do you need a refill?" Antonio queried. "Your order is about ready."

John watched as she smiled sweetly at the man and nodded. "Sounds good, Antonio." And then she licked her lips. Was that for the food or for the man? John wondered.

"You eat here often?" John glanced from her to the man she called Antonio. It really was none of his business, and he shouldn't have asked. This case must have thrown him for a loop, making him act so out of character. And her private life . . . what was it to him? *Change the subject.* "So what kind of pizza did you order?"

"I could have ordered the barbeque chicken pizza had I known you had your heart set on chicken. But you'll love what I did order. Trust me. And if you want a salad, just ask Antonio for one. He'll bring it with the pizza."

Before he could talk her out of the kind of pizza she had ordered, Antonio returned with the drinks and the pizza. It smelled great, but glancing over it, John said, "Did you leave anything off? It looks like everything but the kitchen sink is on it." He tilted his head and teased, "At least you left that off."

"Don't get smart with me. It has everything but anchovies. And if you had been on time, you could have ordered for yourself." Her eyes darted to the pizza and then returned to his face. "They have different salads and great hot sandwiches. Of course, both are covered with cheese — mozzarella and/or parmesan. Your choice! Oh wait." She twisted her lips. "That's right. You weren't here to choose. So quit complaining and dig in." She threw another quirky smile at him and returned her attention to the pizza.

John found himself enjoying their banter. It was nice, relaxing over a dinner for two after a long, hard day of work. "You're right. Let's eat it while it's hot." He picked up a slice to slip onto his plate, then swiftly dropped it and blew on his fingers. "Trust me, it's hot." He blew some more and then grabbed his cold drink. "Ahh," he said as the coolness caressed his fingertips, giving him instant relief. John resolved to enjoy their little dinner and the pleasure of Taylor's company. Why not?

While they were eating, Taylor started talking business. She told him in detail how she'd discovered the connection. She swallowed another bite and took a sip of her drink. As she set her glass down, she said, "I scanned the area for country bars."

"You did what?" The detective dropped the half-eaten slice of his third piece on his plate. His jaw stiffened.

"I decided to see what country bars were near the area in which the girls had been found. Because each girl had the same bumper sticker and it was of a country radio station in town, checking out the country bars seemed like the next logical step. If their bumper stickers had been reflecting jazz music, it would have made things harder trying to trace their favorite hangout and then seeing if it was the same for each

— too many jazz clubs in the Quarter. This was a plus for us."

"Us?" he questioned quickly.

"Yes. There aren't very many country bars down here. Jazz pubs are a-plenty though, so count your blessings as they say."

"You're right, Miss Jaymes. I should count my blessings, and I do every day. But, sweetheart, you getting too close to these cases would not be a blessing." With hands exaggerating what he said, John pointed to himself first and then to her. "You let me do the investigating and you do the reporting . . . but at the right time. So I'll tell you like I told the governor: This is my case, and I'll work it. And a side note to you, Miss Jaymes — I don't need civilians getting involved." His pointer finger waved back and forth in the air.

Things have been going so well, she thought. *Why does he have to spoil everything?* His gestures made it clear he didn't want her anywhere around him or his case. But must she remind him that she found the connection, not him?

Too bad he didn't want any reporter sticking their nose in the middle of his investigation. Like it or not, this nose was staying on top of things. Clasping her chin with her fingers, she rested her elbow on the table.

He had seemed so friendly at the beginning of the meal. Oh well. It was nice while it lasted. In fact, that was the longest relationship she'd had in a while. She glanced at her watch. *Almost thirty minutes.* Then she laughed to herself.

Shaking her thoughts from her head, she decided to focus on the facts, not on the detective. The three victims each had the same bumper sticker on their car. That was a lead and one she would follow. She had found it. Not him, or his police department. The victims all liked the same type of music, so country bars were the starting point of this investigation . . . *her* investigation. If he were as good a cop as the word on the streets suggested, he, too, would see it.

"Call me Taylor, please," she insisted, deciding not to focus on what he had just said.

"What?" He pushed his plate back slightly. "You're trying to ignore what I said. In fact, you're trying to change the subject. Don't get me wrong. I'm glad you found a possible connection, but I don't want you to put your life in danger. Leave that for the professionals." He eyed her closely. "Okay . . . Taylor. Now, did you bring the pictures? I'd like to take a better look."

She nodded as she took another bite. Laying her slice down and wiping her hands on a napkin, she reached for her purse. "I did better than that." She pulled a red envelope marked CONFIDENTIAL out of her handbag. "I made duplicates for you. The three pictures of the back end of the cars, that is."

John reached for the envelope she offered and opened it. He studied the pictures one after the other, his brows furrowing. Glancing up, he said, "What made you aware of the stickers? They aren't that noticeable. On one the sticker is almost faded away." He began flipping through the pictures again.

She felt the blood drain from her face as she recalled the feeling that had overcome her upon her discovery. Clasping her hands together on the table, she said, "One picture kept bothering me. At first I didn't know why. Finally I pulled out my magnifying glass and started going over the whole picture, one section at a time. Then I saw the bumper sticker and knew that was what had called to me." Taking a deep breath, trying to keep her emotions under control, she added, "You see, I have the same sticker on my car." She picked up her glass, swallowed two more gulps, and set her glass back down.

The expression on his face changed, but only for a second or two. What was he thinking? Taylor couldn't decide what that expression meant — it came and went so fast. She only knew it was different, and it only lasted a split second, maybe two. Taylor waited for him to make a comment, but he didn't. She continued. "Anyway, that made me wonder what the other bumpers said about their owners. Then I found the same sticker on the other two cars." She pushed her plate away as she finished her explanation, not bothering to finish her pizza, and then placed her chin on her cupped hands that were braced on the table with her elbows for support.

"So some things do bother you. How about that? After your great heroics on the burglaries in the Quarter that you helped our burglary division solve, it surprises me to see you affected like that by anything. I thought you were tough through and through."

Her gaze locked on him, but she made no comment. Truly, she did not know what to say. He was right. Rarely did things affect her. She was not even sure why this had. Taylor knew she wouldn't be the next victim, but the connection to those women spooked her for some reason . . . maybe just the fact that she could have been one of the victims.

His eyes brightened. "Now that I think about it, I do recall hearing the radio on in two of the three cars when we arrived. I don't recall the first car having its motor running. I'll check that out. It should be in one of the reports; mine or the first officer on the scene. We should have noticed the stickers on all three of the cars, though. I admit the one on the second car is pretty faded, but it's still there."

Taylor felt sorry for the detective. She didn't like hearing him beat himself up about not finding the connection himself. "Well, I'm a trained reporter and I over-looked it, too . . . at first. So obviously they weren't very noticeable." *Cops are human, too,* she thought but didn't dare tell him that.

"We know now, thanks to you. That's what is important." After slipping the pictures into his breast pocket, he finished off the last two slices of pizza. "That tasted pretty good," he admitted. "The spices, the tangy tomato sauce. I haven't had pizza in a long time. Normally, I cook a well-balanced meal and then save portions of the dinners in the freezer for a later date, or I go to a good restaurant near the station on my way

115

home." His eyes glanced around the room. "Not that this place isn't good. Truthfully, I enjoyed it. I'm glad you suggested we meet here for dinner. I mean, for our business discussion."

Her heart skipped a beat. He sounded pleased. She concluded that the blond in the cafeteria at the police station might know him better than Taylor realized. He seemed to have a sweet side after all. Her gaze lifted to his face. His beautiful blue eyes were watching her. She lowered her eyes instantly. Her heart raced. She wasn't sure what caused that. Was it the way he had been looking at her, or the realization that the blond knew him so well? Either way, she frowned.

"Taylor, don't. I like seeing you smile. It makes me think there is something pleasant in this world after all."

Heat rose in her cheeks. He had complimented her again. She had to admit, she liked the feeling it gave her, but then immediately scolded herself for feeling good about it. *Don't get carried away,* she told herself. *This man is apparently taken. Besides, he's had a long day and is probably just too tired to be nasty.* "Well, Lieutenant, do you think those will help you?" She pointed toward the pictures in his pocket, where he had slipped them earlier.

He shrugged. "I don't know, but it gives us a place to start. It's a connection, and that was something we hadn't found yet." He smiled at her. "You might as well call me John. Who knows? Maybe we can be of some help to one another after all." He reached for the check.

Taylor tried to snatch it from him. "I asked you," she pointed out. "Let me pay."

He shook his head. "Not on your life. I'll get it. I think this is the first meal in over a month I actually enjoyed." He raised his brows in a quick motion and added, "Although the food tasted good, I don't — I don't think that was what I enjoyed." He smiled.

She liked the way he had trouble paying accolades, yet she had been given three in a very short time. On that thought she filled her lungs with air as her mind filled with good thoughts.

"I believe it's your happy nature that I like. It makes you enjoyable to be around. I guess you make work not feel so much like . . . work."

"Thanks. It sounded like that was almost hard for you to admit."

John pulled his billfold from his pocket and slipped out some money. "It wasn't that it was hard to say; it's just been awhile since I've relaxed a little and enjoyed myself. Your happy-go-lucky nature makes a person relax. I enjoyed this evening, even though it was business."

That was good. He kept reminding her that this dinner was business and, although he enjoyed it, it was still business. The two never mix, and she knew it. *Yes, keep reminding me that this is work. Keep me straight. Keep me in line.* She smiled to herself. It didn't work. His nice words made her feel all warm inside — and it was his nice words that kept playing over and over in her mind, not the nagging thought in the back of her mind that said he had a girl-friend. *Forget it.*

When Antonio handed John his change, he left a tip on the table. "How about I follow you home to make sure you get there safely?"

She held back a laugh. After all, he was a policeman, and he tended to think the worst of people. "John," she said, trying to call him by his first name. She liked it. Simple. Plain, yet so strong. It fit. "John, I'm a big girl now. I go home by myself all the time. You don't need to trouble yourself."

He helped pull her chair out as she started to rise. "It's no trouble. Where are you parked?"

As they exited the pizza parlor, the warm night air brushed her skin. The humidity had dropped some, and it actually felt pleasant outside. Or was it her company that made things seem a little nicer? "I walked. I live right down the street." She pointed toward her apartment building.

"Then I'll walk you home." He took hold of her elbow and escorted her in the general direction of her place, making their way through the crowds of people roaming the sidewalks in the Quarter. "How long have you lived in the Quarter?"

She smiled at him. It was nice having a man look out for her, even though it was business. "Almost five years — fighting my mom and dad the whole way, I must admit. You would think I was still a kid the way they act. The French Quarter is no place for a single woman . . . alone." She laughed as she mimicked her parents' warnings.

John shrugged. "I've worked the Quarter for a long time, and I have to agree with them. It's the party section for the world. Everyone comes to the Quarter, and a lot goes on here."

"You sound like a cop . . . or a parent. Don't worry, Mr. Officer. I'm a big girl now, and I take real good care of myself." Stop-

119

ping in front of the entrance to her little complex, she asked, "Would you care to come up for some coffee?"

He hesitated only a moment, then said, "Yes. I'd like that."

CHAPTER 10

Did I say yes?

He watched from behind as he followed her into her building and up a double flight of stairs. She seemed strong, a self-reliant type, sure of her moves . . . too sure. She didn't look around as she stepped into the dark area of the entryway or the turn in the stairs. Sure, there were low lights going up the steps so no one should miss their footing, but what about things hidden in the dark corners? Anyone could be standing there, hiding, waiting to attack. Taylor just dashed up the stairs one step at a time as her hand barely caught hold of the railing, paying no attention to anything around her. Maybe it was because she knew a policeman, an officer of the law, was with her.

Then he noticed the hand that hovered above the railing appeared to shake. Was she afraid of something? That surprised him. The woman seemed so self-confident

121

from the instant he'd met her yesterday.

Was it only yesterday?

Opening the door with her key, she led the way into her little apartment. The lights were off in the living room, but the full moon spilled in through the glass sliding doors that looked out upon her balcony. The moonlight supplied plenty of light, but she snapped on the kitchen light as she began to fill a teakettle with water.

"Let's sit on the balcony to enjoy the coffee, if that's okay with you?" she asked as she unlocked and then slid the door open. "The coffee will only take a few minutes. How do you take yours?"

"Black with a teaspoon of sugar," he said, stepping through the open glass doors. Edging near the railing, he gazed out over the courtyard. The villas and apartments in the Quarter hid such beauty. The tourists would be amazed if they saw behind the grungy stoned walls that covered most of the exterior facade. Of course, since Katrina, a lot of the buildings had fresh face-lifts.

Several of the finer hotels had remodeled after the hurricane. Their guests now saw the inside of the courtyards, like Taylor and others who lived full-time in the Quarter. Most visitors who came to the city of New Orleans visited the Quarter but spent their sleep-filled nights in the five-star hotels on and off Canal Street, the area that edged the Quarter. Daytime visitors mostly parked on the edges and walked the streets or rode through on a horse-drawn buggy. Streets were narrow with very little parking. It was a never-ending party in the Quarter with so much foot traffic. The real beauty was behind the walls, in the courtyards of the private homes and apartments. They stayed so beautiful that the city of New Orleans offered a Garden Tour. That was when the probing visitors got to see the flowers in bloom, surrounded by the brick patios with the Spanish-looking decor — a tour worth taking.

In Taylor's courtyard, the stone-covered flooring was lined with large green plants that survived on little to no sunlight. The leaves on some of those plants were huge. They offered great shade to those who sat on the black wrought-iron patio furniture . . . in keeping with the grandeur of the olden days.

John inhaled the fragrance of honeysuckle and gardenias. Raising his eyes toward the heavens, he whispered, "Thank You, Lord."

Taylor joined him on the balcony with two cups of coffee. "I decided to make instant. Quicker that way. I hope you don't mind."

"That's fine," he said, taking the cup offered him. "These apartments seem pretty quiet." *Hopefully they are also safe,* he thought but didn't say.

Taylor laughed. "Quiet? You bet. There are only four apartments and the other three have older retired people living in them. I think their bedtime is before nine. They are all so sweet, and they tend to act as my mother and father sometimes. One is a husband and wife. The other two live alone, having lost their spouses. One is a man, the other a woman. So you see, besides my own parents who smother me, I have two more moms and two more dads. So I'm pretty well looked after. You don't have to worry about me."

"I'm sure they all take good care of you."

"Occasionally, like during Mardi Gras, some have grandchildren who come visit. They get a little rowdy, but not for long." She sipped her coffee. "Oh, I almost forgot, would you like a cookie or two to go with your coffee? Ms. Sadie always bakes, and she never forgets to share with all of us. Now Martha, the married one, still cooks almost every night. She makes sure I get one to two meals a week." Patting her stomach, she said, "I know it shows, but it's a good thing, since I don't cook. First, I don't like to cook. Second, I'm not very good at it. And the most important reason, I never have the time. At least that's what I tell my mom. Chasing the next story always keeps me busy."

As much junk as she liked to eat, it was amazing she wasn't as big as a barn, but apparently she burned off all the calories she took in. "I'll pass on the cookies," he replied. "Still stuffed from the pizza."

"The sweets won't go to waste, I assure you. I'm not the only one who gets fed around here, though. Martha slips Dan, the widower, a meal or two a week also. Sometimes Joe, her husband, gets a little jealous. It's so cute. They're all in their eighties and nineties. Besides, I think Ms. Sadie has her eye out for Dan."

"Life in the fast lane here. You better watch out that you don't get caught up in the love triangle." His laugh boomed out, and she joined in. "You know, if your mom and dad sat out here, they might change their opinion of the place. It's amazing how, even though the streets are crowded, here you feel alone. The peace and serenity is awesome. How easy is it to get into the courtyard from the streets?"

"You can access it from your apartment." She pointed to the steps winding down from the far side of the balcony. "Or as a renter you can use the key, giving you access through the gate hidden behind the stairs. Trust me, the chance of my parents seeing the beauty here is nil, zip, zilch, nada. They never come to the Quarter. Never have and never will. Them be happy for me? That, too, would never happen, 'cause the only way it would is if I'd settle down, marry the perfect man, and become the perfect little homemaker. Hah! Fat chance, and we both know it." She took another sip.

"So you have no plans on taking the big step, aye? Can't say I blame you. With the business you're in, it wouldn't be fair to the man in your life."

"Oh, there's no man —" Her lips closed. "Besides, I'm married . . . to the job."

They sat out for another half hour — sometimes talking, sometimes in compatible silence. John finished his coffee and set the empty cup by hers on the little table that sat between them. He was truly enjoying their time here on her balcony — the quiet, the small talk, and the shared laughter. He found himself surprisingly delighted by her company. No pressure when talking with her . . . so easy.

Slapping his hands to his thighs, he decided he better go before he got to liking his visit too much. He rose. "Well, you're safe at home. I'd best be on my way. I have a lot of work to do in the morning. A lead to follow." He smiled at her as their eyes locked. "Good night, Taylor. And thanks again for your help." He turned to leave.

She followed him into the apartment and passed him to open the door. He stepped out into the hallway and turned back toward the door. He was about to thank her again when she said, "Well, good night, John. I enjoyed dinner and the visit on the balcony." Taylor radiated happiness, and he found himself drinking in her smile, her warmth.

He couldn't tell what she was thinking, but he felt certain she wanted to say something. Her eyes sparkled. If he didn't know himself better, he believed he actually wanted to kiss her good night. Not John. He had no time in his life for a relationship, especially another woman who put herself in harm's way and didn't think anything about it.

The corner of his lips turned up as he thought what her reaction might be if he tried to kiss her. She would probably slap his face. It might be worth the try. Instead, he managed to control his impulses.

John took her hand in his and squeezed but dropped it as quickly as he'd taken it.

No harm in that. "Take care of yourself."

To his surprise, she didn't recoil from his touch. Instead, her smile stayed on her face, even grew a bit larger as she looked at him.

He didn't trust himself, so he swiftly headed down the stairs. When he reached the bottom of the top set, he pivoted and glanced back up at her doorway. She still stood, watching, and gave a slight wave. He trudged down the second set of stairs heading toward the street opening. Out on the sidewalk he strode back toward his car, one block past Dante's Pizza.

John knew leaving was the right thing. He didn't know what had gotten in to him. In the two years since Jennifer's death, John hadn't been interested in any woman, even though plenty had asked him out for the evening. His fiancée had died in the line of duty — a fellow officer, one who had lived for the work, just like he did — like Taylor did. He'd sworn off any woman willing to die for her job. He wasn't able to bear the pain of losing another love. Truth be told, Taylor, although not a policewoman, had a job that could cost her — her life, in fact. That crossed out any possibility between the two of them.

Help me, Lord. Keep my mind on the job and off of this woman.

He didn't need to think about her or yearn for a chance to know her better. It stopped here and now. Stepping next to his Bronco, he climbed in and took off. Mashing the button to lower his window, he let the fresh air blast him. Maybe the wind would blow thoughts of that pretty redhead with the explosive temper and passion for life right out of his mind. He hoped so. It seemed the harder he tried not to think of her, the more she invaded his thoughts, and the clearer the picture of her became in his head.

He had just met her yesterday. How could she consume his thoughts already?

He slammed the palm of his hand down on the steering wheel. "No. I'm not going to think of her. She could mess my life up in a heartbeat," he spat with genuine determination.

Besides, he needed to stay focused on the case.

CHAPTER 11

Tossing and turning all of Saturday night ruined John's sleep. His thoughts drifted to that reporter. *Get out of my head!* He smashed his pillow over his face trying to block the view.

In the past, the minute reporters were out of sight, they were out of mind. That was the way he liked it. John made a habit of talking to all reporters together, giving them the same info. Anything more than that only happened when the captain rode John to make nice with reporters — when the NOPD needed good press. But John didn't like to make nice with reporters. He didn't like telling them anything because reporters sensationalized the news, anything to sell their copy. The updated broadcasts and the newspaper stories made it harder for detectives to do their job. Unfortunately, the captain didn't agree. According to his boss, when the police department played nice with the reporters, reporters worked with the police.

Hmmph. He doubted that. Most reporters were only in it for ratings, either for the television station or for themselves. The sad thing was that they didn't seem to care about the people's lives that were destroyed by the reports they gave as news, along with the images they flashed on the screen. Some were half truths or half-substantiated reports. Whatever worked for the ratings or sold the most newspapers and magazines. John found that, with a lot of reporters, if what they reported wasn't total fact, that was okay. Their follow up story would straighten out the facts, or they would just move on to the next one.

At least that was how John saw it — although he knew he shouldn't put all reporters in one box . . . just like all cops are not the same.

Maybe Taylor Jaymes is different. Who's to say?

One thing he could say for sure: his mind refused to stop thinking about her — or the fact that *she* found the connection, not the NOPD.

Was it luck? Or was she good at what she did? Was it her investigative skills that kept her face coming into view when he closed his eyes?

It had to be. Her abilities impressed him.

Enough about her! He tossed his pillow to the side and then punched it. *Enough!*

He needed to get his mind back on the case and do his job.

There was nothing he could do tonight but try and get a good night's sleep, if it would come. After church tomorrow, he would slip by the radio station that the bumper sticker represented. Do a little background check on their employees and ex-employees. He hoped to find someone with a record or one who was fired and now had an axe to grind with the station. But instead of taking it out on the station, they were attacking the listeners. His thought process seemed far-fetched, but people reacted in strange ways.

Turning over one more time, he thought about the bars. According to Taylor, she had already started identifying the bars in the area and planned to start asking questions tomorrow night when they opened for business. She was right about them being a good lead to follow. John would start by checking out the station and their employee history. That was first on his list. Later, he and his men would hit the bars. It was their off day, but surely they would come in for a couple of hours to help him out. Police work called for that at times. Money was tight, but the job had to come first — getting the criminal off the street. They would see if anyone remembered any of the victims . . . maybe all three. They could have been regulars at one establishment, for all he knew. That would narrow down the search some.

Fat chance. He could only dream.

The French Quarter was a hodgepodge of bars, mostly jazz, as well as souvenir shops, strip clubs, and sex shows, unfortunately. And the partying never closed down in the Quarter or the bars. They stayed open until the last customer left. The activity alone kept their station working 24-7, with rotating shifts that never stopped. But as much as he hated most of the atmosphere in the Quarter, he felt that was where he was supposed to be. Now he needed some shut-eye so he could get up in the morning, refreshed and ready for the day.

Lord, I don't know what's going on in my mind or why her image keeps manifesting itself in my brain, but help me. Help me forget her and get some rest.

John knew he wasn't ready for a relationship of any kind, whether girlfriend or just a good friend. After Jennifer's death, John decided with the kind of work he did, he was better off staying single. He couldn't see putting anyone through the pain he went through with the loss of his fiancée. And if that was the case, why bother to date at all? That way of life he'd put behind him when he gave his heart to Jesus. Now he needed to keep those things behind him.

Sleep . . . help me sleep. He must have rolled around, unsettled in bed, for another half hour before finally managing to doze off.

The next thing he knew, his alarm was buzzing. Hitting the snooze button to silence it, he said a quick prayer of thanksgiving for not having another killing in the night.

Still dressed in gym shorts and a T-shirt, after the coffee dripped its last drop, he stepped out on his front porch and grabbed his newspaper. At the table John laid open the paper and started scanning the articles. After a few minutes of scanning the headlines, he released a pent-up breath. "Great, nothing about the connection. Looks like Taylor kept her word."

He poured a cup of the hot, dark brew and sat at the table again. This time he did some serious reading of the news, local and national. Time passed quickly. By the time he'd finished his second cup of coffee, it was time to get ready for church. He rinsed his cup out, placed it in the sink, and then went off to shower, shave, and change for the service that morning.

With fifteen minutes to spare, he parked his Bronco in the lot and strode toward the church doors.

"Morning, John," said the usher as they shook hands. "How are things?"

Smiling, John said, "It could be better, Timothy, but, as He tells us not to worry about tomorrow and let Him guide us through the day, that's what I have to do."

"We're thankful for men like you in this city. New Orleans is not all bad. Even in the midst of the evil here, we need a sliver of light running through so we know there is still hope for us all. You're that light, John, in the Quarter. Keep up the good work."

John thanked him. As he entered the church, he found a seat near the back. He never sat in the front — not that he didn't want to, but he never knew when his beeper would vibrate, and John needed to be where he could leave without distracting from the message.

God had anointed Pastor Larry Stanford. It showed in his actions, his life, and his messages. The church grew and grew as it reached out to the community all around it and beyond. Like the Word says, "I'll know you by your fruit." Pastor Larry's fruit was plentiful.

The message was uplifting, as usual. It helped John find strength in the Lord and comforted him with the knowledge that he would find this killer. He only had to keep looking, keep pounding the pavement, and God would lead him. John only hoped it would be before someone else lost her life. But only God knew, and all John could do was obey.

Later, down at the station, he sat at his desk. He laid the three pictures Taylor had given him out in front of him on his desk. With his fingertips, he moved his mouse, stirring his computer to action. While he waited for it to warm up so he could log on, he scanned the pictures. Instinctively, he picked up a pen and jotted notes of all he wanted to find on his computer: the country bars in and outside the Quarter within a ten-mile radius of the killings, the name of the owner of the radio station, and if any arrests listed employment at WKRN. Afterward he'd head to the radio station to see what else he could find. On Sunday he doubted someone in charge would be working, but with the right words, he should get some action. This was something he felt he couldn't delay.

In the silence of the office, John heard the *clickity-clack* as he tapped away on his keyboard. When he finished his lists, he printed a copy of each, clipped them in place inside a folder, and logged off.

First stop for him was the radio station, WKRN, the one that had been displayed on each of the victims' cars. When he arrived at the station, only one car was in the parking lot . . . probably because it was Sunday. It was what he had expected.

John entered the lobby, and the light above the inside door flashed *On the air.* He pushed the button on the side of the door and sat down. Hopefully someone would realize he was out there. He'd give them five minutes, ten tops, and then would find his own way back to the DJ on duty.

Waiting wasn't easy, especially with nothing to do. He took out his notepad and glanced over the notes he'd made at each of the crime scenes, as well as notes he had made from the ME's preliminary report at the scene. Probable COD, strangulation: petechial hemorrhaging and hemorrhaging over the back of the larynx and soft tissue over the cervical spine, along with ligature marks around the neck. Also noted were fingernail scrapings, but instead of being

DNA from the perpetrator, the skin was from the victim. Each girl scratched her own neck trying to remove the rope, fighting for air to stay alive. Yet, in failing to do so, their hands fell back down on their purse, as if digging through it.

Suddenly, the door opened and a man, in radio-melodic tone, said, "Hi. Can I help you?"

John closed his pad and stuffed it in his top pocket. In the same move, he grabbed his ID and flashed it along with his badge, saying, "NOPD Detective Bradley. I have some questions I need answers to. Can you help me?"

The man's eyes grew wide as he opened the door wider. "We'll see. You'll have to come back here with me. I have to go back on the air in thirty seconds. I'm by myself for the moment. We can talk during songs. I'll put on a double play."

The detective followed him through the door to an isolated booth the size of a small office. The DJ closed the doors behind John and sat back down. He put his headphones back on, held up his hand is if to say, "One minute," and then flipped a few switches.

Suddenly that melodic voice rang out again, telling his listeners they were in for a treat. Back-to-back Alan Jackson. The man flipped a couple more switches and then removed his headset. "Now, what do you need?"

"I need to know if anyone has been fired in the past two months or if any of your listeners have filed any grievances against your station or any of your DJs."

The man's eyes widened as he sat back in his chair. "That I'm not sure I can give to you, even if I knew it. It would only be scuttlebutt, gossip, coming from me. I just work here and listen to the talk around the station. The head honcho, Monica Williams, will be here tomorrow morning. You can ask her. She can give you all the facts our legal department will let her give."

"I need you to get Mac David, the owner, or Ms. Williams on the phone. This is a police emergency, and I need these answers now. It can't wait until tomorrow. Sorry."

The DJ nodded and picked up his phone. "Monica, darling, you need to get down to the station now. We have a policeman —" he turned toward the detective and asked, "Who are you again?"

"Detective John Bradley with NOPD homicide."

"Yeah, Sweet Cakes, it's Detective John Bradley with the New Orleans Police Department. He said he's with homicide, and he needs some answers now. It can't wait until tomorrow."

"I was told to call you or Mr. David. Do you want me to call him? I will."

John watched the man as his face gave away his enjoyment of hearing probably confusion and outrage from his superior.

"Sorry, Babe, you're the man in charge. Oops. Excuse me. Woman in charge. So you've got to come down here and help the detective, or I call Mac." His dissatisfaction for her being the boss spoke volumes in John's mind. When the DJ cradled the phone, he pointed toward the detective. "You can wait back out there in the lobby. She'll be here, she said, in fifteen minutes. But I'd count it as thirty."

John rose and was about to thank him, but the man focused back on his duties as if John was already gone. The DJ covered his ears once more with the apparatus he used to communicate with the city of New Orleans. Two quick flips on the soundboard and he was talking again in that melodic tone. John shut both doors behind him quietly and made his way back out into the lobby.

He flipped open his pad, but this time to a blank piece of paper and started jotting questions he had for the woman — Monica

Williams, manager of the station. He listed a few questions on the blank paper and then left room for her answers. Flipping back to his notes on the homicides, he started with the first crime scene notes and scanned them to see if he had noted if the radio had been on in the car. He couldn't find anything on the first or the second, but he had noted it on the third. There he had Johnson cut off the radio. Of course, he wasn't first on the scene to any of these crimes. He'd have to check with each officer who had been first on the scene the other two nights. Each, John remembered, had stated in their report they had been driving slowly through the Quarter and around the exterior watching for anything out of the ordinary. According to procedure, both would have noted whether they had turned off the engine or the radio upon their arrival. Had the same man found all three, it probably would have clicked as something of importance. But to three different officers, this wouldn't have seemed important.

Taking a deep breath, he slowed his mind down. John didn't want to get his hopes up too high, but it was the first possible connection that had been found. If this wasn't the connection, where would he turn next? He hoped the sticker meant something significant.

As he was about to look at the pictures on the walls, the outer door opened and in walked a woman clad in tight jeans and a slinky top hanging off of one shoulder. She smacked her gum as she extended long fingers with freshly polished nails, much longer than the norm. They had to be fake. She could kill someone with her fingernails alone.

John rose to his feet and grabbed her extended hand. "Mrs. Williams."

"It's Miss." She led him to her office. "Have a seat, Detective, and tell me what you need."

John took the seat she offered and flipped his pad to the questions he had listed for her. Within half an hour they were through, and he was leaving out the door when she asked, "Do you think one of these people I gave you have something to do with these killings we've had lately?"

"We're just following leads, Miss Williams. I can't tell you any more than that. Thanks for your cooperation."

He had his list of bars. Should he try to cover as many as possible right now, or wait and start fresh on these tomorrow with Brown and Johnson? John checked a few bars out on his own, but to no avail. Giving up for the night, he headed home. As tired as he was now, tonight he would make up for some of the sleep he had lost last night . . . maybe not.

CHAPTER 12

Monday arrived, and John woke before the alarm. At least he'd slept all night this time.

When the coffee finished dripping, he poured himself a cup and strode out onto the front porch. Letting the screen door fall back into place, he slipped over to the porch swing. Lowering his six-foot frame down onto one side of the swing, he relaxed, a cup in one hand and the other resting across the back of the swing. Gently he pushed the swing into a slow, easy rhythm. Taking a sip of the dark brew, he scanned his surroundings, enjoying the light breeze.

A sigh escaped. His neighborhood didn't have the same calming effect that Taylor's terrace projected, but he felt that sense of peace at the moment. It was only because it was still early in the morning. In the next thirty minutes, traffic would grow.

It hadn't started flowing freely yet as he sipped his coffee, so he leaned back in his seat and kept the motion of the swing going with his foot. John had a big day ahead of him. With no luck last night, he prayed today would give him insight into which way to go next.

Trying not to think about work just yet, John noted the thick green lawn that spread everywhere except around the massive roots of an old oak tree. The yard was plain and simple. He had kept it that way on purpose. With his job, he had no time to prune flowerbeds or trim bushes. His yard had one nice shade tree that seemed to reach to the top of the sky. Acorns dropped in masses into the yard. Squirrels gathered their meals and chased one another across the lawn. Watching animals in their natural habitat always brought peace to his soul.

At the corner of his lot stood a black wrought-iron lamp-post with three large round bulbs. These lights illuminated his yard from dusk until dawn. When he had the time, he sat out at night as well. Lately, that free time had eluded him.

Glancing at his home, the peaceful yard, and then the empty spot next to him on the swing, he wondered if maybe he was ready to fill that emptiness in his home, as well as in his heart. He'd thought this two years ago, when he had proposed to Jennifer, but her death caused him to slip back into his old way of thinking: single was the only way for a detective to live his life. But, again, John was tired of coffee for one and coming home to an empty house at night. Should he stay open to finding that one special woman and falling in love — a special someone to fill his free time up with love?

"She's the one."

John looked around. Where did that come from? *Are You talking to me, God? Or is that me fantasizing? Could Taylor be that person?* Could he marry a woman who lived her life in such danger? She lived a life with screwy hours, just like his. Maybe they could coexist and build something special. He knew he was drawn to her looks. He had to admit it even though he didn't want to.

He moaned. Who was he kidding? "God, if that was You, I think You need to rethink Your words."

This case, like others, stole all his free time. John needed to concentrate on that, not on a woman. He needed to find the killer and find him now, for the city's sake as well as his own.

By six he was drinking his second cup of coffee, and the noise level grew, as did the traffic. The turmoil made it hard to stay outside. With the peace gone, the pleasure disappeared as well. Time didn't allow him hanging around outside any longer anyway. Taking that last swig of the black brew, he rose and headed back inside.

Through the windows spilled the first rays of morning light, reflecting on his highly polished wood floor. The bright shine was thanks to his wonderful housekeeper, Mrs. Evelyn Brumfield. She said she kept a bright polish on his floor and furnishings because he left her so very little to do. When she came over biweekly, she wanted to earn her pay. Otherwise, Evelyn felt she was stealing his money with what little work she had to do to keep the place looking good.

He liked his housekeeper. Evelyn was a widow raising her two grandchildren on her own. John never heard the woman complain. Janie, Mrs. Brumfield's daughter, had run off with some guy who came down one Mardi Gras and never came back for her daughter and son. It broke the seven-year-old twins' little hearts, which broke Mrs. Brumfield's. So the woman simply loved them more than enough to heal their wounds of abandonment — first by their birth father, then their mother — and raised them as her own.

The house grew brighter as the sun rose to peek through the windows. John didn't

147

like dark, closed-in spaces, so he kept no draperies or blinds over his windows, except in the bedroom. Sometimes he had to sleep in the daytime and needed complete darkness to fall asleep. On the outside of all his windows, black bars protected his home from unwanted entries, but neither the sun nor moonlight was blocked from entering freely into his home. Some windows had custom stained glass in muted colors while other panes were beveled glass. He liked the openness, yet the privacy they allowed.

Pouring another cup of coffee, he started getting ready for work. In less than half an hour he was backing his car out of the garage. His quiet corner, Bienville Street and St. Patrick, was no longer quiet.

John arrived at the office and turned on his computer. While waiting for the slow connection, he pulled out his hard files from the filing cabinet on the new murder, as well as the two previous murders, and stacked them on his desk. When his system was ready, he clicked open the large new file on his computer where he had stored all three of these killings yesterday afternoon. Today he would get the coroner's report on the latest victim. Then it should be confirmed, as he'd thought after the second, that there was a serial killer in New Orleans taking his anger and bitterness out on unsuspecting, undeserving females.

Making extra copies of the list of country bars he didn't get to yesterday, as well as the information given to him by the radio station, he laid them next to the files on his desk as he waited for his detectives, Buford Johnson and Leon Brown, to come in this morning. Around the station they referred to Buford as "Buck."

Both were usually in by 6:30, so John made a fresh pot of coffee in the large office next door where his men and a few other detectives shared the bullpen. As he fixed himself his fourth cup — but who was counting? — his men strolled into the room, heading straight for the coffee. Leon carried a box of doughnuts that he placed on the table next to the pot of coffee.

"Morning, gentlemen. I have some new info we'll talk over while you eat your breakfast." The doughnuts were a ritual that the two had followed for as long as John could remember. They took turns bringing in the doughnuts, but that was what they ate every morning. It was a good thing they both burned up the calories they took in by going to the academy gym three times a week, when work permitted.

"Chief, did you get another lead? Someone called something in?" Buck poured himself a cup.

John smiled a half smile. "Better than that. We may have a connection between all three victims. Get your coffee and come to my office."

Opening the three folders he had stacked on top of each other, John laid them out with the pictures of the cars on top. Buck and Leon marched in, each carrying a cup in one hand and a doughnut in the other. Both plopped into the empty chairs set in front of John's desk.

"Whatcha got?" Buck asked.

"Without getting any sticky sugar on the pictures, check them out. See if you notice anything."

Instead of handling the pictures themselves, both sat up in their chairs and leaned forward to scan the pictures. Leon took another bite of his doughnut as he sat back, shaking his head. "Sir, we've looked at these before. I still don't see anything."

Buck wiped his fingers and then set his cup down, as well as his doughnut and napkin. Picking up two of the pictures and looking at the third shot still lying on top of the file, he said, "None of them seem to mind messing up their car bumpers with stickers. That's something I won't allow my wife or kids to do."

John slapped his desk as he said, "That's it."

"What? They junk up their cars — that's their connection?" Brown asked with a smirk. "And just where does that lead us? Put out an APB on all junky yards and messy houses?"

"Stow it. That's not it." John lifted a brow. "Well, it is and it isn't. Buck, you were close. I didn't see it at all. It was that reporter, Taylor Jaymes, who noticed the connection."

"That looker with the red hair?" the detective asked as he laid the pictures down. Buck snatched up his doughnut and took another bite.

John ignored Buck's comment. "They all had bumper stickers advertising one particular country radio station. WKRN."

"And that's the connection?" Brown eyed the lieutenant and then Buck.

"Yes, it is. I followed up on WKRN and paid them a visit yesterday. Found out one of their employees was terminated just over two weeks ago . . . about the time of the first murder."

That got their attention.

"We need to take a closer look at Michael Guidry. WKRN's manager fired him with good cause, right before the killings started. It seems this man has a temper and started a couple of fights at the station with his coworkers." Holding his hands up as if in surrender, he said, "I know it's a stretch, battery to murder, and to think he'd be kill-ing women who listened to the station just because he got fired . . . but people have killed for less."

"That makes sense, sir. Did you get an address on the guy?"

"Yes, I did. We're going to pay him a visit. I also made a list of bars to check out. I printed some copies of the victims' photos for each of us. Today, I need us to pay each bar a visit with the pictures and see if anyone recognizes the faces, and if so, find out when the last time was that they were seen at the establishment. Maybe we'll get lucky. The main thing is, we now have a connection."

"So your theory of it being a serial killer is correct," Detective Brown stated, almost in a question form.

"Yes. We should get —"

The buzzing of his phone interrupted him. "Bradley," John said as he answered his phone. He heard the ME in his ear.

"I've got that completed report for you . . . well, some of the test results we are still waiting on, but you know what I mean. You want me to e-mail a copy to you?"

"Yes, please. If you could send it now, I'd appreciate it. We were just talking about it. Did everything match the other two?"

Silence hung for less than a minute. "Unfortunately, they did."

"Okay. Thanks. I'll be watching for your report."

"Was that Bob Jenkins?" Buck asked. "What timing! Almost like the ME has a bug in your office, Chief. Better look out."

Brown flicked his brows up and down and then glanced into each corner of the office as he clowned around. "Hidden microphones or cameras. Big brother is watching."

Comic relief. All stations needed it, and Brown was theirs. He kept the mood light around the station, but sometimes John didn't care for it, especially when they were working a string of cases.

"Yeah. Let me read his report before we talk further. Here's the info on Michael Guidry. You two go talk to him. See where he was on the nights in question and get a feel for his attitude toward the station."

"I listen to that station myself, Chief. I even remember 'The Crazy Cowboy Mikey,' as they called him on late-night air at

WKRN. That was probably why he got fired. Being on so late at night, he thought no one cared how he talked. He got pretty wild and ugly sometimes with his callers." Detective Brown shook his head.

"That's what I was told, and it caused a few heated arguments between him and his relief. Go check him out, and call me when you finish up the interview. If you don't feel the need to pull him down to the station, we'll divide up the list of bars, and I'll help check them out."

"We're on it, Chief," Brown said with enthusiasm. "Come on, Buck."

As soon as the two left, John called his captain to let him know, as promised, what he'd gathered over the weekend. He knew the captain already knew about the third killing, so he was prepared for some more yelling. The good news was, when John gave him the leads they were following, the captain stayed somewhat calm as he said, "Sounds like we're finally making some progress."

Glad to get that behind him, John hung up the phone. Now he could move forward, to the other things at hand. Instead, he thought of Taylor. Heading for his filing cabinet, he muttered, "This is ridiculous."

Pulling out a drawer, he flipped through

the folders, found the one he was looking for, then yanked it out. He thought if he put his mind on another case while he waited for his guys to call, surely he would quit thinking about that nerve-racking redhead. The file he pulled was on robberies in the homes near Jackson Square. She wasn't the reporter involved in writing stories on that case as far as he remembered; that should make a difference. Maybe he could stay focused on the job instead of her. After flipping through the hard copy file, he turned to his computer and searched to see if similar robberies had been reported elsewhere in the city. Maybe these guys weren't just robbing in the Quarter.

Slouching down in his chair, he scrolled through the file one page at a time. Studying the list of items that had been stolen and the way the perpetrator entered each apartment, he thought he might get a clue as to who the perpetrator was. He might figure out if it was a gang of kids or a known burglar with a past history. Sometimes there was a rhyme and a reason that could link these things together or at least lead him in the right direction. They were already watching known markets for these type of stolen goods — electronics, jewelry, and paintings.

But these thieves hadn't taken flat screen TVs, DVD players, or stereo systems — harder-to-trace items for the police department. They could be sold on the streets to individuals or behind the scenes at outlets of used furniture and electronics.

The items stolen were insured by the owners but not by the same agency. John had pictures of most of the items and copies were in the computer file. An active link continued searching, should a similar piece come up for sale on a resale website. Those places were a wonderful way to unload your own items, but little did criminals realize the police department was linked in 24-7 and would be instantly notified, should a stolen piece of merchandise pop up for sale. The thieves would be apprehended within six to twelve hours of the attempt of the sale. The high-end items that were stolen were probably sold through a major fence that handled expensive jewels and pricey paintings. The burglars knew what they were taking.

As he scanned the various pictures of the jewelry that had been downloaded into the computer file, he came to a pair of ruby red earrings that sparkled with brilliance. The brilliance of the red manifested a flash of a long ivory neck supporting a mass of curly red hair twisted up and piled on a head as those dangling red earrings hung from the delicate lobes of none other than Taylor Jaymes' ears.

With more power than was needed, he clicked the arrow and moved on to the next item. It displayed a delicate necklace made of pearls and diamonds. The ivory of the pearls reflected the ivory of her skin in his mind's eye. "Enough!"

He clicked his computer off and rose. As he started pacing back and forth and then around his desk, over to the door, and back to his desk again, frustration taunted every muscle, every nerve fiber. How could she dominate his thoughts like that? He wobbled his head, trying to shove out thoughts of her. "Ooh," he muttered and then followed the same path on the floor again. Finally he gave in to his impulse.

Snatching up the phone, he glanced at her business card on his desk and punched out the number. The receptionist patched his call through to Taylor's desk. He heard the phone ring over and over again. No answer.

"Ugh," he groaned, slamming down the phone. *She's probably out somewhere stirring up trouble, digging up information for her story.*

No sooner had he replaced the receiver in

the cradle than his phone started ringing. Ripping the receiver off the base, he barked, "Hello!"

"Yikes. I hope I have the wrong number," a sweet voice said tenderly. A light chuckle followed her words.

He smiled as he recognized the warm voice, full of laughter. "Always the comedian. What's that old saying? A million comedians out of work and . . . I forget the rest. But you get the message." His voice softened somewhat. "You're not funny."

He heard a soft giggle in his ear and then she said, "You're not as tough as you think or pretend to be, are you, Detective Bradley?"

John's smile fell. "I thought you were going to call me John?" He leaned back in his chair, picked up a pencil, and then twirled it in his fingers. Unfortunately nothing came to mind to say, but he found pleasure in not saying a word, just hanging on the line, knowing she was on the other end.

Yes. This is what I need.

For some unexplainable reason, this girl made him feel relaxed — when she wasn't in the same room with him getting into his business of crime. Friday night, hearing her voice across the table, had done this to him and again now. Somehow, some way, she

158

made him feel a sense of joy. John couldn't explain it. He didn't care to even try to figure it out. It just was.

CHAPTER 13

Taylor laid back in her recliner as she listened to him talk. She traced her cheek as she thought of the possibility of his touch on her face.

He asked her if she had forgotten he asked her to call him John.

No. Of course not.

"I figured it was the pizza that turned your head or the excitement of the moment — you know, me finding the connection. I didn't want to chance getting chewed out for 'insubordination,' or whatever it's called." Her smile broadened as a spurt of laughter filtered through the line.

All right, he does have a sense of humor. She liked what she heard.

"Trust me. I don't say anything I don't mean."

Trust him? Of course she trusted policemen in general and the brotherhood, as well as firemen and other men of authority who risked their lives daily for the people, but him? Just his voice made her think irrationally. How could she trust him? Or was it herself she couldn't trust?

Taylor sighed but covered the mouthpiece so he wouldn't hear her. She'd have to think on that. She trusted what he stood for, but as far as the way he made her feel, she wasn't too sure. "I'll try to remember that. If you say it, you mean it. Okay. Now, for the reason I called. I was checking to see if you were doing anything with what I told you?"

The soft, friendly voice disappeared, and a hardened, clipped tone shot through the line. "Of course. That's what the city pays me to do."

She heard the tension in his voice along with the words he spat, but she couldn't complain. Taylor was the one who brought up business. "Yikes! I did it again, didn't I? I know how to push your buttons. I hope you know I don't do it on purpose."

He cleared his throat. "Sorry. I spent most of Sunday following up on the lead you gave me. Today is no exception. My men are following up on something I found yesterday, and then the three of us will be questioning some other leads . . . thanks to your insightfulness."

"I see."

"By the way, that was good detective work on your part. We hope after today to be able to narrow the bars down to one or two in the ten-mile radius of where the bodies were found. At least now we're moving forward again."

"That's good. I was going to tell you I spoke to Trudy's neighbor, Sally, and she said Trudy went out every weekend. Come Monday, she would tell both her and her daughter about some of the people she'd met and the good times she was having. By the way Trudy described it to Sally, she felt certain it was a bar or a lounge with a nice-size dance floor. Trudy talked about dancing and having fun, but Sally couldn't be positive as to which one it was. Trudy had mentioned the name in passing, but her neighbor couldn't recall it. She's supposed to check with her teenage daughter and see if she remembered where Trudy went clubbing, but I haven't heard back from her yet."

Taylor decided to keep it to herself that she had gone to the radio station Sunday afternoon. She had dropped by the station on the chance he may be there so she could update him on what she found out about Trudy's activities. He was leaving, so instead she followed him.

This morning she went back to the radio station to see what the DJ would tell her. Unfortunately, she didn't get very far, but the DJ did say a detective had been there the day before and talked to the manager. He also hinted he might be willing to talk if she would go have a drink with him after work. Flicking her brows at him, she implied she might get back in touch. Of course, she knew John had been there, so she made no commitment of joining the man later for drinks. She'd get her info from the detective, if she played her cards right. If not, then she'd contact the DJ. Taylor could keep it business, no matter what that DJ thought he'd get out of it. She knew better.

"That's good," John said. "If you ever decide to give up your writing career, you'd make a good detective. That'll help us today as we go around to the various bars in the area. Yesterday I met with WKRN's manager and got the name of a person of interest. So that bumper-sticker connection has given us two leads to follow, in separate directions. We'll see what we find."

She paused. His compliment touched her deeply. She didn't believe he was one to dole out compliments too freely. "Thank you. I'll keep that job offer in mind, but remember, to be a good journalist, you have to be a good investigator, so I'm probably where I need to be. I don't think I could carry a gun." In her line of work, she probably should learn how to shoot one, protect herself, but that wasn't on her to-do list. "While we're talking about the case, have you thought any more on what I asked you?"

He didn't hesitate to respond, so apparently he had. "You're hoping I changed my mind. I know. I hear it in your voice. You want the exclusive and all the details on the investigation."

At that moment, she thought she heard a hard snap across the line. Was he chewing gum? Or had something broken? Maybe he broke a pencil, wishing it was her neck. *Eeek!* She probably should back off and wait on him, but she wanted this story so desperately. She needed this story.

"Ah, come on, Detec . . . John." She softened her voice as she called him by name. "Give a girl a chance," she pleaded, trying to keep the conversation on a more personal level, hoping it would keep the lines of communication between the two of them open.

John tossed the broken pencil in the garbage as he shook his head. When he called her, he had planned to give her the exclusive. So why hold back now? Shaking his head, he knew. He had changed his mind when she didn't answer his call. The lieutenant figured she was off somewhere getting into trouble, trying to get too close to his crime.

He sighed. That wasn't fair on his part to change his mind so easily. She'd earned the story. If they broke the case soon, it would be thanks to her. They'd had no leads until she discovered one. She found the connection; she deserved the story. Besides which, if he made the deal with her, he could control her words to the press. That was a plus. He would make it part of the agreement. The positives and negatives of allowing her into his investigations bounced through his head. Should he give her the exclusive, or not? Could he handle being around her so much . . . or at least talking to her on a daily basis? Could he keep a distance between them? She played havoc on his emotions, but he shouldn't make his decision based on his reaction to her. He needed to do what was best for the case.

"John, are you still there?" a sweet voice murmured into his ear.

"Actually, I've been giving it some thought. In fact, I called your office a short time ago, but you weren't there." He knew it was the right thing to do, and he urged himself forward. He would survive the daily contact. He would make sure to keep an emotional distance between them. The main thing was, this way, giving her the exclusive, he controlled what leaked to the public. For now, he needed her to keep the discovery of the connection under wraps. She found it. It was hers to disclose if she so chose, but if he agreed to give her the exclusive on the full investigation through to the final arrest, he could make her silence part of the stipulation . . . make her hold off on releasing the connection at this time.

"You called me?"

He was about to tell her the news, but her question distracted him. Her voice literally purred. Maybe it was her tone that caught him off guard.

A light laugh sifted through the line. "I'm at home. That's the beauty of being a journalist. Sometimes you're working out of your home office. It's not a nine-to-five job. Of course, sometimes it's twenty-hour days."

"Sounds like you're lucky. And yes, I'd called you. I called to tell you I'm going to give you the exclusive. By that, I mean anything major we discover, I will let you know, but you have to keep those things I share only with you under wraps until the end . . . until I say you can print the whole story. Sometimes it's those little things that help us pull everything together, and we don't want to give the killer a heads-up."

He exhaled. "And anything else you come up with, you share with us as you did earlier. But it also means when we close in on the killer, you'll be given advance warning, if possible, so you can scoop the others as well as have more details from the investigation that you can reveal in your story. For the time being, I have to ask you not to write about the connection. It might signal our perp that we're getting close and make him do something crazy."

"No problem. I promise. Thanks."

"Great. Well, I'll let you go, and I will be in touch."

Taylor sighed. As she hung up the phone, she whispered, "He'll be in touch. I wonder . . ." She closed her eyes and remembered her earlier thoughts, wondering what it would feel like to have him brush her cheek with his fingertips. Warmth spread across her face. His brilliant blue eyes came to mind . . . and the dark waves that crowned his head. Her fingers itched to feel their softness. Taylor remembered the way he had reached out and almost touched her face Saturday night, but then thought better of it.

A man in control of his emotions. Too bad.

He may not have followed through on his desires, but she saw the look in his eyes, the wanting. At that moment, she knew he'd thought about her as a woman, not a reporter.

She wished she'd said something that night and gotten him to stay awhile longer, but she hadn't. Taylor had been mesmerized into silence by that man. She laughed. What was that called? An oxymoron. Complete opposites — Taylor and silence. Taylor was never known for her silence, except when she was slipping around in the dark trying to get closer to a crime going down . . . anything to get her story.

Suddenly she opened her eyes. She was going to be working with him. That thought stirred her sanity.

Surveying her living room, she decided maybe she should pick up while she had a few minutes. Her place wasn't dirty; it just wasn't neat. Maybe she should take the time now to return her mom's call. Taylor never called her mom or Tina back — not the calls they left at work for her or the ones they left on her home answering machine. Instantly, she recalled the stranger's message

168

at work — and then again on her home phone. There was no reason stated as to why any of them called, so what were they up to? She was assuming the three calls were connected. As busy as Taylor had been, she didn't take time to call any of them back. What were they up to? And who was that man? How did he get her home number? A fix-up? It must be, but she hoped not.

That man could have had a lead for her — but that call should have gone only to the paper . . . not her house phone. Could it have been so important that the paper gave away her home number? No. It had to be her family who passed it out freely, with hopes of finding her the "perfect man."

Glancing at her watch, she jumped out of her chair. *No time for my family now or that man. I'll call later. I need to get to the office and update the boss. What a story! Mr. Cox will be so pleased.*

By ten thirty she was in Mr. Cox's office. "He committed the story to me, Chief! I think it was because I found the connection for the victims . . . but a girl's gotta do what a girl's gotta do. The detective even went as far to say it might be the break they'd been looking for."

Mr. Cox leaned back in his massive chair, lifting his feet to rest on the edge of the

169

desk. Pressing his fingertips together across his stomach, he said, "I knew you could do it. I had no doubts."

Taylor talked with him a little longer, explaining the connection and about the promise not to release anything yet. That was the only way, she said, that Detective Bradley would agree to give her the scoop on the story, all the little details he wouldn't be giving to the other reporters.

"I guess I'll extend that week I promised you. As long as you stay on top of it and I can spare you. Of course, you still have to submit something daily for the paper on the killings. We're not going to fall behind. There will be something you can tell the public. So do me proud."

"You got it, Chief."

Taylor left his office full of anticipation for the week ahead.

CHAPTER 14

She returned to her desk to find another note from that same man, Tim Robertson. This time he left his name but still didn't say what the call was about. Who was he, and what did he want? Calling her through the paper again, maybe it was about a story. But why did he call her home phone, and where did he get her number?

Picking up her phone she punched in the numbers scribbled after his name. *Beep, beep, beep* rang in her ear. *A busy signal.* "Oh well, Mr. Robertson, I can't keep trying now. I'll check you later," she said aloud. She hung up, disconnecting the call.

Instead of waiting around to hear what Detective Bradley and his men turned up, she spent the rest of the day doing a little detective work of her own. *Oh yeah, John, not Detective Bradley,* she reminded herself. That she had to work on. John's face leaped into her brain. He was good-looking — and smart. She had to give him credit for being a great detective, too. She'd looked up his record on the force. Before now, only two unsolved cases. Who could blame him on one of them? All the evidence burned up in the fire. He cleared his cases by not giving up. If he had any unsolved cases, he held on to the files and kept returning to them in between working on other new cases, and he did it until he closed the cases. The man was relentless.

Back to the business at hand. Who knows? Maybe I'll find another link to the present case he has pending. John would like that, and so would I.

Stopping at the first country bar that was about ten miles out from the scene, but not in the Quarter, she found the cleaning crew getting the club ready for another night of business. Those guys weren't there working at night, so they would be of no help to her. She needed the bartender or a couple of waitresses to take a peek at the pictures of the vics. They'd be the only ones who might identify them for Taylor. She'd have to come back later to this one.

Next stop, she found a country bar where the band was doing a little rehearsing. They might remember one of them. Taylor sashayed over to the band with a picture of each of the girls. She managed to recover other shots of each of the victims through the paper, looking through their archives. Each girl had been involved with something in the past four years: a wedding, a wake, and a political affair. She found one for each girl. Unfortunately not all pictures were current, but she managed to zoom in on the girls in each photo and make a small replica of all three. The drummer recognized Trudy immediately.

"Yeah, I remember her. She used to come in here every weekend. I remember, because she used to flirt with me. I kind of liked it, but I have a wife at home so I couldn't follow through. Well, I could," he said and then shrugged, "but I wouldn't. So it became just light talk, but still friendly. Then, about six months ago, she quit coming in. I figured she got her a guy or found another bar she liked better."

"So when you let her know there was no possible way you'd be more than a friend, did you notice her hanging out with any other particular guy?"

"Trudy was friendly with everybody, but not in the way you're talking about."

She thanked him for his time and his candor. When Taylor left, she drove around some more and found three more bars in the vicinity of where the bodies had been discovered. After checking each out, she decided she'd have better luck at night, so she turned her car in the direction of Trudy Walker's. She figured it was late enough for Sarah's daughter to be home. Maybe she could help pinpoint the bar Trudy went to toward the end of her life. That was what they needed to find. She knew that there they would find what they needed to get a handle on the killer — their next lead at the least.

Sarah opened the front door wide and called out behind her, "Annie, that reporter I told you about is here." Turning toward Taylor, she said, "Please come in."

Taylor stepped inside and waited. There was no need to take a seat. "This should only take a few minutes."

Suddenly, rushing into the front room was a cute little blond, a younger version of her mom. She came to an abrupt halt once inside the doorway. Her cheeks blushed as she looked down and said, "Hi. Momma said I might be able to help you find Trudy's killer."

"Well, by telling me this, we might be able to help the police find the killer. I appreciate your help. Do you recall the name of the club Trudy went to in the last few weeks of her life?"

"She used to go to Mudbugs and Mustang Sally's, but lately she had been going to one she found in the Quarter. She didn't tell me the name of it, but she said it's one that bought out two businesses, side-by-side, and knocked out a wall to make the place roomy." The young girl glanced up when she finished talking and then looked away as quickly. "It's a fairly new place."

Immediately, Taylor thought of the one near Rampart and Bienville. She'd hit that one tonight. "Well, thank you Annie, for your help. And Sarah, I appreciate you sharing with me as well about Trudy. I almost feel like I know her, and that always helps when we write about victims. It adds a more personal touch. I think that's important."

When she left Sarah's, she took some time to research the third victim, like she had done with the first two: workplace, family members, neighbors, and friends. Trisha McIntyre had been recently divorced and lived in a condo in the Warehouse District. She had legally reclaimed her maiden name. Taylor noted to check out the ex. He may be holding a grudge . . . a big one. Who knew? This could be a copycat killing just to cover up another murder. When married, she was Trisha McIntyre-Matthews. The brown-haired woman had never had any children, so she was alone, just like the other two.

Next, Taylor took time to visit with some family members of each of the first two girls. She liked to give family members a little time to grieve before detailed interviews. First off, their minds would be clearer, and secondly, she wouldn't upset them as much. Especially when she explained she was working with the police.

Trudy's mom explained they didn't know how Trudy spent her nights or where. They only talked occasionally — not that there was a rift between them, but just neither had the time to get together often, even on the phone. Boy did Taylor know how that was. She didn't have time to get with her mom and sister as much as they would like, but still they kept calling. Wasn't Trudy lucky that her mom understood?

Mrs. Gauthreaux, on the other hand, was very helpful. Although tears rimmed her eyes as she spoke, she answered all of Taylor's questions. She said, "Stephanie had recently broken up with her boyfriend, Larry David. Spelled like the boy who slew the giant, David, but pronounced *Da-veed,*" she explained. "So now when she went out . . . I mean so lately when she went out, it was with the women in her office. I think they met up at the lounges. Some were even in the Quarter, but you'll have to ask her coworker, Janie Goudeaux, the names of the places they went. I have no idea."

After wiping at her wet cheeks with the back of her hand, she continued, "I never approved of her going to nightclubs, but she was a grown woman and had to make her own decisions. I wish now I had argued with her instead. Maybe she'd be alive today. You raise them, teach them morals, but today's generation feels like they need to party all the time. I don't understand it." She pressed her fingers to her temples and whispered, "I'm sorry. I don't mean to burden you with my feelings."

Taylor touched the woman's hand gently and squeezed. "I understand. I don't have any more questions right now, Mrs. Gauthreaux, but I want to say that you can't blame yourself. Like you said, she was old enough to make her own decisions. And you can't even blame her. It was the killer who was in the wrong. No one deserves to be murdered."

"Thank you."

This time, Taylor reached out and hugged the woman. *Where did that come from?* Taylor wasn't one who showed emotions. Not a hugger or a kisser . . . just a talker. She didn't even hug her own mom much. What had gotten into her? She thanked the lady for being so helpful.

"No problem, Ms. Jaymes." Mrs. Gauthreaux reached out and grabbed both of Taylor's hands and held them tightly. "I recognized your name from the paper. You have quite a reputation with helping the police solve crimes. I hope you can do the same for my daughter's murder." Another tear slipped down her cheek.

Squeezing the woman's hands, Taylor thought maybe that was why she felt connected to this woman. Stephanie's mom already knew Taylor through her writing.

Yes. "I'll do my best," she said.

"They ought to be very grateful for all the work you do to help them."

"Thank you, Mrs. Gauthreaux, for helping me get more information. It helps me to write better stories on the victims. Making them more human to the reader. Helps them know your daughter's heart."

"I don't worry about you and how you write Stephanie's story. I know it will be done well. And I hope you help the police find Steph's killer. Thank you for caring."

From there, Taylor decided to pay a visit to a neighbor of the third victim. This woman, Wendy, had the condo next door for as long as Trisha lived there. In fact, they moved in only a week apart from one another. Maybe they had connected.

"As a matter of fact, Trisha and I became fairly tight friends recently. We didn't connect in the beginning. We were both married and lived our own lives. But since each of our divorces, we kind of connected. We both had similar problems with our husbands. Mine was an emotional abuser while hers physically abused her. But the pain was the same on the inside."

"Had her ex-husband been physically abusive to her since their divorce?"

"No, not that I know of. Not physically, anyway, but it's because she wouldn't let him near her. Over the phone he played a lot of mind games on her, trying to get her to take him back. It was stressful for her in the beginning, but what could she do? Report him to the cops? For what? Not being nice on the phone? As long as he stayed away from her, she said she could handle the mind games. She planned to get rid of her house phone and go to only a cell. She'd never had one of those before. With a cell, he wouldn't be able to get her number, and it would have made it harder for him to agitate her. At least now he won't be able to torment her at all."

Taylor wondered if the police knew about her ex-husband. This again could be the copycat she was thinking of earlier. Instead of following that line, Taylor decided to stay on the track she'd been following with the other victims. "Did Trisha go to bars at night?"

"No. Usually we'd go out to places together to eat and then to the movies. Neither of us was looking for a new man in our lives and truly didn't feel like faking a good time . . . until this Friday night, anyway. I don't know what changed her, but Trisha decided she wanted to try out this new place someone at work told her about. She loved to dance and hadn't done it in years. I had a bad headache so chose not to go. She said she was going to go check it out anyway. She couldn't explain, but she felt it was important to get out again. Trisha even said it might work out better if she went alone, since it would be her first time out in a long time. She'd be around people who didn't know her, and I think she thought she could relax better. Maybe she even felt it would be a way to be free of all the past. What a mistake! I urged her to be careful, but it didn't help." Wendy's shoulders dropped as she talked about her neighbor. "Maybe if

I'd gone, she'd still be alive."

"You can't blame yourself," Taylor said as she rose to leave. "Thank you for your help." Taylor handed the woman her card, and Wendy promised she'd call if she thought of anything that might help.

On the ride back to her apartment, adrenaline flowed. A good story always excited her. She thought this might be the best of her career so far. Maybe this would be the one to bring her one step closer to attaining that Pulitzer Prize she so wanted. Who knew? Wouldn't her dad be proud . . . maybe even her mom? No. The only thing that would make her mom proud would be to find a gold band on the third finger of Taylor's left hand.

"Sorry, Mom," she whispered in the car. A man was the last thing she wanted or needed.

Suddenly she turned right. *Why not?* Since she was near the Garden District, she might as well swing by her parents and pay them a short visit before going home. She'd be busy from now until this killer was found, so she had better take the opportunity while she had the chance.

CHAPTER 15

Late that afternoon, after talking with Buck and Brown, Detective Bradley discovered the three girls had been seen in two of the clubs near the area. The nightclubs outside the Quarter he interviewed had seen one of the victims and another had seen the other two victims, but no one club had seen all three of the women. So this was a step in the right direction.

"Sorry to say, Lieutenant, but we couldn't find Guidry," Buck admitted. "Although his rent is paid up till the end of the month and all his clothes appear to be in his apartment, he is nowhere to be found."

"Maybe he skipped town?" Brown suggested.

"Maybe," John said, and Buck nodded in agreement.

"Or maybe he took off to clear his head or went looking elsewhere for a job. Maybe he has nothing to do with the killings."

Brown sounded like he didn't want Guidry to be found guilty. Of course, if the man enjoyed the DJ, as a policeman he would want the guy to follow the law.

"But it wouldn't hurt to be sure," John reminded him. "It only takes a second to turn people's thinking around. You never know what will set someone off. And being fired from a job is at the top of that list of things that set people off."

"True," Buck said.

"Yeah, I know," Brown said as he rose from the chair with his head and shoulders drooping. "We'll check harder, Boss."

After the two detectives left his office, John wanted to call Taylor and ask her to scope the bars out with him tonight — mix a little business with pleasure. Not that he would find any pleasure in it . . . well, no, he would find plenty of pleasure in being near her. At least he had the other night at Dante's. He truly didn't mix pleasure in with business. That was the work code he lived by, and he wouldn't change it now. It would be strictly business. They would go as a couple simply to help people open up more to him. He felt certain people would talk freely if they only thought they were gossiping. Sometimes police made people nervous. Why? He didn't know. They did their job with the intent to serve and protect private citizens. Why wouldn't they want to help?

John's stomach growled. Since he'd be working tonight, he wouldn't have time to cook. He decided to run down to the cafeteria and eat a hot lunch. That should hold him through the night.

In the lunchroom, Gloria waited on him immediately, bringing him plenty of roast and gravy, along with an ample portion of green beans. "Here you go, Sugar. You don't have to wait in line. I fixed you all up. I even added a slice of that strawberry pie you love. Ponchatoula's finest."

Although John never gave her more than a few pleasant words that he could recall, she always seemed to make a beeline to him when he entered the cafeteria. At times she appeared to be offering herself to him with her eyes. Kind of gave him the creeps, but because Jennifer had called her a friend, John tried to be polite and overlook her brash ways. "Thanks," he murmured as he took the tray and headed toward the cashier.

Before making his way to checkout, he stopped to pour himself a cup of hot tea. "I'll get that for you, Hon. Go take a seat, and I'll have it right out."

Pulling money from his pocket, John paid for his lunch and then found an empty table. He'd barely unwrapped his eating utensils and laid them down on a napkin before Gloria swished her way over to his table and set the cup of steaming hot tea down in front of him, along with a little cup of cream. The sugar was already on the table. "Here you go, Handsome."

"Thanks."

"Does that woman at your table the other morning having breakfast with you mean you're back in circulation? I thought you'd never get over Jennifer. You two were quite a pair. Glad you finally remembered you're not dead." She dragged her hand back slowly across the table as she leaned in toward John. "Glad you're back in the land of the living." Her lips curved into a smile.

Without thinking, John said, "That was a reporter, not a date. I don't think I'd bring my dates to the cafeteria."

"Ah, Sugar, didn't mean to offend you. Just you and your lady friend Jennifer used to eat in here all the time. I always hoped you'd drop her and give some of us other girls a chance."

How do you answer that? He thought they were friends. Instead of replying to her question, he said, "Thanks for the tea."

She took the hint and left without another word.

As he ate, he again pondered the idea of calling Taylor and getting her to go with him to a couple of the bars tonight to ask a few questions and snoop around. Bars were not his normal hangout anymore. He'd grown to enjoy going straight home from work, turning on a little Harry Connick Jr., Michael Bublé, or Frank Sinatra and then fixing himself a glass of iced tea. He would then relax out on the swing or in his recliner in the living room. There he enjoyed the music and the peace and quiet. That was how he spent his free time. It worked well for him.

Tonight the bars would be crowded, noisy, and the rooms full of smoke. He looked forward to none of this. Now, if he could persuade that reporter to go with him, maybe it would make the night a little more bearable.

Shaking his head, he decided against that. He didn't need to enjoy work. He needed a clear head. He needed to be able to focus. There was a purpose for his job, and he needed to be at his best. That was the only way to fight crime. He knew that was his purpose here on earth — to keep the peace and share the Word, wherever and whenever he could.

After lunch, he went back to his office and

186

told Brown and Buck what he planned to do.

"Me and my old lady could hit a few as a couple and see what we could find out. My sister-in-law could watch the kids for us. This would make Maddie excited about my job for a change." Buck stood, waiting for the okay.

"Lucy would get a kick out of it, too. Count me in, Boss."

That sounded like a good plan. In fact, it was what he'd thought about doing with Taylor. "Good idea."

So it was decided. Each would go to a different bar and see what they could find out. They'd meet in the morning and share the info. If anyone found something worth meeting together sooner and discussing, they would beep the other two and then all would meet back at the office.

John was the only one going alone tonight. He didn't mind. He was used to being a loner. Not that he was really alone. The Lord stayed right with him, giving John direction wherever he went. Tonight would be no different.

He ran home, showered, and shaved. His place was still clean from Ms. Evelyn's visit yesterday. With nothing to do for a couple of hours, he made himself lie down and try to take a nap. He'd need it so he could stay up as late as necessary.

Four hours later, his eyes popped open. Stretching his arms wide, he rose from the bed. The nap worked wonders, even though he didn't think he would fall asleep. At eight he was donning his jeans and a T-shirt. To hide his gun in his shoulder holster, he slipped on a dark blue blazer. It was made to dress up jeans or relax a pair of slacks. It did its job tonight. Looking in a mirror, he saw that it hid his weapon well and would help him blend in with the rest of the crowd. No one need be suspicious of him. In the movies the cop always stood out, but John always tried to blend in. He discovered more that way. People were more willing to talk.

By the time John walked through the front door of the bar, smoke filled the room. The music screamed out live and loud. The band's rendition of George Strait's "Ace in the Hole" blasted his ears.

Glancing around, he saw the place was packed, so he found a seat at the corner barstool for the time being. John wondered if Buck or Brown were at their locations yet. At least they had someone to talk to while they worked away the hours. He watched for a table to become free and ordered a Coke.

"With what? Whiskey? Gin?" the bartender replied.

"Coke over ice. Nothing extra."

"Still get charged for the alcohol whether you drink it or not."

John nodded. "I understand. Coke straight," he repeated one more time.

Looking around, he thought, *This would be so much easier if I had a woman on my arm.* Too bad Taylor wasn't with him. It wouldn't be a date. It would be business. She wanted the same thing he did — to find the killer. So why didn't he ask her to join him?

When the bartender set the filled glass in front of him, John laid three pictures on the table. Of course, these were headshots from the morgue, not a beautiful sight, but the women didn't look that bad . . . just dead.

The man's eyes rested on the pictures very briefly, one after the other, and then he looked back at John. "You a cop?"

He flipped open his wallet and revealed his badge. "Have you seen these women in here before?"

"That one," he said, pointing to Trudy Walker. "Not every weekend, but probably once a month. A friendly sort; that's why I remember her."

"What about the other two?" he asked as he handed the server a five-dollar bill and said, "Keep the change."

"A quarter. Thanks." The man glared at the five and then John. If they come in here, they don't get their drinks from the bar. Maybe they're always at the tables where the waitresses take their order. Check with them."

"I need another beer down here," a man already having had a few too many hollered to the bartender.

"Thanks," John told him, even though the man had already turned his back to go serve the other customer. Probably figured he'd get better tips from the drunk.

John sipped on his Coke as he waited for each waitress to come order her drinks for her tables. As they did, he took the opportunity to ask, "Have you seen these women in here before?"

The first two barely glanced at the pictures before shaking their heads and turning their backs on John.

What has come of this world today? No one seems to care anymore.

By the time he had a fresh cold Coke, he spotted a different waitress and approached her with the pictures as she stood next to the bar waiting for her order. "Hi, Miss. I'm Detective Bradley with NOPD, and I was wondering if you've seen any of these three women in here lately?"

She turned her head toward the dance floor, and he followed her gaze. *What is she looking for? These women are dead. They aren't in here tonight.*

"I haven't, but I'm new. They could be here now."

As she spoke, he started to look back toward her but caught a glimpse of beautiful red curls out on the floor and did a double take instead. Was that Taylor? Was she here? What was she trying to do, get herself killed? That was how she worked, if he remembered. She tried to get too close to the story. What better way than to be bait for the killer? Was she a fool?

He scanned the floor again and couldn't find the redhead, but he knew what he'd seen. He'd never seen hair so pretty before, so inviting, wanting a man to run his fingers through it. It had to be her. But where did she go?

"Sir? Did you hear me?"

Returning his stare to the waitress, he said, "Yes. Thank you for your time." John slipped back over to his stool and turned so he could watch the floor. He would find her, if it was the last thing he did.

"Ten-minute break. We'll be back soon," he heard over the speaker as the lights in the place rose to the next level, making it easier to look around.

Where was she?

Suddenly, two hands rested on his shoulders and he jumped. Swiveling, he rested his eyes on soft, shimmering red curls and luscious green eyes. "Taylor," he whispered, forgetting he was angry.

"John! I couldn't believe that was you." Excitement pealed from her voice. "I was out on the floor dancing and thought I saw you over here, but I told myself it couldn't be. You don't relax. You don't go clubbing. So what are you doing here? Are you alone, or do you have a date with you? The blond bombshell from the cafeteria?"

Remembering he was perturbed at this reporter right now, he spoke harshly. "What do you think I'm doing here? I'm working! The question is, what are *you* doing here?"

CHAPTER 16

Taylor slipped onto the barstool next to John and spoke in a voice barely above a whisper, so he leaned closer.

"Lower your voice, and I'll be glad to tell you what I'm doing here. But the world doesn't need to know our business."

Music started up again as the band returned to the stage. He barely heard her last words as they opened with the lively tune of "Boot Scootin' Boogie" blasting through the air. John attempted to block out the band and the people around them as his gaze locked on her lips. He watched her speak more than he heard "our business." He knew by the tautness of her lips she wasn't too happy with him. Well, the feeling was mutual, so he scowled back at her. He didn't have to see his face to know what was written on it. He only hoped she got the message. Chasing a killer was *his* business, not hers.

Every cell in his being wanted to shout at her, telling her what a fool she was to come here on her own. He knew what she was doing, trying to catch a killer. Mentally shaking his head, he corrected that. Chasing a story was what she was doing, even if it might cost her, her life.

Didn't she care? Humph! He grunted.

Why should he lower his voice? Because she said so? He was a cop. He had every right to be there and ask questions. He could yell if he wanted to, and everyone in this place had better listen to him.

Blowing out a gush of pent-up air, he admitted he didn't want them to listen right now. He wanted her to listen. In fact, he wanted her to know he was angry because she thought so little of her life. Was that the cop in him? Or the man in him that held this concern?

Seeing her pleading expression, he changed his mind. Lowering his voice, he said again, "Okay. So what are you doing here?" Taylor could have it her way for the moment. He listened for her answer, but it had better be a good one. John straightened stiffly on the barstool, giving her space.

When Taylor didn't answer him swiftly enough, he urged her along. "Well, I lowered my voice, and now I'm waiting." He watched as Taylor brushed a few strands of hair off her face. Part of him wanted to reach out and brush them away for her, but no, he couldn't do that. Averting his gaze for a second, he cleared the thought.

"I'm here working, too. The sooner we find out the bar they all three went to, the sooner we find the killer."

"That figures." John rolled his eyes as he threw his hands up into the air. "Are you alone? Or did you at least bring a date to protect you?"

This time, instead of brushing her hair back softly, she tossed that long mane that hung over her right shoulder roughly behind her back and glared in disgust. "Look, John, I don't know what your problem is. I've been doing my job for ten years or better, with no difficulty whatsoever. Tonight I'm following up on a lead. Which I'm sure you're doing as well. So what is the big deal? You're chasing a killer, and I'm chasing a story. Sure, we're going to work together — but not together, together. And to answer your question, of course I'm alone. I work better alone. I don't need a man to protect me. Besides, he'd get in my way of finding out information. And to tell you the truth, it's none of your business." On those words, she rose from the stool, turned her back on him, and started to storm away.

Rising quickly, he grabbed her by the arm and turned her back toward him. This was ridiculous. They fought like they'd known each other forever. He knew that what she did was none of his business, so why was he trying to make it his business? Regaining control of his emotions, he admitted, "You're right."

That surprised her, he could tell. Suddenly her chin came up, and a large smile started to spread. She must not be used to winning so easily. Not that she had won, but he did know he'd crossed the line. Keeping it on a business level, he said firmly, "This is my case. I am the detective. You are the reporter. I investigate the case. You write the facts." With each sentence he would point to himself, and then to her, and then back again to himself, emphasizing his every word. "If you continue to try and do my job, which may hinder my investigation, I'll pull you in on charges of obstructing justice so fast it will make your head spin. Do I make myself clear?"

She looked but never said a word. The smile wiped from her face.

"The least you could have done was brought a date with you for protection."

"Again, I don't need protecting. A date

would interfere with my job. I can't snoop around and worry about keeping some man's ego happy at the same time. Without a date, I've been able to walk around, look at people, ask a few questions here and there, and got some good answers." She dropped it there, not bothering to share any information.

He balled his hand in a fist, restraining his anger. As he was about to speak, she added, "I might have gotten another lead tonight, for all you know."

"You're right. I don't know. But what I do know is that if you ask the wrong question to the wrong person, you could be the next stiff I get called to the scene for." Leaning his face closer to hers, he said, "And I don't want that." Straightening his stance once more, he said, "Stick to reporting while I do the investigating. You write the facts we give you. Don't interfere. Don't take chances that are unnecessary."

When those big green eyes started to stray from his face, he caught her chin in his hand, drawing her attention back to him, but not as roughly as he'd grabbed her arm earlier. "You're not listening to me," he said to her as her eyes still looked over his shoulder.

"John," a familiar female voice said as she

rubbed his back gently.

Turning quickly, he wanted to bark, "What?" at whoever interrupted the important conversation he was having. Instead he tightened his grip on Taylor's arm so she couldn't run away and looked down into the eyes of the woman from the cafeteria at the station. "Gloria," he said, nodding slightly.

The woman glanced at John and then looked around him at Taylor and his hand holding her. "I thought you told me you two weren't an item. That she was a . . . what did you call her?"

Great! Now what? "I —"

Before he could speak, Taylor extracted herself from his hold and reached out to shake hands with the female intrusion. "Hi. I'm Taylor Jaymes. A reporter from the *Morning Tribune.* Nice to meet you."

"Gloria." She filled in her name.

"Nice to meet you, Gloria. And don't you worry. Your man is safe from me. We're talking business here. I have no claims on him whatsoever, and he has *none* on me. Let me leave you two alone. Have a great night." She turned and smiled up at John as she said, "Nice to see you, Detective. We'll speak again soon."

And she left him there, standing with

Gloria, like that was how it was supposed to be. Should he run after her?

"John, I didn't know you went to bars. I thought that went against your values."

With his back still to Gloria, John watched Taylor disappear into the crowd onto the dance floor. Finally, he twisted back around and faced the woman he had no desire to talk to, but with the question she had asked, he knew he must respond. "Yes, Gloria. You're right. I don't come to bars, except on official business. I hope you realize what is going on in our city right now and know the possible danger you are putting yourself in by going out alone to clubs. You are alone, right?"

She smiled, apparently thinking he might ask to accompany her. "Why yes, John. I'm alone. But I don't have to be."

Grabbing both of her shoulders, holding her in front of him, he looked straight into her eyes, making sure he had her full attention. "I'm telling you this for your own good, and I hope you listen. Go out in groups, if this is the life you choose for yourself."

"What are you talking about? Those killings didn't happen at a bar. Those women were murdered on the side of a street. I'm not going to stop on the side of the road for a stranger. Give me a little credit, John. You guys talk about some of the stuff you see at the tables over your lunch. I hear enough. I don't want to be the one y'all are talking about."

At least she holds a grain of sense in her head. "Well, be safe tonight when you go home. Good night."

He walked around her, heading for the door. There was no need for him to linger any longer. The waitresses had already let him know only two of the three had been seen there and neither in the past month. As he stormed for the exit, he found himself glancing over the crowd.

What was he looking for? Taylor? He knew he was, but why?

Chapter 17

Taylor made her way through the crowd and slipped off to the other side of the dance floor. Striding to the front door, she grumbled to herself the whole way. "What got into him? I wasn't doing anything wrong. Only my job. What's it to him? Our agreement has nothing to do with me doing my job." Rolling her eyes, she said, "And just think: I was beginning to like the guy." She pushed the door open.

Plodding down the sidewalk, she headed for her Mustang. Yanking the door open, she dropped inside and strapped on her seat belt. With a *click* the belt locked, and she jammed the key into the ignition. Slapping the steering wheel with the ball of her hand, it hit her. "I know where I know her from." Suddenly that blond rubbing all over John came to remembrance. "She's that little waitress in the cafeteria who kept eyeing him the other morning. She has it bad for

him, and I don't think he even knows it."
She laughed aloud. "Tonight she may make
her move." Putting the gear into DRIVE, she
eased out of her parking space.

Edging her car into the street, she steered
for home. It wasn't far. Just a few blocks
down and a couple blocks over and she
would be home. Passing the late-night visitors strolling in the Quarter, she didn't take
time to study them, as was her norm. In the
few years she had lived in the Quarter, that
was what she enjoyed the most — people-
watching.

Tonight her mind was on other matters —
the detective and the way he reacted to seeing her tonight. You'd think he'd be grateful
for all the help she gave him.

After unlocking her front door and stepping into her apartment, she tossed her
purse and keys on the table and slammed
the door closed behind her. Stretching and
twisting, she found she was wound up
tighter than a spinning top. *Why?*

Probably because of the story. She wished
she'd found out more tonight, or at least
gotten some important tidbit like she'd
indicated to John. Unfortunately she hadn't
truly found out anything. She'd alluded to
it, just to make him mad. Taylor hoped it
worked.

Tonight promised to be a long night for Taylor. She knew she wouldn't go to sleep if she went to bed, so she opted for rummaging through all her notes and pictures. Maybe something would jump out at her or fall into place. If nothing else, her eyes would grow tired. Then she could go to sleep. Start fresh tomorrow.

In the meantime, Taylor took out her files on the three girls and glanced over them again one at a time, not seeing anything new. As she tried to focus on the case, her mind wandered to the thorn in her side . . . the detective. Her thoughts smoldered on that devastatingly attractive man who drove her crazy. Why had he behaved that way? He told her she could work on the case with him. What was the big deal? Besides, she didn't blow his cover. Of course, he almost did with his big mouth. She was surprised no one seemed to hear his loud, irritated voice shouting at her. She sure did.

Enough about him. Think about the case, the victims. Who would do such a thing? Why these three women? And who was next? She wondered if the police had worked up a psychological profile yet. Or did only the FBI do that sort of thing? It was definitely a serial killer, so if the FBI weren't in on it yet, they would be soon. How would Detective John Bradley handle that?

She had come full circle. Her thoughts were back on him again. Not where she wanted to be.

Throwing open the top file, Trisha McIntyre-Matthews, she forced her mind to focus on the subject at hand. She had been married to Robert Matthews, but as soon as she applied for a divorce, she'd returned to using her maiden name. Had the police checked him out? Had he been cleared? Or was he a person of interest to them?

The only neighbor who had known Trisha had been Wendy. They both lived in the Warehouse District and had been neighbors for some time. Both were married to abusive husbands. Wendy's divorce was final, whereas Trisha had four more months to go. According to Wendy, Robert didn't want the divorce and was fighting it.

Three months ago, with Trisha's father's influence, Robert had been forced to leave their home. Her father had bought the condo, and it was still in his name. He wanted to make sure his little girl had a roof over her head. Part of him had never trusted Robert from the beginning, but little did her father know how much her husband couldn't be trusted. Mr. McIntyre hadn't known for a long time what went on beneath the roof he supplied. Wendy said Trisha didn't tell her parents how he abused her. Robert had made sure the marks were hidden. Their two families were friends. She didn't want her rotten husband to ruin that for her parents, whom she dearly loved. But when Robert twisted her wrists so hard, one snapped, that was the last straw. Then she told Mom and Dad everything.

At Trisha's workplace, Taylor heard a little different story, but not so different that it made Robert seem innocent. If anything, it made him look worse. According to fellow workers, Trisha never exposed her personal life to them, but within a few weeks of her marriage, her smile had gone. Trisha's joyful spirit had turned quiet, and she kept to herself. Then they noticed marks that appeared to be covered with makeup — nothing obvious, but enough for coworkers to wonder. And some days every step seemed to be filled with agonizing pain as she moved slowly, cautiously. When someone would ask if she was okay, Trisha always pasted on a smile and said, "Wonderful. Thanks for asking."

Normally the husband would be the first person the police would look at, but because of the similarities, Taylor felt certain the police were primarily focused on the work of the serial killer. She hadn't discussed details on the third victim yet with John.

Mr. McIntyre made his views clear to everyone who would listen. He believed Robert Matthews had killed his daughter. He believed it was a copycat killing.

Taylor hoped the police had questioned Robert Matthews well and checked his whereabouts. You never knew. If nothing else, he deserved punishment for what he had put Trisha through.

Taylor wanted to talk to him herself — to see how he portrayed himself. As the suffering widower? She'd catch up with him tomorrow, she hoped. He was at the top of her to-do list.

The only possible dissimilarity between Trisha and the other two victims was the fact that Trisha was separated, not truly single. She had four months left before her divorce would be final. This was enough in Taylor's mind to look deeper into Robert's alibi. Of course, the killer might have known Trisha had split from her husband. Maybe they should look closer at men who knew Trisha well.

All of this whirled in her brain, making her feel like she was going out of her mind. She needed to talk this over with John. See what they truly knew about Robert and

Trisha. What had they found out? Had they cleared him and was it with enough true evidence?

"John, I need to talk to you."

Why did they have to argue at the dance club? Pounding her fist on the table, she uttered, "John. Why does everything have to come back to you?"

She'd never needed help before. Why now?

It was late and she was tired. Maybe if she gave the whole thing a rest, tomorrow she'd have a better perspective. At least a good rest might get the thoughts of her friendly neighborhood cop out of her mind . . . she hoped.

CHAPTER 18

John revved the engine of his Bronco and took off. On the way home, he took a slight detour, not even thinking about it — three blocks over and two down. There he slowed his car and looked for lights in the high windows. Maybe he hadn't seen her on the dance floor when he glanced around the club because she had already left and gone home.

He hoped that was the case as his gaze lifted to her windows.

Darkness.

Disappointed and frustrated, he lowered his gaze and gritted his teeth.

John pulled over to the curb and killed his engine. He needed to know Taylor made it home safely. Sure, she'd been taking care of herself for a long time. He knew that. How could he forget? She kept reminding him. But still he had to be sure.

It's not that I'm trying to take care of her.

No. He was looking out for her because now she was a part of his team . . . well, sort of. Not that he would ever admit that to her.

By peering into the darkness, into the shadows of the parking area, he could see the rear corner of her Mustang.

He grunted. That didn't prove she was home. As close as her place was to the bar, it wouldn't surprise him in the least if she hadn't walked tonight. That girl was afraid of nothing.

Either he needed to slip into the courtyard and look up onto her balcony to see if any light spilled out of the glass sliding doors or slip up the stairs and listen through the door for noise inside. The chance someone left the gates to the courtyard unlocked was slim to nil. He doubted it seriously that one of her good neighbors would do that.

What would happen if he followed his second plan of action? Wouldn't that look good? Someone see him, call the police to report a prowler, and then find him as the perp? That would be tragic . . . one of his own coming out to arrest him. How would he explain that? He'd never live it down.

"That's a chance I'll have to take," he murmured to himself as he climbed out of his parked car. Quietly, he slipped inside the hidden parkway. Squinting, he shot little daggers toward the lock on the gate and decided not to waste time trying to pick the lock. That wouldn't look good either. Stepping softly, he climbed the stairs and eased his way up one step at a time. Delicately he eased over to her front door. Pressing his ear against the wood, he listened.

Nothing. She wasn't home. *That woman!*

Then it hit him. *What if she walks up and catches me?*

He shoved that thought to the back of his mind. Otherwise, he'd have run off right then.

Finally, he heard a loud pound, like someone slamming their fist down on a hard surface. Was she being attacked? His muscles tightened. Instantly, his body made ready to kick in the door and save her, but then the pounding was followed by her voice grumbling aloud about something. Sounded like she was fussing at herself. He released his held breath.

That was good enough for him. She was home safe and sound.

Swiftly and silently, he made his way back down to his car and headed home. The short time it took him to drive the twelve miles, he tried not to think about Taylor in any way, shape, or form. To help him, he turned off his radio, lowered both front windows, and let the fresh air blow through his car. The wind sliced through as if fingers were raking his hair. Taylor's, he thought. In his mind, he heard her laughter.

He shook his head to remove that thought. Instead, a quick flash of her gorgeous smile bolted out in front of him, and he gave up the assignment of forgetting about Taylor. For the next fifteen minutes, he relived this past week with her, recalling each time he had seen her and how she made him feel.

Finally, he pulled into his garage and parked. Before killing the engine, he raised his windows.

What a night!

John unlocked his back door. As he entered his home, he hooked his key on the curved nail by the kitchen door and then made his way to the bedroom. There he slipped off his blazer and hung it on a rack in the closet, smoothing each wrinkle out before shutting the closet door.

On the ride home, all he could think about was Taylor. Was she still arguing with herself? Had she found a better way to spend the rest of her night at home? Someone needed to talk some sense into that girl. She had to be nuts checking out the bars by herself. Taylor was looking for trouble. What if she'd run into the killer and he figured out what she was doing and why? The dispatcher would be calling him at three in the morning to come view another crime scene, this time with her behind the wheel.

Shivers raced down his spine.

Speaking of morning, it would be here way too soon. Time to hit the hay. Five would be there before he knew it. Sitting on the bed, he removed his shoes. Rising, he placed them in the closet and dropped his socks in the dirty-clothes hamper. After he laid his wallet and change on the top of his butler, he hung his jeans on the rod attached for pants. He hadn't had them on but for a couple of hours. Why throw them in the dirty clothes?

John pulled out a fresh pair of gym shorts and a T-shirt to sleep in, dressed, and climbed into bed. Feeling the need to sit up but having no energy to do so, he realized he forgot to set the alarm.

Relaxing, he closed his eyes and murmured, "No problem. I always wake before the alarm. This time I just have to make sure I get up when I wake."

No snoozing raced through his mind as he felt his body start to rest, unwinding at the end of a very long day.

Turning on his side, he released a long sigh. His nerve endings tingled as his body started to relax even more. *Help me, Lord. Lead me to this killer. We can't have another person die.* His prayers slipped out as sleep tried to overtake him.

As he sunk closer toward sleep in his mind, he saw those soft, long, red curls. His hands reached up and rubbed his eyes as he muttered, "Go away, Taylor. I'm trying to sleep here. . . ."

The next thing he remembered was waking up to a pitch-dark room, all but the red glow of his clock showing 4:45.

Time to get up.

He tossed back the covers and headed straight for the shower. The cool blast of water woke him the rest of the way. As he lathered himself with soap while water continued to pour down over his head, a glimpse of that redheaded reporter flashed through his mind.

She had dressed sharp last night. In all his anger, he had failed to take in her looks, but this morning was another matter. Tucked into those brown snakeskin boots were tight-fitting jeans. She fit right in with the crowd wearing that kind of top girls wore with the cowgirl fringes hanging across the back of the shirt. A cowboy hat would have sat perfectly on that crown of red hair, but who would want to spoil the look of those tresses falling free all around her head, down to her elbows, and around to the back. If John didn't know better, he would have believed she was all cowgirl.

Of course, he really didn't know better. In fact, he didn't know Taylor at all, except what he read written by her in the paper. And none of that spoke about her. It only showed the girl had no fear for her life.

What *did* he know about her?

His mind wandered as he dressed for the day. He knew she was a hardworking reporter. Anyone who would give up a night of relaxing at home or going out on a nice date to a movie for her job was a dedicated worker. Quickly he reminded himself how she almost got herself killed on the case of those thefts in the Quarter. How dedicated could a person be?

Suddenly he recalled her face plastered across his television set when that case had come to resolution and the criminals had been locked behind bars. His eyes had been drawn to her; he couldn't look away. She had a pull on him even then when she wasn't flesh-and-blood in front of him. He'd better be very careful now not to let the flesh rule his life. He knew better.

At the time that case was brought to a close, the police got the credit; however, the news media played her part up big. That probably wasn't good for her future incognito investigations. It had to hurt more than it helped, but it was always nice to be recognized. That he knew for a fact, even though he wished they would keep his picture out of the paper. A little good press went a long way. His name was one thing, but pictures gave criminals a heads-up on him, and that he didn't need — as he was sure Taylor didn't, either.

Knowing he was attracted to her against his better judgment, he admitted, "She is one amazing woman." He had to give her that, but he'd better watch out for himself. His attraction for the reality of her seemed to be growing too quickly. That wasn't good.

Get your attention back on the case and keep it there.

He growled, "I give up. I've got work to do. No time for you, Miss Jaymes."

Off he stormed to make a pot of coffee.

CHAPTER 19

Determined to know everything on this case, Taylor got up early so she could beat John to the station.

"He can call me his shadow," she whispered to her reflection in the mirror as she wiggled her brows. The good thing was, this time it was with his blessing. A smile warmed her lips as she scrunched her curls slightly at the scalp, trying to give her hair some lift and bounce this morning.

"Oh well." She gave up the battle with her hair. The red curls always won out. They did what they wanted to do.

Snatching her beeper off the dresser, she clipped it to her jeans. After stuffing her pockets with some cash, her cell phone, and her ID, she grabbed her keys, ready to hit the road. As she started for the door, her landline rang. Taylor glanced at it with the thought of ignoring it, but her steps faltered.

It might be John telling her he changed

his mind. Did she want to hear that?

No.

Shaking her head, she continued toward the front door, passing the phone. It rang again. Slapping her hand against the doorframe instead of grabbing the knob and turning, she frowned. "I can't do it! I can't just let it ring. I have to answer it. It might be important," she mumbled to herself.

The inner struggle was twisting her into knots. A third ring pealed out.

Closing her fingers into fists, she said, "It might be the city desk with a breaking story they need me to cover — a rape, a missing person, another homicide."

Arghh, she groaned.

Pivoting on her heel, she took three steps and snatched up the receiver. "Hello."

As soon as she heard the voice on the other end, she regretted answering the phone. *This could have waited.*

"Morning, Sis." The cheerful voice on the other end of the line floated into her ears, so smooth, so sweet.

"Yeah, morning, Tina. I was just heading out the door. Whatcha need?"

"I won't keep you long. You sure are a hard one to track down. I've called you at work, on your cell, and on your home phone leaving messages, but you haven't called me back at all. Have you been working too hard lately? You'll never get a life if you keep doing that." Taylor's sister sounded just like her mom.

Give me a break, she thought but didn't say. Instead she rolled her eyes because she knew when her sister said she wouldn't keep her, it meant, "Sit down. This could take awhile."

"What's up?" she asked again, trying to push Tina into a response.

"You know next week is Mom and Dad's thirty-second wedding anniversary. Rodney and I thought we might throw them a little party Friday night. Invite some family and friends. I wanted to make sure you marked it down on your calendar and in your Blackberry so you'd be here." Taylor heard the command in her sister's voice.

Chewing her bottom lip, Taylor thought about it. This was probably some set-up between her mom and Tina. A blind date thing they'd cooked up. She knew them. Knew how they thought and what their priorities in life were. Number one: a husband to take care of her. Number two: a husband to love her. And number three: a husband to give her children. This all boiled down to a man in Taylor's life. She had no time for a relationship, and her career had no need of a husband. Taylor had known since she was a small child where she wanted to go in life — and it wasn't walking down any aisle to say, "I do."

Glancing at her watch, she realized she needed to get to the bottom of this phone call and get to it fast if she was going to beat John to the station.

"So do I bring a date?" This should get the truth out of her sister.

Excitement bubbled through the line as Tina said, "You mean you have a man you could ask? Who is he? How long have you been dating? Tell me the story. Mom will be so delighted. This could be the best anniversary gift you could give her."

Taylor scoffed, pinching her lips together. *I knew it. I knew it.* "No, Tina. There is no boyfriend in my life. I was just testing you to see if you and Mom had someone lined up for me. I don't want any more fixer-uppers from you two. Do I make myself clear?"

"Yes, Sister dear, I promise. This really is for Mom and Dad. They don't even know about it. Actually, it was Rodney's idea."

Tina sounded sincere. Taylor had to give her that. Either Tina was becoming a better actress, or she was telling the truth. Taylor twisted the phone cord around her fingers as she thought of what to say. "Mom always did say Rodney was the perfect son-in-law. In fact, she wants me to find someone just like him."

"Well, you would be happy. And —"

"Don't tell me." Taylor cut her sister off as her nerves tightened from head to toe. She dreaded hearing what Tina was about to say, so she said it for her. "You happen to know someone you could introduce me to, and he's just like Rodney. In fact, you could have him come to the party. Thanks, but no thanks. If I come up with someone, I'll bring him to the party. If not, I'll be alone. You and Mom better learn to accept me the way I am. My job doesn't leave much time for socializing. And I like it that way."

By now the telephone cord had tangled so tightly in her hand it was cutting off the circulation to her fingertips. She was tired of her mother and sister playing Cupid. "And I especially don't have time to form a relationship with some man who would need me to devote myself to him. No one understands my drive for being the best reporter I can be. Only Dad has a glimmer of understanding."

Taylor heard Tina's giggle cross the line. "Dad made a comment the other day you might be interested to hear. If not, I'll tell you anyway. He said since my two little girls seem to be so much like me, he couldn't wait until you settled down and started a family. He could see a couple of grandsons, or tomboy granddaughters, running around with printer's ink staining their fingers, just like you, Taylor. You and Dad, that is."

"For your information, we don't get ink on our fingers anymore. Computers do wonders."

"I'm sure Dad was just being cute with that remark, stressing how much you are into your job as a reporter."

"And what makes him so sure my kids would be boys or tomboys?"

Tina's laughter grew stronger as it filtered through the line. "He said you wouldn't dare give him two more little sissy granddaughters. That was something only I would do."

A part of her heart broke. She felt betrayed by the one man who always seemed to understand her. Now it sounded like even her dad was going against her wishes for her life. "Tina, I really have to go. When is the party?" She listened to her sister's response and made a mental note. Later she would key it into her Blackberry.

She wasted no time getting out of her apartment before another phone call slowed her down. She climbed into her car and eased out onto the road. The only reason she drove her car to the station instead of walking was because she couldn't be sure John would allow her to ride with him. It was a police matter, and she was a reporter. The detective probably wouldn't want anyone to know they were together. With her car, she could at least follow him.

Soon she was at the station, parked, and headed toward John's office.

His office was empty, so she walked in and made herself at home in the spare chair she sat in not too many days ago. How she beat him in, she'd never know. Tina had definitely kept her longer on the phone than Taylor had wanted. After sitting and tapping her fingers silently on her lap for several seconds, which seemed like long minutes, she glared at her watch and mumbled, "It's almost nine. He must have stayed out late last night. He probably had a really good time with Blondie." She made a face as she imagined him and that Gloria woman huddled together on the dance floor.

Standing abruptly and shaking free that image of the two of them pressed together, she said, "I did enough of that last night."

"Enough of what?" The question came from the doorway.

Spinning around, Taylor discovered John's frame filling the space at the open door. Her pulse raced as she took in the dark circles under his eyes. *It must have been one night to remember for him.* She clenched her teeth, trying to restrain her first response. Asking him what kept him out so late last night was none of her business — and part of her really didn't want to know.

After holding her tongue for a minute or two, she said, "So you decided to come to work after all. I didn't know cops got to come in so late in the morning." She was satisfied at the way she approached him. "Maybe it's not too late for me to consider a career change. Your hours seem more conducive to having a life. Wouldn't my mother be proud?"

He grumbled something under his breath that she couldn't understand. "Have a seat. What are you doing here? Did you discover something new last night *in your investigation?*" Sarcasm oozed from his last words.

"I'd ask you the same thing, but I'm not sure I want to hear about you and Gloria." Taylor loved to aggravate him. She didn't know why, but she felt sure that remark would do the trick.

His face broke into a wide smile, and he started laughing.

That wasn't the reaction she'd expected. What was going on? She wasn't trying to be funny. Her intention had been to irritate him just a little, rub him against the grain.

He swallowed his laughter as he said, "So what do you think happened with Gloria last night? No. Never mind. You're too young to be thinking what you were thinking, so let's get down to business."

Taylor felt her face redden. Why was she getting angry? *You don't want to know what they did,* she reminded herself.

Then it hit her. He called her *young.* In the beginning, he insinuated she was too young and inexperienced to be getting so close to her cases. It was dangerous for her. She wanted him to treat her like a woman, a woman worldly enough to do her job well. She also wanted to be treated with the respect she'd earned over her years of experience.

"Young? You talk about me as if I'm a kid. I'm all grown up, in case you haven't noticed." She placed her hands on her hips as she punched out the words.

His eyes studied her carefully. After looking her over from head to toe, he said, "You can't be more than twenty-three, twenty-four tops. You're barely out of college. It's your job that makes you feel old." His words were said with a hint of laughter.

With a toss of her hair over her shoulders, she stood erect. "I'll have you know I'm what is known in some circles as 'an old maid.' Talk to my mom. She'll tell you. I'm twenty-eight, almost twenty-nine."

His blue eyes widened in surprise. Taylor could tell he was truly shocked. Maybe he had thought she was young and fresh out of school. Well, he was in for a wake-up call.

"You're not joking, are you?" He shook his head. "No, I can see you're not."

Taylor shot daggers at him and then sat back down in the chair in front of his desk. As he walked around his desk to sit down, she said, "I don't know whether to take that as an insult, saying I look like a baby, or assume you meant it as a compliment, saying I look young for my age."

He shrugged like it didn't matter to him one way or the other.

She reached in her blazer's hidden pocket and pulled out a pad and pen. "No comment? Just for that, I'll take it as a compliment. Let's get down to business, shall we?" She grinned as she crossed her legs. "What did we find out last night . . . anything?"

CHAPTER 20

John leaned back in his chair and chewed the inside of his cheek slightly as he watched Taylor swing one leg across the other. He knew he needed to reverse the direction his mind was headed.

The mind is where the battle first begins, he reminded himself.

Releasing a heavy sigh, he said, "I think you're jumping the gun here. Or maybe you just misunderstood what I meant when I said you'd get the exclusive on this investigation. I didn't mean I'd be reporting our every finding to you the moment we found something. I meant I would tell you everything we learned at various intervals, keeping you abreast of our findings . . . with the promise from you that it stays out of the paper until I give you the go-ahead. I'll contact you. You don't need to come by my office daily and hang out for the next update."

He watched her shift in the chair. "So, you see, we won't be working together, together." His hands interchangeably stretched out to her and then pulled to his chest and then back again — almost like a seesaw while stressing his point. He hoped she got the message. "Don't worry. I'll keep you filled in on the various stages of the investigation at different points along the way." He picked up his pencil and twirled it through his fingers, like a lot of people did with coins. He found this relaxed him sometimes. "You don't need to come down here as if you're going to ride along with us as we follow our leads."

A spark shot through her green eyes as they narrowed. Her back stiffened. It seemed she now understood their relationship on this investigation, but he detected a slight sensation that Taylor didn't like the way he explained the particulars.

She sat up straighter in the chair, leaned slightly forward, and as her brows lifted, she said, "You're right. I don't understand."

So much for hoping, he thought.

"Yesterday you called me to say we would work together. *Together* in the dictionary I have says 'with one another.' " She flung her hands up into the air with a confused expression. " 'With one another' does not mean you by yourself." Her open hands moved with practically every word, expressing her frustration. Stabbing a finger in his direction, she added, "And then occasionally you call me?" She slapped her hand against her chest, her words choppy as she balled her hands into fists. "And then you fill me in with a tidbit here and tidbit there? That's not going to work."

"You seem very upset. Sorry." John rose and strolled over to his filing cabinet. "Taylor, these murders aren't the only crimes in the Quarter I'm working on. I have other cases I'm handling at the same time. You and I will not be spending every day together working on this one case." He pulled out two files as the phone rang. "Like these active ones." He emphasized his statement to her by tossing the files on his desk, glancing her way, and then answering the phone. "Bradley," he said, speaking into the mouthpiece. Maybe, just maybe, she understood now. He hoped, anyway.

Buck's voice pricked John's ear as the detective said, "We found him, boss. Michael Guidry. If his story checks out, he was out of town when the first two murders took place. We're going to follow up on his alibi. See if it holds."

"Sounds good. Let me know what you

find." It didn't. Not really, but he wasn't going to say that out loud. He had hoped Michael Guidry would be a strong suspect. Without giving any of his conversation or his thoughts away to the redhead watching his every move, John hung up the phone.

He didn't want to give her any more clues to chase. John looked up just in time to see Taylor slipping the strap of her purse over her shoulder. Rising to her feet, she was ready to depart from his office.

Good. Maybe she wasn't even listening to his conversation.

Guilt flooded his heart and mind. The woman worked so hard to get her story, and she had helped them so much. Without her, they wouldn't even have a lead. And this was how he repaid her? He told her they would work together, so why try to slip out the back door now and keep her out of it?

He knew why — in his heart and in his mind. He didn't need the distraction. For his own sanity, he needed to keep her as far out of his sight as possible. John's scrutiny followed her frame as she moved toward the door, proof of point. He couldn't pull his gaze away, no matter how hard he tried.

Why not let her ride along with him today when he checked on Eddie Thomas, the ex-con who was seen at two of the bars last night? His rap sheet was a mile long for physical abuse against women. Maybe he had escalated in his assaults. Maybe he needed to go further than just hurting women. Maybe he needed to see them die now. John had checked with Eddie's parole officer first thing this morning and found that Eddie was always right on time for their meetings, but that didn't make him innocent.

With her hand on the knob, pulling open the door, she turned and said, "I guess that means I continue my own investigation and tell you what I uncover. Does it mean you will show me the same respect? Or is this a one-sided deal?"

Before he could respond or even share what he was thinking, she added, "Is the police department going to tell me anything they uncover? I presume it does work both ways, right?"

"Miss Jay —" he started to say, but it was as if his answer truly didn't matter, for she was out the door, slamming it behind her.

He did hear her say over her shoulder, "You really disappoint me, Detective Bradley. I thought you were better than most." The rest of what she said was cut off when the door closed behind her, but he didn't think she really cared if he heard her or not.

"Taylor," he called out, wanting to tell her to be careful. He wished she would let him do his job instead of chasing the story herself. She could just report what he gave her. Wasn't that what a reporter did? She didn't need to go investigate on her own. It was not a game. She could get hurt.

Get your head straight, man.

He rubbed his face hard and then raked his fingers through his dark hair, trying to push his concern for her investigating on her own out of his brain. Reporters investigated and reported what they found all the time. That was their job. That was her job, so what did he care if her investigation put her in tight corners? She was a big girl. She could take care of herself. Right?

John opened the top file on his desk. *I need to get back to work. I really do have more cases than the pre-dawn murders.* Thumbing through the papers in one of the files, he muttered, "In fact, I have to be in court tomorrow to testify against this guy to make sure he goes away for a long time for his crime. That's my job!" John almost tore the page in his hand as he flipped it over and grabbed the next one in the file while completing his thoughts aloud. "Getting scum off the street."

After studying the file and refreshing his

memory on the case of Donald Smith, arrested for kidnapping his son, John set the file aside, but the memory of the case lingered. The man had lost his visitation rights because of his addiction to drugs, and while under the influence, he had harmed his child. His ex-wife took him back to court, and they changed his visitation to supervised visits only. That set Donald Smith off on a tangent, yelling in court about the unfairness of it all — having some stranger hanging around him the whole time he was with his son. Security had to restrain the man.

John knew it was more than him wanting to see his son. When the man used to pick the boy up from his ex and then bring him back, he always stretched out his time with her. Smith always tried to convince her to take him back. Truth be told, Smith was only trying to hurt his ex-wife when he took the boy. The man knew the best way to get at her was through the kid, so he wanted to hold on to his rights to agitate her . . . since she wouldn't come back to him. And even if she would, he only wanted her back for a punching bag.

It broke John's heart for the boy to be used as a tool for Smith's pleasure. He remembered the sad look in the kid's eyes when they caught up with the two of them. They were at a dirty, disheveled house that Donald's mother owned and where she allowed him to stay for free. He was supposed to keep it up, but did the man care? No. He didn't care about his mom's house any more than he did about his son. All Donald Smith cared about was himself.

Sad. Do the crime, pay the time. Maybe ten to fifteen years would wake the man up to reality.

Tomorrow John had to give the facts in court. He was ready. Glancing at his watch, he decided it was time to pay Eddie a visit.

Driving over there, John didn't pay attention to his surroundings as he usually did. He was too absorbed in the guilt he felt for betraying Taylor's trust and the way he treated her. She wasn't even with him, and his mind had stayed on her. At this rate, he may as well have let her tag along.

Eddie lived in a small, one-room efficiency over on St. Phillip Street. The outside wasn't too clean, so John didn't expect much on the inside. He wasn't disappointed. When John flashed his badge, Eddie backed up and let him in. John saw dirty dishes spread around on the counter, as well as the table. Clothes were tossed here and there. The couch covered by a blanket thrown over it in disarray didn't disguise the filth in the room. A musty odor hung in the air, mixed with the scent of stale cigarette tobacco and ashes, as well as rotted food. The stench gagged John slightly. *How can people live like this?*

Eddie rubbed his eyelids as if trying to wipe the sleep, or booze, out of his eyes. He grumbled, "What do you want? I ain't done nothing wrong."

"Just a few questions. That's all." John didn't bother to sit.

Eddie plopped down on the couch. "Go ahead. Fire away. Like I said, I ain't done nothing wrong."

John pulled out his note pad. "Where were you Friday night from midnight until 5:00 a.m.?"

"Where do you think? Right here sleeping, of course."

"You got any proof, any witnesses?"

He smirked. "Yeah. I picked up this chick and brought her home. Didn't bother to get her name, though. Who needs a name to do what we did? I paid her, and she was happy when she left."

John made a note. "Get a name, Eddie. I mean it. I'll be back to check. Another question. Where were you a week ago Saturday night?"

The ex-con squinted his eyes. Through cuss words he asked, "What are you getting at? Are you trying to pin me with those murders going on in the Quarter? Forget it! I didn't do them, and you ain't gonna lay the rap at my door. Go find some other sucker."

John knew he was wasting his time with this one. The guy wasn't smart enough to hurt someone and walk away without leaving any evidence behind. In fact, in the past, Eddie loved leaving proof that he was the one who hurt his victims . . . and he was proud of it.

"I'm not a killer! I just like to hurt those who hurt me. If I killed them, they wouldn't feel the pain."

His expression changed. It appeared he was seeing someone he was torturing in his mind's eye as a sick smile touched his lips.

John wanted to punch him in the face one quick time. If nothing else, it would make John feel better. "Come on, Eddie. Do you want to do this at the station, or are you going to cooperate and answer my questions here and now? Where were you a week ago Saturday?"

"All right, all right. Man. Let's see . . . I'm not sure. I got off work around midnight that night and went drinking. Tried to pick up some action, but wasn't lucky. Guess I was too late 'cause usually my money is good with any of those wh—"

John cut him off. He may have to work with the evil in this world, but he didn't have to listen to their foul mouths. "Who were you drinking with? Can you give me a name? Anyone who can corroborate your story?"

Nodding, he said, "Oh, yeah. Old Curtis . . . Curtis Miller. He works with me. We clean shrimp all night over by the docks. My parole officer has the info."

John closed his pad. "Your story better check out. If not, you'll be seeing me again. But next time, I won't be as pleasant. And don't forget to get me a name for the other night. Your lady friend." Stepping out, as hot as it was, John was glad to be out of the disgusting odors and rubbish all around, even though the man's air conditioner worked well at keeping his crib cool. John hated filth, and that was what surrounded Eddie.

Not wasting any time, John called the parole officer once again. He did it the minute he climbed into his car. John didn't want to give Eddie any time to contact this Curtis guy and line up an alibi. Not only did John get the exact location where Eddie worked, but the parole officer gave him some info on Curtis as well. Both were parolees.

After getting the address, John eased on over to the landing. The fish market on Decatur hired anybody who could clean shrimp and gut and clean fish. Eddie was one of the night crew, along with Curtis Miller.

John addressed the owner. "Don't you ever worry about having so many ex-cons around, Mr. Patin?" Down here in the South, the man's name was pronounced *Patan*. Everywhere else, it would be said like patent leather shoes. New Orleans was Cajun country — Acadian exiles, French-speakers from Acadia.

"Not really. What's to steal? I ain't got nothing but fish and shrimp. Besides, they work cheap," Patin said. He wrote down Curtis' address and handed it to John. Patin also backed up Eddie's story as to how late he worked a week ago Saturday. Friday was his night off, so he couldn't vouch for him there.

John paid Curtis a visit. He basically told the same story Eddie had given, but in his own words. In fact, he filled in a few more details, none that John cared to hear, but he took notes and thanked Curtis for his time.

The detective decided to slip by his house

and shower. Tonight he would be checking out one of the two bars left. He would see what low-life he could turn up there. With more paperwork gathering dust on his desk, John decided he would go straight from work. And since both bars were in the Quarter, if he had enough time, he'd cover both tonight. So far, all they'd come up with were dead ends. They needed another break. Hopefully tonight would give him one.

CHAPTER 21

Taylor followed John from one place to the next. Writing down the addresses didn't tell her who he was talking to or what the conversation was about. A lot of good it did her. These stops could deal with one of his other investigations he so proudly stuffed under her nose. How could anything take priority over these murders?

When he pulled into his own driveway, she knew it was time to call it a day. Turning her car around, she headed toward her place. Today was probably a good waste of her time.

If only Detective Bradley . . . John . . . had kept to his side of the agreement.

Tucking her curls neatly around her ear, she strategized her next step. Now that she was back to investigating on her own, she would continue checking the bars out tonight. But she needed a little time to relax before a night on the town . . . for work.

Taylor opened the french doors to the balcony, allowing a breeze to flow into her apartment. The air conditioner was on the blink again. Just what she needed! And of course the landlord would get to it "as soon as possible." It was a good thing her rent was cheap and she loved the place; otherwise, she wouldn't put up with the cavalier way he fixed things. After Hurricane Katrina, her rent had gone up a hundred a month, but it was still low compared to the outrageous prices surrounding the Quarter.

A cool shower later, Taylor slipped on a pair of cut-offs and a T-shirt. Lying on her couch, she brought the telephone with her and punched in her mother's number. It started ringing.

"Hello."

"Dad! Hi. How are you?" She was surprised but pleased to hear her dad answer the phone. Usually he let her mom get it. After retiring, he kept his distance from the outside world. That saddened Taylor. As a reporter, he was always on top of what was going on in and around the world, but when he quit working, he seemed to lose interest in the world.

"Taylor, sweetheart. What are you doing? Trailing another hot lead? I haven't talked to you in days. Tell me about it. Catch me up!"

Taylor closed her eyes and smiled. *Yes. He still loved her work. Tina probably embellished the story about him wanting grandchildren from Taylor.* She quickly told her father the story she was working on, as well as how the police department promised her an exclusive because she came up with the important link in the case. Something they had overlooked. She didn't tell him what she'd discovered . . . because she had promised John. Her dad understood the importance of not revealing certain things to the public, so he didn't press her for the details.

They talked awhile and her father praised her over and over. As they were hanging up, Taylor said, "Give Mom my love. Tell her I called and I'll see you two again soon. I promise."

Hanging up the phone, she glanced around the room as a slight breeze touched her skin. Newspapers were stacked in the chair. Paper plates and napkins sat on her desk and her kitchen table.

While I have the time, I should take a few minutes and pick up. Sighing, she closed her eyes and decided the sleep was a little more important. . . .

241

After almost three hours of shut-eye, Taylor woke with a start, excitement stirring within. Tonight her investigative reporting kicked into high gear as she mulled over the possibilities of what she would uncover. By the time she was dressed and walking out the door, the reporter blood in her stimulated her senses. She was determined to catch another lead. Tonight that lead would give her a name or a motive . . . something.

At nine straight up, Taylor left her apartment and walked the six blocks to the Wild Horse Saloon on Burgundy. It was a small place with a counter along the total length of the room to the right and stools cramped against one another for maximum capacity. To the left was the actual bar with more stools for the customers. The bar also ran the full length of the wall. In the middle was the dance floor, and at opposite ends were small tables with two chairs at each. The dance floor wasn't very big, but it appeared more people sat around drinking and talking than dancing. The stage for the band was smaller than the dance floor. It could be why it was only a three-piece band — keyboard, drums, and guitar.

Clad in tight-fitting jeans tucked into ankle-high black leather boots and a black and aqua blue-printed cowboy-cut shirt covered slightly with a black leather vest sporting fringes, Taylor was relaxed and comfortable, ready to dig into her work. Of course, tennis shoes would have been even more comfortable, but she couldn't have everything.

After ordering a drink at the bar, she flashed the pictures of the three girls to the bartender. He didn't recognize any of the women. Taking her drink, she made her way to the far end of the bar, where the waitresses turned in their order. While each woman waited for their drinks, Taylor showed them the victims' pictures. Two recognized one of the girls as a customer before, but they couldn't be sure how long ago it had been. Another waitress recognized all three but thought it was from the TV news and the newspapers. She didn't recall any of them being a customer, but she had a suggestion.

"What you should do, when the band takes a break, is go talk to the drummer, JR. He watches all the women." She gave a knowing smile. "If anyone noticed them, it would have been JR."

Taylor followed up on the waitress's idea. She was right.

JR pushed his hat back on his head as he studied the three pictures. "I've seen this one before. She started coming by for a while about six months ago, but I haven't seen her for at least . . . two, maybe three months."

Taylor took all this information in but made no notes yet.

Pointing to Stephanie, he said, "She had just split up with some guy and was —" JR stopped midsentence. He eyed Taylor as he chewed on his words.

"Go ahead," Taylor urged.

"She was looking for a good time with no strings attached. My kind of woman, if you know what I mean." JR lifted his hat and wiped his brow with his shirtsleeve. "You're not going to tell me something I don't want to hear, I hope."

As he slipped his hat back on, she said, "No, Mr. Sneed. This is much worse. The woman was killed a couple of weeks ago. We're trying to help find her killer."

JR looked relieved, but then a little sad. "I'm sorry to hear she's dead. She was a nice woman. Her so-called boyfriend had been cheating on her. I was trying to restore her faith in men by giving her a little attention and some lovin'. The night we got together, she came by here feeling really lonely and depressed. I haven't seen her in a couple of months," he assured Taylor.

"Did she tell you her old boyfriend's name?"

"Probably. But I didn't care to listen. Sorry."

Handing him her card, she said, "Thanks for your help. If you think of anything else, please let me know." At least he sounded honest — a real loser, self-absorbed, but truthful about his encounter with Stephanie.

Downing her watered-down drink, she slipped off of the stool and headed for the door. She believed she had found all she could at this little hole-in-the-wall.

Within fifteen minutes, she made her way to Six-Shooters, the biggest western lounge in the Quarter. For a weeknight, the place was packed. Of course, more than locals visited the Quarter. People from all over the world came to enjoy the history, as well as the partying. It was known as The Big Easy, The Crescent City, Sin City, and probably other nicknames as well.

The noise level was high and the smoke thick. She doubted she'd find out much tonight, but she would give it her best shot. Taylor found a table as far away from the band as possible. *That helps some.* Maybe the distance would help her hear the answers to her questions. She hoped, anyway.

A waitress came to take Taylor's order. She flashed her press pass at her and said, "I just need to ask a few questions."

"Can't you see we're too busy for that?" She turned nervous eyes on Taylor after glancing around the room.

Taylor reached into her vest pocket and pulled out the three pictures. "I'm doing a follow-up piece on the three girls who were found dead in the Quarter. Do you recognize any of them? Have you seen them in here?"

"I've only been here two weeks. You need to speak to someone else. Look, I gotta wait on customers. Do you want something to drink or not?"

Slipping the pictures back into the pocket of her vest, Taylor asked, "Is there anyone who works here that's been here awhile?" She understood the woman was busy and doing her job, but didn't people care anymore?

"Ask her," the waitress said as she jabbed her finger toward the tall blond waiting on the next table over. Then she marched away.

Taylor hoped the next waitress would be a little more helpful with a dash of that good old Southern friendliness. Shifting her weight to her feet, she started to rise when a voice stopped her.

"I thought I'd find you here."

"What are you doing looking for me? You should be looking for the killer." She continued to rise to her feet.

"I am. That's why I'm here. I'm not looking for you, I just knew in my gut I'd find you doing your snooping around tonight."

"What do you expect? I'm not getting anything from you like you'd told me I would. So I've gone back to doing my job, on my own. I thought we were going to work together on this, but you made it plain this morning that we're not." She hoped her disappointment in the police department and in him came through loud and clear. Taylor didn't realize how much so until she started spilling her pain to John.

He lowered his eyes as he said, "I tried to stop you this morning."

Taylor almost believed he sounded sorry for the way he let her down, but she wasn't going to fall for that again. If he truly had planned to let her be a part of this investigation, he would have let her go with him today . . . or at least told her what he was doing and promise to share what he found, if anything. "I have a job to do. I'm still on this story, so I go where it takes me."

He raised his blue eyes and locked on hers. He scraped his bottom teeth, almost as if he was trying to stop the words from coming out of his mouth but couldn't. "I had every intention of having you be a part of our investigation — only not on the rough, dangerous stuff, mind you. I can't put a civilian's life at risk. But for interviews that may lead somewhere, I see no harm in you tagging along."

"So what did you find out on your interviews today?" If what he was saying was true, he would share right now with her.

"What?"

"That's what I thought." She nodded slightly, knowing he was leading her on. *So much for sharing.* Quickly, she stepped around him and started for the ladies' room. She needed to get herself together before she started approaching the workers. Get her game face back. For some reason, John Bradley had a way of rattling her very last nerve.

John caught her by the elbow and held on tight. "If you'll calm down and sit with me, maybe we could talk about this."

Her skin tingled where his fingers touched. She wanted to walk away and leave him standing there, but she couldn't. She felt trapped, like she had to stay. Was he ready to discuss business? Was she?

"This had better be good," she muttered,

as if it really mattered at this very moment. She didn't dare let him know where her mind was. It needed to be on her story. She needed to write the best investigative piece ever if she wanted to win the Pulitzer. No man was going to get in her way of following her dream. "I don't have time to waste."

John turned Taylor back to the table, then sat across from her. Leaning toward her, he looked deeply into her eyes. "How did you know what I did today?"

John saw guilty secrets shoot from her eyes, but she didn't say a word.

"Never mind. I don't want to know." She was a regular spitfire. He took a deep breath and started sharing. "I followed a couple of leads that came my way. So far, neither has panned out, but we're still looking into both men. My men have been asking questions at this bar and two others in the area. The only one that all three have been seen in is this one."

Her shoulders drooped. "I just left Wild Horse. Only Stephanie's face was recognized in there. In fact, the drummer, JR, had been intimate with her. I was just starting to ask here. I haven't been as lucky so far. I've spoken to one girl and she's new. She's only been here two weeks. Glad your guys had better luck."

John liked the way she shifted from indignant anger to work mode at a drop of the hat. Obviously, she was dedicated to her work. At least she wouldn't let her emotions interfere with her job. Maybe that meant she would be able to concentrate on what she was doing. "If you had come back when I called your name instead of storming off in a huff, you would have been with me today. You'd know the two I spoke with were persons of interest. They both had alibis we will need to corroborate. We did find one thing out today. If you'd been with me, you would have known."

A smile started to cross her lips but quickly it disappeared as she said, "How was I to know? I'm not a mind reader. You ran me off this morning. You could have said something in the beginning instead of stressing over all the work you had and that not all of it was about these murders."

Her eyes sparked. He could tell she wanted to know what he'd found out but didn't want to ask.

"Well."

Yes. She wanted him to tell her but didn't want to ask. Why was he toying with her? He knew why. He liked the way her green eyes ignited when she got agitated. And the way her cheeks grew rosy red when she tried to hold her tongue.

"Are you going to tell me or not? I thought that was what you said. You wanted to share with me the investigative results. So start talking."

Laughter tickled the back of his throat, but he held it in. Only a smile escaped. This teasing a reporter, sharing with a reporter, was not him. Open and honest with a reporter went against the grain of his makeup. Not that John was ever dishonest with a reporter. It never seemed right to share with reporters what they had found. It wasn't the thing to do — talking to a person who could ruin a case faster than anyone he knew.

It wouldn't be right to share his thoughts so openly with her. Besides, it would put their relationship on a different level than that of cop and reporter. He wasn't ready for that to happen . . . at least not right now.

"We got a match on the tire cast. It was found at two of the scenes. The first and this last one. We know the brand of tire, and it has a spot of really worn tread. Both matched. So, if we catch the killer, that will be one more thing to tie him to the killings."

He watched Taylor mull over the informa-

251

tion he gave her. It looked like she wanted to smile but fought against it. She seemed to be deciding how to respond. As a reporter, he saw the desire to know more flash through her eyes, but then as quickly a veil covered the excitement, revealing a reserved, patient, characteristic determination to let him spill all at his own pace. She appeared to fight every muscle in her mouth to keep it shut.

"You sure get upset easily. If you want to know more, why not just ask? Like this morning. If you hadn't stormed out of my office, you'd already know all of this. I tried to stop you then —" Before he could defend his actions again, she cut him off.

"You could have come after me."

"I don't run after anyone."

"Then you could have told me up front that you were going to let me go with you. No. You told me I misunderstood our arrangement. You led me to believe your word meant nothing."

John reached across the table and laid his hand on top of hers. "Let's forget about this morning. Let's go someplace where we can talk."

Her hand burned where he touched her. She hadn't forgotten how her skin tingled when he grabbed her or how her heart fluttered when he said he had called after her this morning. Why was this man affecting her so? She knew it was strictly business, but something about him excited her. "What do you have in mind?"

"Could we go somewhere so we could talk without all the noise around us? Besides, we don't know who's listening."

Taylor glanced around the room. No one seemed to be paying any attention as far as she could see. "Okay. Let's go." They rose and she followed him out to the sidewalk. "Okay. Where do you want to go?"

"How about the Café du Monde? This time of night we should be able to find a quiet spot. Besides, I know you love beignets."

"Sounds good to me. You know I'm on foot."

It was several blocks back toward the river, but John took her by the elbow and led the way. She loved the feel of the light breeze in the air. Groups of people meandered through the Quarter. It was "the city that never seemed to sleep," and Taylor loved it.

After John got his coffee and Taylor her hot chocolate and beignets, they found a table away from the crowds. To the average eye they would look like a couple wanting to be alone, but Taylor knew it was to keep their conversation private.

"At least now I know how you stay so slim. You walk everywhere you go."

"I don't walk everywhere I go — only when my story is in the Quarter do I get to do that. I'm not that lucky all the time. My job takes me all over the city of New Orleans."

John smiled but said nothing.

Taylor didn't let that bother her. Instead she turned her attention to the white powdery concoction in front of her. She smacked her lips as she lifted one and pulled it toward her mouth.

"I thought we came here to work, not eat," John quipped.

"You're the one who mentioned beignets, remember?" Taylor's gaze crashed into his. "Besides, I'm sure you had your well-balanced meal tonight, but I haven't eaten since breakfast and I'm starved." She took a bite, looked away, and sat back. After chewing and swallowing, she dared to return her eyes to John.

He was watching her.

"What?" she asked.

He smiled crookedly. "You have white powdered sugar on your nose and chin." His grin widened.

Swiping it off of her nose with the back of

her hand and then grabbing her napkin, she dabbed her chin. After tossing the white paper on the table next to her beignets, she said, "Go ahead. Tell me. What are your plans for this investigation?"

"It's simple. Since each of the three victims had been seen at Six-Shooters the night they were murdered, I suggest you and I go to the place together like a couple. We'll be able to watch without people being suspicious." John took a sip of his coffee, all the while watching Taylor. "How does that sound?"

It sounded like a date to her. She picked up her mug and swallowed a mouthful of hot chocolate. "It's a plan that might work. Count me in."

He smiled again.

Her heart raced in anticipation. The only thing Taylor didn't know was if the beating of excitement was because of the investigation or if it was the thought of being together with him every night for a while.

Maybe it was a little of both.

CHAPTER 22

For the next two nights John and Taylor were together from nine until one in the morning. They visited Six-Shooters both nights, undercover. Each night, they sat at a table for two tucked away in the corner so they could watch the people coming and going. They acted like two lovers, cuddled together in the corner. At times, to authenticate things, they made their way out onto the dance floor, usually barely moving to the slow numbers so they could continue to keep their eyes peeled.

Taylor found herself enjoying the play-acting. Occasionally she'd forget it wasn't real, and then she would have to reprimand herself.

When they parted Thursday night, Taylor said, "John, I'll have to meet you at the bar tomorrow night, because I have to go to my parents' anniversary party."

"Why don't I take you to the party and

then we can go to Six-Shooters from there?"

"I don't think that's such a good idea." The last thing she wanted to do was put ideas in her mom's head.

"Why not?"

What could she say? Because her mom would see them as a couple, or she would see her daughter was finally attracted to someone? She sighed. "Okay. Be at my place at seven. But watch out for my mom. She has a mind of her own. She'll have the two of us married before winter if you're not careful."

John laughed. He obviously thought Taylor was joking.

"It's not funny. I promise. I already told you my mom wouldn't be happy until she sees me, her eldest child, married. You think it's a joke. She's dead serious."

John walked Taylor to her apartment door. "I think I can handle her. I don't know too many women who want to see their daughters marry police officers. Trust me."

Closing the door as John walked away, she pondered his words. *It might not be such a bad idea. This might teach Mom and Tina both a lesson and keep them off my back — if we can pull it off, that is.* Taylor would love to pull one over on her sister and Mom, although she doubted that would happen.

That night, she slept well.

Friday came quickly. She rose and cleaned up a bit in her apartment. Not much, but at least enough not to be embarrassed should John actually come in when he picked her up tonight. By the time she was finished putting her place in order, she wished the night were over. Unfortunately, it hadn't even begun.

The afternoon started lousy with a phone call at three.

"Hello."

If she had known who the caller was and what he wanted, she wouldn't have bothered to even answer the phone.

"Taylor?" After her automatic yes, he continued. "My name is Tim Robertson. I've tried to reach you several times at work. I even left a message on your home phone. You've never returned any of my calls."

Taylor remembered the two messages left for her at work. She truly meant to return the call in case he had a lead for her, but she got so caught up in her investigation with John, she forgot. "What can I do for you?" she asked as she hoped maybe, just maybe he had something new to add to the investigation. Her heart doubled in beat.

"I'm sorry to be calling so late, so last-minute, but I wanted to escort you to your

258

parents' party tonight."

Taylor's head snapped, and she felt her eyes bulge slightly. "You what? Where did you get my number?" She knew the answer before she asked, but she still wanted to know for sure.

"Actually, your sister gave me your work and home numbers."

She stood, one hand balled up in a fist, wanting to strike her sister, while the other gripped the phone tight. Her grip was strong enough to choke a horse. Instead, she said, "Thanks. I already have a date." Then she slammed down the phone. It wasn't his fault, but look out, Tina!

Her blood pressure rose, as the thumping grew louder and stronger in her ears. "How dare she! A complete stranger and no warning. At least in the past she usually gave me a warning. A description. A heads-up. Something."

With pent-up energy she started pacing back and forth. Taylor knew she needed to calm down. She wanted to, but just thinking about her sister plotting her life kept her piqued. Suddenly the phone rang again. She snatched it up. "You heard me. I'm not interested, so don't call back!"

As she was about to hang up, she heard, "Not interested in what?"

Recognizing the voice as John's, she instantly pulled the receiver back to her ear. His voice seemed to calm her anger somewhat. At least enough for her to be civil. "Sorry. What did you want?"

John snickered. "You think you can answer a phone like that and leave it in the air? I think not. I want to know what that was all about?" he insisted.

If she'd been smart, she would have told him it was none of his business. Instead, she fell back on the sofa. Deciding this conversation might take awhile, she made herself comfortable. "That remark, believe it or not, was meant for some man I didn't even know. He called, asking me to let him escort me to my parents' party tonight."

"Why did he wait so late to call you, and how did he get your number?"

Taylor started playing with the phone cord, wrapping it around her finger and then releasing it one wrap at a time. "My dear, sweet sister. Who else? I knew this party was a setup. I tried to make her admit it. She swore she wasn't trying to set me up with anyone. She said this was all about our parents. Tina promised she was not trying to find a husband for me. She did admit Mother would be happier if I came with a date. I told Tina if I brought someone, I would. If I didn't, they would have to live with it."

Taylor hated spilling her guts to John, but she grumbled of all they'd done in the past two years. Blind dates unbeknown to her until — *boom* — there he was. John didn't need to hear all of her family problems, but she was mad. She needed to talk to someone. Unfortunately for him, he won the lottery — got the whole spew. The more she said to him, the madder she became. Taylor didn't even know how John was handling all of her personal stuff being dumped in his lap, but she poured it all out.

"Can I make a suggestion?" he finally said.

"Sure, but I can't swear I'll follow it." He got her attention, though. Taylor sat up to listen intently. *He thinks he knows how to get my mom and sister off my case? Great. I want to hear it.*

"We're going to this party, right?" Apparently that was a rhetorical question because he didn't wait for an answer. "Why don't we give them something to think about? You and I have been playing lovers for two nights straight, and if you don't mind me saying so, I think we've gotten pretty good at it. If we do it tonight and they fall for it, it will solve two problems."

"Two? What two?" Taylor was puzzled.

"First, it will get your mother and sister off your back for a while. At least until they figure out it was a fake date. And second, it will let us know if we're doing a convincing job at the bar for the killer, should he or she be watching. That is what we hope is happening; otherwise, we're wasting our time."

The part of his theory that caught Taylor's attention was getting her mom and sister off her back. She loved that! But could she chance playing his lover in front of them? She knew she was already physically attracted to the man. Pretending in front of strangers was one thing, but pretending in front of family was another. Part of her wouldn't be pretending, and they would see through it. When they found out later it was play-acting for their benefit, her family, at least her mom, would know the truth and would know how deeply it would hurt Taylor when the job was over.

"Come on, Taylor. Don't think about it. Just do it. It would teach them a lesson about sticking their nose in other people's lives. I know. I've been through it myself."

John sounded like he really wanted to help her. How sweet. "Okay. Let's do it."

"Now, back to why I called you to begin with. How should I dress for this party tonight? The same way I've dressed the past two nights? Casual?"

"Yes, John. By all means, dress casual. We're not fancy." What a guy! He was worried how to dress for her parents. Most men wouldn't care. "Don't forget to pick me up at seven." On that, they said good-bye.

It was almost six. Taylor hadn't eaten lunch yet, so she fixed herself a quick ham and cheese sandwich. With it she tossed back a few chips and chased it all with a glass of milk. She figured at Tina's she wouldn't have much of an appetite. Taylor ate while she finished watching an old movie on TV. By the time the credits were rolling, it was six thirty. Jumping up, she ran to get dressed.

After her shower, she dried off and dressed for the night. She wore knee-high black leather boots with jeans and a T-shirt, one with a country singer sparkling across her chest. Taylor dabbed on a bit of makeup and a quick splash of perfume, then took a minute to try and tame her wild curls. When finished, she glanced at her reflection in the mirror. "You don't look too bad." Normally Taylor would find all kinds of faults, but not tonight. She chose to bolster her morale in order to face her sister with a smile and not a .45.

That thought brought a half smile to her

face. She couldn't even tell her sister how mad she had gotten today. She and John were going to play the happy little loving couple. What a joke!

Walking out of the bedroom, she heard a knock at the door. "Coming," she called. Grabbing her purse and the present she had bought for her parents, Taylor reached for the doorknob. Pausing, she said, "John, is that you?"

"No. I'm the crazy guy on the phone." He laughed.

Soon they were in his Bronco, heading toward her sister's home. "They live in the Garden District near my parents," she explained.

Glancing his way, she studied him as he drove. He sure looked good tonight. His face was clean-shaven, and he smelled heavenly. Taylor wished what they were about to do wasn't a joke.

"You up for your part tonight?" he questioned her in clipped tones.

Taylor's left brow furrowed. "Sure. I've made it through the last two nights playacting with you. What's one more?" She knew the difference. Tonight it was in front of family, but she didn't dare let him know she was a little nervous about the next couple of hours. She continued to direct him until they pulled into Tina's driveway.

Getting out of the car, John walked around and opened the door for Taylor. As she started to step out, he reached for her hand. As she placed her hand in his, she climbed out of the Bronco. When her feet hit the ground, he wrapped his arms around her and pulled her close. Suddenly he kissed her hard, on the lips.

Taylor's heart leapt into her throat as it beat uncontrollably. As soon as she could speak, she said, "What was that for?"

Slowly he slackened his hold on her but kept one arm draped around her waist and then directed them toward the front door. "In case someone was looking out of the window. Besides, you needed to look like you've been kissed. You were too stiff-looking, almost frightened. Now" — he paused — "now you have the look of love."

She smirked. "Yeah, right." She had a hard time catching her breath but didn't want him to know how much he'd rattled her.

Her sister must have been watching, for the minute their feet touched the first step, the door flew open and Tina filled the doorway. "Taylor. You made it." Tina's voice sounded surprised.

John pulled her a little closer, making Taylor look up at him before she answered her sister. She couldn't help but smile. Taylor knew that was a warning from him to be sweet to Tina.

"Yes, Tina. I wouldn't miss this for the world. I have someone I want you to meet." They stepped into the foyer.

Tina smiled at John with open admiration. Taylor knew that look. John had better hurry up and tell them he was a cop if he knew what was good for him.

"John, this is my baby sister, Tina." After greetings were exchanged, Tina led the way to the family room.

As Taylor started to pull out of his grasp, he caught her hand in his, keeping them touching one another as they entered the living room where everyone was seated.

Taylor's father and Rodney, Tina's husband, immediately rose to their feet. "Taylor, sweetheart," her father said as he approached her. John released her hand, giving her freedom to hug her dad. She then kissed her mother's cheek, hugged Rodney, and laid her parents' present on the end table.

"I'd like all of you to meet a . . . a friend of mine, John. And this is my family." She then called everyone by name as she pointed toward each. "Where are the kids?"

"They're upstairs. They'll join us for dinner."

"It's a pleasure to meet all of you," John said. "Taylor has told me so much about each of you these past few weeks." He gazed at Taylor. "It's only been a couple of weeks, right, darling?" Then he turned his blue eyes on her mother. "It's been the best weeks of my life. Your daughter is something special."

Needless to say, Taylor's mother ate that up. "We've always known that. It's just been hard making Taylor see it."

John slipped his hands over Taylor's shoulders and said, "I tell her that all the time — she's something special." Then he topped it by leaning down and kissing her cheek in front of everyone.

Taylor couldn't believe it. She knew her cheeks turned red. She felt the heat rise. Was he ever putting on a show! He deserved an Oscar.

Rodney interrupted Taylor's thoughts as Taylor and John sat on the loveseat. "Are you working on a new story? Dad said you were covering those murders that have been happening in the Quarter. I've seen a few of your articles, but they don't have the details you usually share with the readers. What's going on?"

"Yes, I'm covering the murders, but I'd rather we not discuss them tonight."

John took over before she could say any

more. "Actually, that was how I met your sister-in-law, Rodney. I'm the detective in charge of that investigation. We're working closely on it." He smiled sweetly at Taylor. "But I'm keeping my eye out for her. I don't want anything happening to her."

Taylor's mother spoke up. "This is refreshing — a young man who wants to protect our daughter. Taylor usually won't allow anyone to protect her." She squeezed Oliver's hand, vividly showing her enthusiasm.

John smiled at Mrs. Jaymes. "I know what you mean. She gets mad at me if I put too many protective barricades between her and her story. She wants me to believe she is as tough as any man." John winked at her dad. "But I know she's as fragile as a piece of porcelain."

Oliver cleared his throat. "Well, I imagine she is that, but Taylor has taken very good care of herself, and I believe she will continue to do what is best for her."

Dear old Dad. How sweet. "You know, y'all don't have to talk about me as if I'm not here. I am, and I hear everything you're saying." Taylor nudged John in his side.

"Well, I, for one, think she's done wonderfully for herself, picking a policeman as a boyfriend," Tina chimed in to the conversation as her eyes laid to rest on John in awe.

Theresa agreed with her daughter, but neither Oliver nor Rodney voiced their opinions. Not that they didn't have one, Taylor felt certain. Her guess would be their opinions reflected their wives — so much for John's theory, them not wanting her to be with a cop.

The conversation continued and Taylor could tell her family was eating him up. They were falling for John hook, line, and sinker. Boy, had she made a mistake! Her mother didn't care that he was a policeman. In fact, she sounded like she loved it because she figured he could take better care of her daughter. Her mother was probably right, but that was beside the point. Before Taylor could pass her thoughts on to John, Tina insisted Taylor help her in the kitchen.

As they entered the other room, questions fired out of Tina's mouth, one after the other. Taylor knew it. Helping in the kitchen was merely a ploy to get her alone.

"Where have you been hiding him? He's perfect. How long have you two really been dating? He said a few weeks. Why didn't you tell us? I hate to admit this, but I did have someone I was going to set you up with tonight. Boy, would he have been a disappointment compared to John." Tina went on and on about John's perfections. His looks. His manners. His knowledge. And she didn't even know him yet.

The only way this charade would work is if her sister would learn a valuable lesson when she learned the truth. Would she? Taylor hoped it didn't backfire. But if Tina did, she would never interfere in Taylor's life again.

Tina and Taylor put dinner on the table and everyone gathered around, including the girls, Shelly and Sheila. They, too, were instantly taken with John. The food was great, but Taylor couldn't swallow a thing. It was a good thing she had eaten a late lunch.

Part of her felt bad for what she was pulling over on her family, but the other part of her was wishing all of this was for real. Everyone liked him so much, and John fit in so well. And admittedly, she liked him, herself. Taylor hadn't heard one lull in conversation tonight. And everybody was getting in on it; everyone except her, of course.

If Taylor didn't know better, she thought John was having the time of his life. He wasn't that bad of an actor. He even had Taylor believing him.

After the presents were opened, it was getting close to nine. John said, "I hate to end this great party, but Taylor and I have something we must do tonight. It's with the case. It has been a delightful pleasure being here with you all. Thanks for including me. It was wonderful meeting everyone. I certainly see where your daughter gets her grace and charm."

Mrs. Jaymes walked them to the door and her dad followed behind. "Thank you for stopping by. The two of us have had a wonderful thirty-three years of marriage. It really is something to think about." She squeezed Taylor's arm as they walked to the door.

Her mother wasn't too obvious, was she? Taylor eyed her mom and then shook her head. Giving them another hug, she whispered, "I love you two. See you soon."

John said bye again, and the two of them left. Once inside the Bronco, he said, "Your family was very nice."

Taylor nodded. "Of course they were nice. I never said they weren't. But didn't you feel my mother measuring your chest for your tuxedo?"

"They did seem to like me, didn't they?" John's face looked surprised and yet a little self-satisfied. "And I caught that hint about marriage being wonderful. Rest assured."

Taylor rolled her eyes as she fell back

against the seat. "Of course they liked you. They think you will make a wonderful husband for their wild daughter who won't settle down. You're perfect. You're a cop. You'll be able to keep me in line. Don't you see?" She huffed. "And you thought they would be turned off by your profession. I should have known better."

John remained silent for a few short minutes, almost as if he was reveling in the attraction everyone felt for him. Why should that surprise him? He was wonderful.

Taylor was worn out, and the night still wasn't over. Actually, it had only just begun. Would she make it?

She flashed her eyes in his direction. Her stomach squeezed. Tonight was wonderful, but she had to remember it was all an act. The big picture was the story, and that was where they were headed now. She had to stay focused on the prize . . . Pulitzer Prize.

CHAPTER 23

Friday night was no different at Six-Shooters than the two nights before; no leads, and no approaches. Toward the end of the night, in fact, the last dance of the night, as the two stepped around the floor holding each other close, John whispered in her ear. "Are you too tired for me to come by for a little while? I think we need to rethink our plan of action. This isn't getting us anywhere."

His warm breath caressed Taylor's neck as she listened intently. They might not have accomplished anything for the case, but these nights with John on his best behavior had done something wonderful to Taylor. She couldn't help but feel slightly guilty. She loved every minute of it.

Earlier tonight, Taylor enjoyed having her mother see her with a date. In fact, she delighted in the feeling it gave her to have a man interested in her, even if it was pretend.

Her heart broke a little inside as she thought about the lie she led her mother to believe, but seeing the joy on her face filled Taylor with hope. Maybe one day she could fall in love. Too bad this wasn't the real thing.

Taylor expected her mother to be on the phone first thing Saturday morning drilling her about John. Tina had her chance earlier that night. Taylor could hear her mother now. "What's he really like? Is his job more dangerous than yours? You two looked serious. Are you?" Taylor smiled at the thought of her mother's excitement. It would be nicer if their relationship had been true, but Taylor knew better than to even fantasize.

"Did you hear me?" John's voice jolted her back to the present. "May I come by?"

"Sure. That's a good idea. I was thinking the same thing myself, and time is running out before the next kill if his MO hasn't changed," she said, keeping her voice low.

In fifteen minutes, they were at her apartment. She had done her version of cleaning that morning, but as usual had left her dirty dishes in the sink after eating that late lunch. Her gaze caught the T-shirt she had slept in tossed on the chair in the living room. Not too bad. The rest of the room looked fairly neat. She swooped the shirt up and tossed it in the bedroom, behind the door. *He won't be going in there, so no big deal.*

When she turned her gaze back toward John, she realized John had noticed the few things out of order. His eyes glanced at the newspaper she'd left open on the coffee table, as well as her Coke glass from before she took off for the evening.

Flashing an awkward smile, she said, "The maid didn't make it today. Have a seat. I'll go put a pot of coffee on for you." She grabbed the empty glass and nonchalantly waltzed into the kitchen.

When the coffeemaker was set and water started dripping, she returned to the living room. The newspaper had been gathered together and left folded neatly on the coffee table, as neat as it had been when it was dropped on her doorstep. Maybe even neater, if that was possible. She noticed her throw pillows had even been straightened, along with the cushions of the couch.

"Sorry if my mess offends you." *Good.* She noticed color wash over his face as if she had embarrassed him.

"I was killing time. I thought I would help you out. Let's get down to business." He pushed a pillow out of place and leaned back against the sofa.

She laughed to herself. "The coffee will be ready in a minute. Two sugars, right?"

He nodded. As Taylor went back into the kitchen, she mumbled under her breath, "Maybe I'll throw in an extra teaspoon full. He needs it."

Taylor returned with the coffee and found no other move had been made to right her living room. In fact, John had leaned his head back against the sofa and looked to be napping.

As soon as she set the cups down, he sat up. "Smells good." As he sipped it, his smile showed it tasted as good as it smelled.

Taylor curled up in her overstuffed chair and watched him as he drank a bit of his coffee. When he placed it on the coffee table, Taylor took that moment to start their discussion. "You're right; we're not getting anywhere, and it's been another week. Any day another woman could end up dead. It could happen tonight."

John heaved a sigh as he rubbed his whiskers and thought about his new idea. *This will put Taylor in more jeopardy, but I think it's the only way. I won't — we won't — let anything happen to her.* He leaned back and draped his arm across the back of the sofa as he said, "I know we've been watching everyone, and we've run background checks on any and everyone who appeared suspicious or even said anything out of the ordinary. In fact, we've checked out all the workers, including the band members, and nothing new has jumped out at us. We're still keeping close tabs on one of the band members, who had a record and a couple of customers we recognized with rap sheets a mile long. But we have to do something to flush out the killer — hopefully before he kills again."

John's gaze traveled around her living room, but he saw nothing. His mind was preoccupied with what this would mean to Taylor's safety. He needed to find the words to approach her about his new idea. As much as he hated it, it seemed to be the next best option.

Taylor smirked. "Let me save you the words. I see it on your face and now I know why you were so nice to me tonight. You're planning to send me packing. It's time I went back to checking out information in the light of day, and you and your men do the heavy lifting, the dangerous parts, on your own at night."

He covered his mouth, trying to hide the smile. *If she only knew how far from the truth that was. She'll know soon enough. Spit it out and be done with it.* "I think you need to go as a single woman, and I'll go keep my eye on you from a distance. The killer is not going to say anything to give himself away to a couple, but he might to an appealing single woman. And in this case, I mean a trained investigator, undercover. I must be out of my mind because I know this could be dangerous. So think it over carefully before you decide. I probably should use a policewoman, but you're more aware of what to listen for, questions to ask without sounding like a reporter or a cop. I just think you're our best bet."

Her eyes lit up.

"I knew it. The minute the word *danger* came into the picture, the light in your eyes started dancing around, doing flips. You get excited over the possibilities of danger." He raked fingers through his hair. "Maybe I'm making a mistake."

"I'm just . . . I —"

John stood. "I knew I didn't want to suggest this to you, but my gut tells me you're the one to get close. But I should really use a policewoman — not you." He shoved his hands in his pockets and walked over to the window. As he let his thoughts overtake him, he stared out into the darkness.

He was asking too much of her, and she

seemed to love it. Why was he encouraging her to continue? More so, why was he putting her in a more dangerous position? Maybe this was his way of making himself lose his desire for her. He hated to admit it — it wasn't working.

Taylor watched his silhouette in the window. His back faced her, but she knew he was deep in thought, regretting his plan to work with her, his plan to use her to draw out the killer.

She eased over to the window and stood behind him. She couldn't let him change his mind. Gently she reached out and touched his back. "John," she whispered. "My eyes danced in delight, as you said, because I was delighted — excited. Not by the thought of the danger. When that thought comes to mind, which I'm sure it will, I'll shudder."

Slowly he turned to face her but said nothing.

Taylor continued. "I was delighted because you didn't exclude me from the investigation. I truly thought you were going to tell me to go back to pounding the pavement during the day and leave the night work to you." Her voice became husky as she continued. "It excites me that you realize I have enough detective instincts about me to listen and watch and discover something to help you out on your case."

Still, he stood watching, saying nothing.

She raised both her hands and shook him gently by the shoulders. "Don't you see? I know it sounds crazy, but coming from you I take that as a compliment and it makes me feel so good." She bit her bottom lip, shocked that she shared her deepest feelings with this wonderful man. When he still didn't respond, she gave up and turned to walk away.

John caught her by the arm. Turning her back around, he sat on the edge of the windowsill and pulled her in front of him, holding her still by clasping her hands in his.

"Taylor, you do realize how dangerous this will be, not to mention it's probably against every police regulation there is. I think I'm out of my mind to allow you to do this, but it feels right . . . here." He tapped his fist against the middle of his chest with her hands still in bondage.

A knot formed in her throat as she felt the beating of his heart. Swallowing hard, she whispered, "No, you're not out of your mind. It shows you have good instincts. We can work together — just not together." She smiled.

Releasing her hands so they could drop to her side, his hands gently rubbed her arms. "You have to promise me something."

Looking up, their eyes locked. "Anything."

"Three things, actually. One, you can't do anything stupid. Two, I have to be able to see you at all times — don't leave the bar with anyone." His glare hardened. "Under any circumstances. And three, you'll do exactly what I tell you, when I tell you, and I'll be watching you like a hawk. Others will be watching you, too, and what's going on around you, too. The way people react to you and so forth. Do I make myself clear?" His words were stern, but his voice gentle.

Warmth spread over her. He would be watching her every move. The only bad part? She wouldn't be in his arms anymore. She would be dancing with other men and wishing it was John. Sighing and shaking her head clear of all romantic thoughts of him, she said, "Whatever you tell me. I understand. I promise I'll listen to you."

"Listen to you. Sighing because you have to do what I say. You don't take orders well, do you?"

A crooked smile twisted her lips. He misunderstood her sigh. *Good.* She didn't want to let him know she was falling in love with him.

John dropped his hands. Glancing at his watch, he said, "Get some rest. It's late. Sleep in tomorrow . . . no. Forget that. It's already tomorrow. Be at the bar at nine thirty tonight. Look for me and try to sit near, but not too near. We don't want to give ourselves away." He smiled, lifting his brows. "Can you handle that?" He rubbed the pad of his thumb softly over her cheek and then placed a soft kiss on her forehead. "Be careful. Good night."

Her heart jumped as his lips brushed her skin. Keeping control, Taylor murmured good night and then watched him walk out the door.

The warmth inside her was quickly replaced by a cold chill. She had felt so good when he was around, safe even . . . secure and desired. At times anyway.

But it wasn't real . . . or was it?

He stirred feelings in her she had never felt before. It scared her. And to think all this time she never believed she could find a man who was right for her.

Her career had been too important to her to even think of settling down. The story she was working on always took precedence over some guy. That was probably why noth-

ing had ever come of any of her relation-
ships. Would a connection come of these
feelings stirring in her?

Probably not.

She still had her goal, and it was still
important to her. Somehow, she thought,
maybe John could fit into her life. Maybe
their careers could work together. He was
different. That was what made him so special.

She felt certain she wouldn't be able to
sleep tonight, but within minutes, she was
fast asleep.

Taylor woke by ten that morning. After her
morning cup of coffee and some scrambled
eggs, she decided to do something she rarely
did. She had an overwhelming desire to
super-clean her apartment.

By three she had her place sparkling, the
best it had looked in months. It even smelled
fresh. Still dressed in a pair of cut-offs and
a pink T-shirt, she ran down to the local
market and stocked up on groceries —
another thing she didn't normally do.

The desire to play homemaker really blew
her away. By the time she finished shop-
ping, she had enough food to fill her cup-
boards and refrigerator. Surprisingly
enough, some of the food she bought was

actually healthy.

"I hope I manage to eat all this before it goes bad." She closed the produce drawer after stuffing a bag of apples inside.

Feeling tired and dirty, after spending most of the day playing house, Taylor decided it was time for a shower. But as she stepped into the hallway, her doorbell rang. "Who could that be? Probably Mom checking on me." She never called, which surprised Taylor. Her mom showing up on Taylor's doorstep truly shocked her.

Before her hands turned the knob, she heard a familiar voice call out, "Taylor. Answer your door. I know you're home."

"John?" she whispered. *What's he doing here?*

Wiping the back of her hands against her cheeks, trying to remove all traces of dirt, she headed for the door. Excitement stirred within her as she reached for the knob. "What brings you here? I thought I wouldn't see you until tonight."

John's gaze slid over her head and behind her into her apartment. His brows wrinkled. "Do you have company?" As he asked the question, he took a step inside.

Taylor frowned. Looking down at herself, she asked, "Do I look like I'm entertaining company?" Backing up, she asked, "Would you like some coffee? I'm sure eventually you'll let me know why the surprise visit."

John stepped into the living room. Glancing around, he paused. Stepping back out, he looked up at the apartment number. "It is the same one. Did the good fairy come clean your apartment for you? Oh, no, I forgot. You said the maid. I guess your maid showed up today." His eyes danced around the room as he teased her. "Looks like you've been cleaning. Expecting someone special?"

"Of course not!" she snapped. "Have a seat. I'll start the coffee."

She slammed the front door shut and darted for the kitchen. What was going on? Why was he here? And did he have to be so aggravating?

Instead of returning to her company once the coffee started dripping, she chose to wait for it. When it finished dripping, she couldn't put it off any longer. "Be nice," she whispered aloud. *Remember. Just last night you had seen a different side of him.* She didn't want him to ruin the pleasant mood that he had set the night before. She poured him a cup of coffee, and Taylor fixed herself some iced tea.

John had made himself comfortable on the sofa. After placing a cup of coffee in front of him on the coffee table, she slipped into the recliner to sip her tea. "What brought you this way?"

Raising the cup, he sipped the brew and then set it back down. "I thought we should go over again what you are to do tonight. I don't want any slip-ups."

"Do you always have to sound so . . . so . . . I don't know what to call it — uncertain? Why don't you just trust me? Trust yourself for that matter? You're the one who thought I could handle it to begin with," she snapped. Calming herself, she determined to put a smile on his face. Softening her voice, she said, "I remember what you said. Stay in your sight at all times. Don't leave with anybody, and above all, don't do anything stupid." Taylor turned her lips down in a pout. "Is that right?"

John shook his head. "All right. Be smart. But still do as I told you — for your own good."

Taylor stood before he could say anything else. "I was about to take a quick shower, then eat. Have you eaten?" She answered for him. "I doubt it. Whatever happened to your good eating habits?" Before he could answer, she continued. "Relax and you can eat with me. I promise. It's healthy food."

He smiled, warming her heart. "Is this

another 'Trust me' remark of yours?"

She shrugged. "Suit yourself. But if you leave, you'll miss a tossed salad and baked fish." She flipped her hair behind her shoulders and sashayed past him. "I'll be out in a few minutes."

Taylor wasn't sure if he would wait or not, but she hoped he would. Her shower didn't take long. Maybe it was because she was anxious to get back out to John. She slipped on her favorite pair of old jeans and a T-shirt.

Using the towel, she worked at drying her hair some. After combing it out and letting the curls and waves manifest themselves, she headed for the kitchen. Taylor passed through the living room and found John looking through an old photo album of hers.

"Looks like you made yourself at home." She smiled but kept heading for the kitchen.

Bending down and pulling out her casserole pan, she heard steps behind her. He followed. A grin etched in her face. "I hope you're hungry."

John sat down at the table still holding the album in his hands. "You and your dad look to be very close by these pictures."

"Uh-huh," she murmured.

John turned the page. "Your sister is always in a dress, and you are always in

287

pants. Did you want to be a boy?"

Turning her head so she could see him, she said, "Don't try to analyze me."

He was still looking at the pictures, not paying her any attention. "You were definitely Daddy's little girl. You're always on his lap or holding his hand. Even when you got older."

"We were close, still are in fact. Just my life doesn't leave much time to go visit him, and he doesn't call often. He leaves that up to Mom. Why? Is there a problem?"

He ignored her again. "What are these awards around your father?"

He seems to enjoy snooping into my life. For some reason, though, it didn't seem hard for her to talk about her personal life with him. She smiled. "He won the Franklin Press Award and the Pulitzer Prize for investigative reporting. Every journalist wants to win that, and my dad did over ten years ago. I only hope I can win at least one major award for my writing — make him proud of me." Taylor's eyes lit up as she thought about what she was saying.

John looked up at her. "So you're trying to be like your father?"

"No. I'm trying to accomplish something in the field I chose to follow, which happens to be the same field he chose as a young

288

man." Taylor sprinkled the fish with garlic powder and a touch of Tony Chachere's, then poured lemon juice over it. Next, she topped it with Worcestershire sauce and a couple pats of butter, and then popped it in the oven.

Turning back to John, she pleaded, "Please don't analyze me and, above all, don't criticize me . . . just be pleasant. Is that so hard for you? You're making me sorry I asked you to stay and eat with me." Taylor turned back to the sink and started washing the lettuce.

John slipped up behind her. Leaning close to her, he whispered, "Man, you smell good. So fresh and clean." His warm breath caressed her skin.

Goose bumps covered her arms, sending shivers down her back. That was better, she thought, but didn't say a word.

"I'm glad you asked me to stay." He touched her damp curls lightly and then rested his hands on her shoulders. "I'm glad you cleaned your place for me, too."

She dropped the lettuce in the sink as she turned off the water. "What makes you think —" Her question was cut off when she turned around.

A smile spread to his lips. His hands had fallen to his sides when she turned so unexpectedly, then he started to put them back up on her shoulders, as if he was about to pull her to him and kiss her.

Placing her hands flat against his chest, she shoved him back. "What did you say?" It was a rhetorical question. She didn't expect an answer. In fact, she didn't want him to answer her at all. "I know what you said. I did not clean my house for you. What do you think I am — a slob? I clean it occasionally. And today just happened to be the occasion. I didn't expect you here today, and you know it. You are so full of yourself!"

John dropped his hands to his sides, stepped back, and laughed. "Come on. Why is it so hard to admit you cleaned it for me? I made a comment last time so you wanted to make sure it was clean the next time I came by. Hey, that pleases me." He grinned.

"Wipe that look off your face, please. I didn't do it for you." She pivoted back to continue rinsing the lettuce.

"Taylor, why is it so hard for you to admit you did it for me?" His voice was soft and gentle. "Look at what you're cooking — fish. That's healthy. You don't eat healthy. It appears by the salad and fish you're trying to eat healthy now. I'm sure if I look," he walked over to the refrigerator, "I'll find other healthy foods inside." He opened the refrigerator door and eyed the plastic bag of apples sticking out. Pulling on the drawer, he said, "See."

Before he could look any further, Taylor stormed over, shut the drawer, and slammed the refrigerator door shut. "Get out!" She pushed him toward the living room. "Get out and stay out! You are uninvited. So leave. I did not clean for you, nor did I shop for you." Rushing around him, she stomped over to the front door. Pulling it open and holding it, she continued, "I'll see you tonight. Don't be late." Her eyes flared with anger. *The nerve of him!*

"But . . ."

"No buts. Get out! Now!" She glared him down.

John didn't say another word. Scratching his head, he left with no more arguments.

Taylor slammed the door behind him. "The nerve of that man," she spat at the closed door. Throwing herself down on her overstuffed chair, she sat and fumed. When the fish was ready, she was no longer hungry. She had lost her appetite right after her temper.

The smell of garlic mixed with lemon wafted in the air. Taylor wrapped the entire meal and stored it in the refrigerator for another day. Then she put the dirty dishes in the sink and ran water on them. She wasn't in the mood to clean another thing today.

Choosing her outfit for the night's work, she considered her outburst with John. Why had she gotten so mad?

He was right. She had done it for him. She'd cleaned her place in case he came by so she could impress him and show him she was capable. Also all the food . . . surely she hadn't bought all of that just for her to eat.

Looking at her reflection in the mirror, she squinted her eyes. "You just couldn't admit it, could you? Although, if he had been a gentleman, he wouldn't have said such things anyway, other than maybe comments on how good it looked."

It's all his fault. . . .

Oh well. Enough of that.

The story was more important than a fight with a deadbeat cop. She'd never cared for cops anyway.

CHAPTER 24

"What got into her?" John headed back to the office thinking all the while, *What's the big deal?*

For the next couple of hours he tried to work but found it hard to concentrate. He couldn't accomplish a thing. Tossing his pen down, he leaned back in his chair and tried to make sense of the earlier disaster with Taylor.

No matter how many times he replayed it, which he did several times, he kept coming up with the same conclusion. "There's no mistaking it. She did it for me. She had to. Didn't she? So why wouldn't she admit it?"

Had anyone come by, they would have thought he was crazy talking to himself, but right now he felt a little crazy. He threw his hands into the air. "Women! What does it matter? I didn't want to get tangled up with her anyway."

A knock at the door brought John out of

his reverie. "Excuse me, sir. Are we still staking out the club tonight?" Officer Brown asked him.

John glanced at his watch. "Darn straight we are. Thanks," he said as he jumped to his feet. "Yeah. Get in plain clothes and get on over there. Where is Buck? He knows what to do, right?"

Brown nodded affirmatively. "By the way, that was Guidry you saw at the club last night. We watched the film today, the one the club cameras produce nightly. We also spotted another known felon for sexual abuse of women, our old buddy Frank Simpson."

John remembered him immediately. Not only did he sexually abuse his women, but he also got a kick out of choking them while tormenting them sexually. He would tie a cord around their neck, then tie that same cord to their ankles and watch them try not to move and choke themselves to death while he had his way with them. Luckily for him, none of his victims died. He had been given five years in prison for what he had done. Five lousy years. That wasn't much for what those two women had suffered.

"Five years goes by fast, doesn't it?"

"Yeah. I checked his rap sheet. He's been out for five months and has stayed clean the whole time . . . as far as we know."

"One of you keep your eyes on Guidry while the other stays with Simpson. Guidry might have had an alibi for the first two killings, but the alibi hasn't been verified yet. He's still a suspect. I'll keep mine on Taylor. Between the three of us watching the three of them, and the others that come in contact with them, maybe we'll get lucky tonight."

"See ya there, Lieutenant." Brown left and John followed him out of the building.

John headed home mumbling to himself, "I can't believe how late it's gotten." He rushed in, showered quickly and changed into a fresh pair of slacks and a neatly ironed shirt. Next he slipped on his shoulder holster for his Walther PPK. The .380 was an easier weapon to hide. Then John put on his sport coat. He would stash his automatic in his glove box for backup.

Glancing around his clean home before leaving, it seemed so empty . . . so cold. "Where did that thought come from?" he asked himself before heading out the door.

On the drive to the club, he found himself thinking of Taylor again. He was running late but hoped she remembered rule number one. Don't do anything stupid. Pressing the gas pedal harder, he rushed to get there, hopefully before her. Tonight he would apologize for their squabble. Maybe she wasn't ready to admit she wanted to impress him, so he shouldn't have pushed it. Before that, though, he needed to concentrate solely on what was going on tonight.

Looking in his rearview mirror, he spotted flashing red and blue lights. His eyes darted down to his dashboard and saw the needle holding steady on sixty. Slowing down, John pulled over, came to a quick halt, jumped out of his vehicle, slamming his door, and trampled over to the police unit. "I don't need this." Flashing his ID at the policeman, he said, "I'm in a hurry here. I'm on a case."

The uniformed officer got out of his car. Recognizing the lieutenant, he started rambling apologies. He was a new policeman and apparently hadn't recognized the detective's Bronco. "Lieutenant Bradley. I'm sorry, sir. I didn't mean to delay you. I thought you were a kid joy riding. Sorry —"

John interrupted him. "It's okay, Findley. Don't worry. I've got to go." He returned to his car and was back on his way instantly. John was late now for sure. All he could hope was that Taylor hadn't done anything foolish. He never liked using civilians for undercover operations and this was why. Unfortunately with Taylor, to him, it was a little worse.

Taylor dressed in a pair of jeans and an off-the-shoulder black fitted top. With this, she wore her black boots with the silver tips on the toes. She took special pains with her hair and makeup tonight. "All part of the job," she told herself looking into the mirror, but she knew better.

Entering Six-Shooters at the scheduled time, she glanced around. He had told her to sit near him. *Can't do that if you're not here.* She double-checked the time to make sure she wasn't early. "Right on time," she murmured to herself.

She found a stool that seemed to be in the center of the long bar down one side of the place. That looked good. She sat down and leaned over to place her order. After ordering a screwdriver easy on the vodka, she told the bartender she wanted to run a tab. Then she sat back and began looking for faces she'd seen in there on previous nights. Recognizing a couple of regulars, she started watching them, trying to catch someone's eye.

Taylor managed to get noticed by several men in the bar. She danced with a couple of cowboys who asked her, names exchanged sometimes, but not always. None made her feel like they were the one she was looking for. She dropped a few remarks, watching their response. Nothing seemed to make them react strangely. So she decided not to waste any more time on them.

The bartender stopped in front of her while she sat on her stool and scanned the crowd, looking for another one to set her sights on. "Is something wrong with your drink? You've barely touched it."

She smiled. That was nice of him to notice. She would have to leave him a good tip. "Oh, no. Everything's fine. I'm just sipping slowly."

"I noticed your boyfriend's not here tonight. Did y'all split up?"

So he had noticed her before. "Yeah, we sure did. That's the breaks. You win some, you lose some." Taylor flashed him a big smile and then took another sip of her drink. She had to get back to work. "Thanks again. I'll let you know when I need another one."

Taylor glanced around the room. She still didn't see any sign of John. She thought she recognized one of the detectives from the other day, but she couldn't be sure. Before she knew it, on each side of her sat young men dressed in jeans and western shirts, wearing boots and cowboy hats, but still no John. What could be keeping him? She turned back to the bar; giving one of her neighbors a smile in acknowledgment. That was all it took. He struck up a conversation.

John rushed to the door but slowed his stride as he entered. He didn't want to draw attention to himself.

Strolling into the club, his eyes trained for searching out small details in an instant, he spotted Taylor at the bar. Two men sitting on either side of her were vying for her attention. It was all he could do to keep his composure and walk on to a table as far away as possible, yet still in view of the bar.

Finding the right table, he took it. As soon as he placed an order, he sat back and started watching Taylor work without looking straight at her. She seemed to be getting into the swing of things, from the bar to the dance floor and back to the bar. At this rate, every man in the place would have danced with her by closing time.

After nursing a Coke for almost two hours, he found himself tired of watching Taylor dance with every dude in the room. She seemed to be enjoying it, giving him even more reason not to like it.

Ordering another Coke, he reminded himself he wasn't interested in Taylor. He was on the job, protecting her. This was a case he wanted to solve before another woman was senselessly murdered. But it was still hard to watch her dangling the bait for the killer. Especially when one of the men she danced with was Simpson — that pervert.

By midnight, Taylor felt that if she danced one more time, her feet would drop off. She at least had the satisfaction of knowing that as bad as her feet hurt from dancing, John appeared to be worse off. He looked down-right miserable having to stay seated in one place all night long. He had slipped in shortly before ten, so Taylor felt safe to turn on the charm with every stranger she met after that. After all the men she danced with, shot pool with, and just talked to, she still felt no closer to finding a possible serial killer. One was very strange, but she didn't get the sense he would kill for his sick pleasure. She knew they needed to check into him, but in her heart she felt he would be a waste of their time.

Her feet throbbed. She wasn't used to dancing so much since she rarely went out. Over the past few nights, keeping up the charade, she and John only danced a few times each night. She was nursing her second drink of the night, more water than drink because she'd let it sit so long.

At the stroke of one, she called it a night. Glancing at John, making eye contact for the first time, she tried to let him know she was leaving. Since she hadn't looked directly at him all night, she hoped he got the message.

Dropping a twenty to cover the two drinks she had, she said, "Keep the change." Then she flashed a brilliant smile his way. The bartender's eyes looked at her but didn't react like the rest of the men. It didn't matter, she told herself. She was too tired to be nice, had he chosen to speak to her.

Taylor walked the few blocks home. No sooner had she walked up the stairs and let herself in, she collapsed on the couch ready to take off her boots. A pounding sounded at the door.

John, of course. She rushed to the door. Before throwing it open, she called out, "John, is that you?"

"You know it is. Open up!"

"Quiet. You'll wake my neighbors."

John stepped in and quickly shut the door behind him. His temper seemed to be riding high. He knew it, and he knew why. He didn't like the way she made herself so accessible tonight.

His anger didn't seem to faze her. Taylor sat down on the sofa and pulled her boots off one at a time.

"I'm glad you checked who was at your door before opening it." He made another attempt to make Taylor think about her own safety.

"Of course I did. I'm not going to open my door to just anyone, especially this time of night." She started to rise but flopped back down on the sofa. "If you want coffee, you'll have to get it yourself. There's instant in the cupboard if you want."

Dragging his fingers through his dark waves, he decided to speak his mind. "I don't want any coffee. You need to be more careful. Even though I wasn't the killer, I could have been one of those doting fools you left at the bar with their tongues hanging out in anticipation. You weren't supposed to be a tramp and score with every man at the bar." He moved closer and closer to the couch as he spoke. Soon he was towering over her. John wanted to pick her up and shake some sense into her . . . but then he wanted to hold her and make sure she was safe. Instead, he just stared down at her.

"You're crazy. I was doing my job. What do you think those women were doing the night they were killed? You think they had gone in just to have a drink, unwind, and go home? No. They were lonely women looking for a one-night stand probably."

That blew the wind right out of his sails. He had no idea women went looking for one-night stands. He thought only men thought that way — not that he would do that anymore. "Is that what women want? A one-night stand?"

"Some."

"Well, you did a great job sending out those signals. I'm just glad no one followed you home to give you what you wanted."

"John. Please. I was doing my job. Hopefully you were doing yours."

She was right. What was he doing here in her apartment? He had come by to make sure she got home safely. Okay. She had.

But when he saw her, he saw all those men who wanted her tonight. He wanted her. No. Even more. He loved her. Could he let her continue this charade?

She didn't give him a chance to figure things out. Instead, she opened the door. "Go home." She glanced at her watch. "I'll see you later tonight. Don't be late — this time." With cold eyes, she dismissed him, double-locking the door behind him.

What had he done?

At 5:00 a.m. the ring of her phone woke her. It was John. She didn't want to open her eyes; she felt she had just gone to sleep.

"We have another victim. I thought you would want to be there."

Her eyes felt like sandpaper running over her eyeballs as she tried to blink them open and hold them there. Forcing them open one more time, she said, "Tell me where. I'm on my way."

Shell-shocked, confused, disoriented, and a little perturbed — all of these emotions raced through her. How could she face him so early this morning after what went down between them only hours ago — their own personal war? She had to go to the scene of the crime, though. She was tough. This was her job. Taylor could handle it . . . herself. She would show him.

It had been a week and a day since the last victim. They should have expected another one. Actually, they had. Only they had expected the perp to follow Taylor last night, and they would have caught him.

She arrived at the scene as quickly as possible. When she stepped out of her car, the police had already roped off the area with the standard tape. The forensic crew and officers were doing their jobs. John was talking to the medical examiner. Her body chilled for a moment. No way would she let him know how upset she was over last night. How confused she was with her own feelings toward a man who probably didn't even realize she was a woman with the same needs and desires of most women. Pasting her business face on, she grabbed her camera and headed toward the detective.

John felt her presence before he saw her. Her cold expression stopped him in his tracks. Why had he behaved so stupidly last night? They were doing a job together. Why did he have to make things harder than they needed to be? He knew why he behaved the way he did . . . he was jealous. Jealous men did stupid things.

"Was she killed like the others?" Taylor asked. "I noticed the bumper sticker is on her car, too."

When John didn't respond right away, Bob answered her question. "She is our fourth . . . same MO."

"Do you have a name yet — that you can give me?" She turned to John. "I won't be printing it. I know you have to notify next-of-kin. I just thought I would get it now, to save having to come down to the station later today."

"According to her license, her name is Lisa Efferson. She lives in the Garden District." John searched her eyes for a spark of that old reporter spunk she always had before but could not find it. She was like a walking zombie, doing her job like a robot, with no emotion on her face at all or in her voice.

John felt certain she was trying to give him the impression she was fine . . . but inside he knew better. He hoped he knew better. John knew how bad he felt.

Would things ever improve? Was there anything between them? He thought so. He hoped so. Was this part of God's plan for him? He had given up on women, on love, on pain, but then Taylor swept into his life.

I didn't ever think I could feel this way again, Lord, but I do. If it's not supposed to be, shut off these feelings I have for her.

Maybe after this investigation, if it was meant for something between the two of them, they could give it a try. In the back of his mind he felt like he was setting himself up for a fall. Somewhere down the road she would get herself hurt or killed. Could he go through that again?

How do you have a life and do a job all at the same time? Was it possible? Things were simpler when all he did was bury himself in work. Since Taylor came into his life, he hadn't been able to stay on track.

He would have to decide that later. Right now he needed to crack this case wide open and get the killer behind bars.

CHAPTER 25

As soon as the team gathered all the information at the crime scene, John headed back to the station. When he entered, the noise level bombarded him. The building was already filling with arrestees and arrestors, as well as people filing complaints.

Heading down the hallway toward his department, John passed one culprit handcuffed, waiting to be booked and printed. John apparently was more sensitive today. Another death and he was still no closer to solving the case. His mind was so focused on what he hadn't done yet that he failed to notice the all-time high on the X-rated scale of the words being batted around the station. Criminals, loud-mouthed cops, and bad language were par for the course, so much so that most policemen let it go in one ear and out the other.

Not John. Usually he took a moment to pray they'd see the light. A lot of people had to drop very low in life before they reached out; only today John wasn't hearing the cries. He was too obsessed with stopping this killer. He had failed again. Was it because his mind had been more on Taylor than his case?

Help me, Lord. Give me direction.

Taking the victim's ID, he ran a check on her. The nearest relative he located was an ex-husband, so he called and set up a meeting with him.

The ex-husband was already waiting for him when John arrived at Tim Efferson's place of business. Mr. Efferson hadn't been sure he would be there by noon, but since John told him how important it was, he must have made special arrangements.

Tim opened the office door for John. "Come in and have a seat. Would you like a cup of coffee? There is no secretary here today, but I took a chance and made a pot. It might be a little strong."

Strong coffee? He could use some. "Thanks."

After they were both seated, John gave him the bad news in as much detail as he could share at the moment. "I realize you are no longer married to her, but you were the closest relative I could find."

The man's eyes grew wide as he stared,

listening to John. When he spoke, Tim gave the answers asked of him but in almost robotic form. The reality was still trying to soak in, John believed.

"Her parents live in California. She was an only child."

"Sorry. You can give me her parents' information, and I'll gladly contact them."

The man rubbed his mouth as he shook his head. "No. That's okay. I think I'd rather let them know myself. It's going to be hard on them." Tim fell back in his chair, still stunned.

"I'm sorry to do this, but I have to ask you a few routine questions. When was the last time you saw her? Where were you last night? Do you know anyone who would want to harm your ex-wife?"

He answered one at a time as the questions were asked. Slowly but surely the veil over his eyes started lifting and when he answered the last question, he started firing off a couple of his own. "How did it happen? Did she suffer?" Tears started to form in the man's eyes. "Oh, Lisa, Lisa." Burying his face in his hands, he sobbed. "If only I'd tried harder to make it work."

When his sobbing subsided, John said, "I wish I could give you those answers, but the autopsy hasn't been completed. The best I

310

can do is tell you that we believe she was strangled at approximately two in the morning. She was found a few blocks away from Canal Street under the interstate in her car. We're trying hard to find her killer and bring him to justice."

After several seconds of silence, Tim said, "The sad part is, she hadn't been going anywhere since we split. In fact, I think she went out last night to spite me. We had words over the phone. Now I get to live with that for the rest of my life. We had talked about getting back together, but yesterday I wouldn't make a commitment. She said she wasn't going to wait around anymore. The next call would be mine." Sighing, he added, "I guess there won't be a next call." His words choked him as sobs racked him again.

After a few more minutes, John stood. "Mr. Efferson, if you learn anything we can use, please contact me right away. Again, I'm sorry for your loss."

Taylor stopped by the *Tribune* on the way home and wrote a short article for the paper's evening edition, noting the Predawn Strangler had struck again. Then she listed the details, all except the victim's name. Before she left the paper, she called the station and spoke with Buck to see if they had any information on Lisa Efferson.

"The lieutenant is speaking with the family now. Why don't you call him back before the press release? Call him about twelve thirty or one." Buck seemed a little reluctant in helping her this time.

"I'll do that. Thanks." She slowly hung up the phone. Did she want to face him again so early . . . even if it was over the phone?

No. Tonight would be soon enough. She would have them fax her a copy of the press release. She already had the details she could release and her story written so she was ahead of the game.

After attending the crime scene this morning, she thought about what she had done wrong. Why hadn't the killer selected her? The same thought crossed her mind again, but this time the answer came with it. Her car. Taylor had walked. Tonight she would drive.

The first thought that crossed her mind was, she needed to call John and tell him. Touching the phone, about to pick it up, she shivered and then a warmth flooded her senses. "No. Tonight will be soon enough."

Taylor could not understand her emotions. Up and down. The need to see him followed by a fear of seeing him. Was this love? Had she finally, at the age of twenty-eight, found a man she could love? Before meeting Lieutenant John Bradley, she was content with life . . . even had a purpose. Now her purpose wasn't even enough to fill the void John left in her heart.

One thing Taylor learned from all this, love wasn't something you chose. It chose you. And boy did it hurt!

Later that day she received the fax confirming everything she'd stated in the article. *Great. We'd better get the killer soon before someone else loses her life.*

Several hours later, sitting at the bar in her short skirt with a brown fringed shirt tucked in, wearing soft brown suede cowboy boots, she hoped to send out the right signals tonight. She noticed John hidden in the distance and wanted to go to him, tell him she'd fallen for him.

Instead, her eyes danced around the room as she pretended to be cheerful and looking for love. After each dance with a different man, still no one seemed to make her suspect them. Some even wanted to take her outside or home with them, but she knew the killer didn't work that way. He caught his victim by surprise — in her car. Tonight she would leave in her car. She even left her key by her purse on the bar, not too obviously letting whoever know she was driving tonight. When she left tonight, she would head toward the Garden District. Maybe, just maybe, he'll go after her tonight,

This past week she hadn't missed going to the *Tribune* every day as she normally had. She'd been too tired to think about missing the hubbub. Usually she looked forward to going in, hearing the latest news, and listening to the hum of the giant printers downstairs. Tonight she was so tired, she was heading to the ladies' bathroom to get a little rest.

Before she could push the door open, she was caught by the arm and dragged to a dark corner of the bar. If she hadn't known John's grip, she would have screamed bloody murder, but she knew he did everything melodramatically.

"What now?" she snapped.

"That's what I want to know. Have you seen anything, or do you suspect anyone? I know I haven't seen anyone suspicious looking. Are we wasting our time?"

"Is that all?" She pulled her arm away. "Do you mean to tell me you took a chance that someone might see us and blow our cover just to find out if I saw anyone acting strange? I thought you were good at your job," she growled.

John's eyes darted around the room. "If you keep your voice down, no one will suspect a thing. I'm about the only single guy you haven't been with tonight, and I thought I better hit on you . . . to make it look good."

"For the record, the bartender recognized me as being the girl with the same man for so many nights in a row and then alone last night. He asked me if we had split up."

John squinted as he regarded the bartender but didn't say a word.

Taylor put her hands on her hips. "If you're so sure, everyone will think you're only hitting on me; then maybe they'll think I turned you down." On those words she smacked him hard across the face, but not too hard. "Now you can go back to your table and do your job." She turned her back on him and went into the ladies' room.

After taking care of personal matters, she splashed her face with cool water. John angered her just by talking to her. He had made no attempt to straighten things out between them. Had she truly fallen for him? She didn't know how much more she could take. Smacking him in the face only felt good for a moment. The joy left her as fast as it had come. She wanted to reach out

315

and caress the red handprint she'd left on his cheek.

We are here to work. She glared her reflection down as she dabbed her face dry with a paper towel. After running her fingers through her curls and then adding a touch of fresh lipstick, she returned to the bar.

Taylor tried to put a smile back on her lips but found it hard.

"Was your old boyfriend giving you a hard time? I noticed he doesn't fit in with all the cowboys you've been dancing with. He looks out of place in here." The bartender placed a fresh drink on a napkin in front of Taylor. "I thought you looked ready for another one, Barbara." He turned away before Taylor could respond.

He called me Barbara. That's strange. I never gave him my name or a fake one for that matter. In fact, we hadn't really even spoken, other than to order a drink. Yet he just talked to me like he had known me for quite some time. That was peculiar.

A chill danced across her shoulders. She would have to tell John about him later.

Breaking her chain of concentration, another man stood next to her. "Wanna dance?" This guy looked more to be the heavy metal type, dressed in black leather and chains draping across him in various

316

ways. *Where did he come from? And what's he doing in a country bar?* Something about him seemed familiar, but she couldn't put her finger on it.

Strange — that was what she was looking for, but would he be that obvious? She agreed to dance with him.

The minute they hit the dance floor, he practically spilled his guts to her. "I wanna be up front with you. I just got out of jail five months ago, and do you know what I came home to?"

Taylor shook her head.

"I'll tell you. My old lady left me for another man. She said we didn't like the same kind of music anymore, so I'm here trying to learn to like this junk. I was here the other night and tried to dress like the others, a little bit anyway. But tonight I thought I would be myself and try to soak up the music that way. It ain't working."

She listened with interest, asking just the right questions to keep him talking. They danced more than once. Taylor thought at first she was onto something, but by the third number, she decided this was another dead end. He was only a broken-hearted fool.

"Thanks for the dances. Good luck with your girlfriend. I hope you straighten things out." She touched his shoulder softly, actually feeling sorry for him.

A tight smile touched his lips as she left him on the dance floor. Taylor could feel the sweat dripping down her back. She was hot and tired. This had been a nowhere night — again — on top of very little sleep. It was after one in the morning, so she gave the sign and then headed out the door. Taylor hoped John would come over after he left or at least give her a call tonight. They needed to talk.

If not, she would give him enough time to get home and then give him a ring. They had to work things out if they were going to continue to work together. She also needed to tell him about the bartender so they could check deeper into his background. Something about him didn't fit. He talked a little strange, noticed weird things, and called her Barbara. If they had talked a little on the side, she wouldn't have thought much of him getting her name wrong. The way people acted and reacted was what made Taylor suspicious. He had her antennas up. This was best not to ignore.

On the out-of-the-way drive home, she didn't feel John's presence behind her. Glancing in the rearview mirror, she said, "Silly girl. You're not supposed to see him.

He stays out of sight."

No one. Nothing. Finally she headed back toward her apartment. She parked her car and headed up the stairs to her place. She unlocked the door and twisted the knob to step inside. Before she could close the door, she was shoved down across the floor, and the door was slammed behind her. Falling to the floor she hit her head. "What the — ?"

She didn't finish her question when she was yanked by the arm and pulled to her feet. The keys were still in her hand. Frantically she tried to feel through her keychain and find the mace. Before her fingers wrapped around the little can, the keys were knocked out of her grip. Fear rose in her throat. She wanted to scream for help. Glancing around for her purse to pull out her .22, she found it on the floor across the room. No way to get to it.

"Don't worry, sweetie," the man said as he threw her on the sofa. "I'll be gentle. I could tell you wanted to help ease my deflated ego." His mouth formed a wicked grin as he fell on top of her.

That guy, Frank, from the bar. Oh, my gosh. "No!" Taylor tried to scoot away from him. She closed her eyes and opened her mouth to scream for help. The second her scream deafened her ears, she felt the weight on her lighten.

Opening her eyes, she found the man in leather in John's grip. He released it only long enough to form a fist and smash it into Frank's gut. Then his other fist came across with a cut to the jaw. In seconds, the man in black fell to the floor.

John flipped him over onto his stomach and held him there with the man's hands behind his back. John eased his automatic out of his shoulder holster. "Move a muscle, and I'll blow you away."

When the man didn't make a move to fight anymore, John reached behind him and whipped out his handcuffs. In one easy motion, keeping the gun pointed at him, John slapped the cuffs on the perp's wrists.

Taylor sat frozen through it all. It happened so fast. If it hadn't been for John, that man would have raped her.

Her bottom lip trembled as she watched John stand Frank to his feet again. Brown and Buck were standing in the doorway. John must have given them a heads-up on the drive over. She was so grateful.

John turned Frank over to his fellow detectives and said, "We'll be down shortly, so Taylor can press charges. Thanks." Turning to Frank, he said, "I hope you enjoyed your six months of freedom, because it's over now."

The cuffed man appeared to be in a daze as he tripped out of Taylor's apartment between the two detectives. John sat next to Taylor as she continued to sit motionless. How had she let that man in? It happened so fast.

He placed a warm hand over her cold, shaking fingers. "It'll be all right." His voice sounded soft and reassuring. "You'll be all right."

Drawing in a deep breath, she said, "Thank you for saving me." Taylor rose to her feet quickly and stepped away from the couch . . . away from John. "Do you think he's the one?" She shook her head. "I didn't think so when I danced with him. I had written him off as just a man angry with life, with his ex, and with the world." Quickly she repeated the story the man had shared with her on the dance floor.

"We do know Frank Simpson has a long rap sheet. He's been convicted and served time for sexual abuse. The man's only been out of prison for six months."

"Do you know he told me that? I guess he thought it was a turn on." She shivered as she thought about him.

Rising, John moved close to Taylor and

reached out.

Taylor backed away again. "I'm fine. Really. I don't need your sympathy. I'm tough — that's my job!"

John stepped back as if he'd been slapped in the face. With a hard expression, he said, "That's so true. I almost forgot. It's your job. I won't forget again." He headed toward her door. "You need to come with me down to the station and press charges. I told them we'd be right behind them."

As much as she didn't want to go with him, she knew she had to file the complaint. The man was sick and needed to be off the streets. "I'll follow you in my car."

The minute she stepped out the door, she was bombarded with her sweet neighbors' concern. Of course all the flashing lights on the police units woke them. "Everything's fine," she assured her friends upstairs. Each stood hunched close together, clad in pajamas covered by their robes. "Truly. Go back to bed. I'll tell you the juicy stuff later." Taylor figured if she made light of it, they would quit worrying.

As she made it to the bottom step, she found Mr. and Mrs. Leblanc also needing assurance that everything was fine. Giving hugs as she passed them, they accepted her quick guarantee with the promise of filling them in later. Climbing into her Mustang, she started her car and made her way out to the street.

Alone in her car she recalled how John said he wouldn't forget. Well, that was his problem. Her job was what it was and she loved it. If he couldn't handle the danger she found herself in, he didn't need to be in her life.

Earlier she refused to let him comfort her, but it wasn't because she didn't need it. She needed it all right, but she had to be tough. Normally no one was around to assure her she was okay. Now she was glad she stood on her own. Her career was her dream, and she wasn't about to give it up for anyone. No man is worth that. If he cared about her at all, he would accept her job.

Turning into the station's parking lot, she whispered, "So much for even thinking I had a chance for a real relationship. Not with my job."

CHAPTER 26

Down at the station, she filled out the complaint form and signed where she needed so charges could be brought against her attacker. Frank Simpson would now go back to a familiar place. Taylor hoped this time they would throw away the key. They would, for sure, if they could link him to the predawn murders.

A chill swept through her as she turned in the completed complaint form to the police-woman at the desk.

The noise level was not as loud as she remembered from her other trips to the station. Probably the early morning hour had a lot to do with it. Most arrests had already been made for the night, and a lot of people were in their beds fast asleep.

What a night! As she headed down the hall toward the exit so she could go home and get in bed herself, John stepped into the hallway and blocked her exit. "Come to my office. We need to talk."

From head to toe she tensed. "What if I don't want to listen?" Maybe he was ready to make things right between them, but she wasn't sure she was. Besides, she already knew a relationship was not going to work between the two of them.

No. He was ready to end the investigation — with me.

"You'll listen." He took her by the arm and headed toward his office, giving her no choice in the matter. Once in his office, he let her go. "Sit," he commanded.

She eyed him wearily, but obeyed.

"You'll want to hear this." John raked his fingers through his hair and sighed. "I hate to tell you this, but he's not our man."

"How can you be so sure?"

"He's worked on a barge for the last month, and it just docked here three days ago. Several people can verify his alibi."

Disappointment engulfed her. Taylor had hoped they had found the killer. She squeezed her eyes into narrow slits as she thought for a moment.

Her head snapped up as her eyes popped open and pinned John. "I just remembered something I needed to tell you tonight . . . last night . . . but with everything —"

"He's still going back to jail for what he

did to you. And with his history, he'll be there for a long time."

"Great. That's good." She waved her hands in the air like it didn't really matter. What she was telling him was more important. "Listen, John, I forgot to tell you about the bartender in all the excitement." She told him her suspicions and how she had written Frank off earlier. "What Frank did wasn't typical of the Predawn Strangler. He was just a crazed idiot. But the bartender seemed demented, like, I don't know. It was weird the way he called me Barbara."

Scratching his chin, he said, "We checked him out earlier. Let's see," he murmured as he flipped through his file searching for Jack Williams. "Here it is. No record of him ever breaking the law. His wife left him. He quit his job at the bank and has been working at the bar for about six months." John shrugged. "We didn't think anything of it, but we'll look into his activities more closely."

John glanced at his watch. "It's late. I'm going to see you home." He didn't let her argue. Actually, she didn't even try.

Once they got to the apartment, John talked her into letting him come upstairs with her. "We've got to talk about . . . us."

Taylor hesitated. She didn't think she was

ready to discuss *them,* even though that was what she wanted him to say all night. It was one thing to admit to yourself you were in love with someone, but it was an entirely different story to admit it to that person. No. She wasn't ready to talk about it — with him or anyone else.

"I insist. You may not want to talk about us." He walked up behind her, pushing her gently into her apartment. "But you're going to listen, because I want to talk."

She kept walking until she reached the kitchen. She let John shut the door. "I've got to fix some coffee. It's late, and I'm very tired."

John didn't stop her. "It's just what I need." He eased over to the table and dropped down in the chair.

"Go ahead and talk. I'll listen while I make the coffee." She grabbed the glass container, rinsed out the pot, filled it with water, and then poured it into the coffee-maker. After cleaning out the filter, she filled in the coffee grounds and turned on the pot.

"I'll wait."

It started making gurgling noises instantly. Taylor pulled out the cups for lack of something to do to keep from thinking about who was with her and what he wanted to talk about.

After two cups were poured, Taylor sat across from John. "Go ahead." She took a sip of the hot brew.

John's eyes caressed her as he stared into her eyes.

That wasn't fair. She swallowed, averted her eyes, then said, "Okay. I'm ready to listen."

John took another sip before he spoke. "I think I'm sending you mixed signals. I can't help it. You have me so confused."

As butterflies swarmed her stomach, he had her attention. This was exactly what she wanted to hear — needed to hear.

"I was engaged once, to a fellow police officer. She was killed in the line of duty. I swore when Jennifer died, I would never become emotionally involved with a career woman again. I only got through her death by the help of God."

Seeing the pain shooting through his eyes, she touched his hand.

He covered hers with his. "There's more. When I saw you, I felt something that I tried to fight. But I heard a voice inside, telling me you were the one. I don't even know if you are a believer, but I am. So I was ready to see where our relationship would go — until you were almost raped because of your job."

Do I believe in God? I did pray, asking God to send John to my rescue. She pulled her hand back as these thoughts ran through her mind.

"Boy, are you a career woman or what? My head says stay away from you, far, far away, but my heart wants to know you more."

Taylor's heart pounded like a demolition ball crashing against a brick wall. He had admitted his attraction to her . . . against his better judgment. Hiding her smile, she hoped he cared for her as much as she cared for him. If that was the case, they could find the answer.

John reached out his hand. Hesitantly, Taylor placed hers in his. His thumb caressed the back of her hand as he held it. "I hope you understand what I'm trying to say. I'm scared, confused, unsure." Inhaling a deep breath, he raised his eyes to hers and she saw the fear in them.

Hope grew a little more within her.

"All day today, I kept telling myself there was a way around your helter-skelter life." Raising her hand, he pressed his lips on her skin. "But tonight told me I was wrong. Had Frank done what he wanted to you, I wouldn't be able to live with myself. Do you understand what I am saying?"

Excitement, desire, love, and plain old-fashioned lust raced through her veins. He was asking her to understand what he was saying, but how could she even think while he was touching her this way?

"My heart says yes, but my mind says no." John stood and opened his arms to her. "Right now I'm going to let my heart lead."

Taylor didn't hesitate. That was where she wanted to be, and she stepped eagerly into his embrace.

"I'm not making any promises until I know we are right for one another and we can commit to each other forever. In other words, I don't want a casual affair. I don't believe in them. I believe in until-death-do-we-part kind of love." He kissed her upturned lips gently. "Can we take it one day at a time?"

She answered with a hungry kiss. Warmth and security blanketed around her as his arms held her tight. She knew what she had to do. She had to make him forget how dangerous her job could be. Let him see most of it was fairly safe. Taylor needed John to love her like she loved him. If she could accomplish that, he wouldn't let her career stand in their way.

A marimba rhythm rang out. John's cell broke further conversation . . . and kissing.

Pulling his iPhone from his pocket, he pressed it against his ear. The smile wiped clean from his face as he dropped his phone back into his pocket.

"They found another body."

CHAPTER 27

Not again. Taylor wanted to break down and cry. She wouldn't be so tough then, would she? "We've got to catch him, John. He can't go on killing. I really think you need to check deeper into that bartender. He looked a little crazed last night. Can't you bring him in for questioning?"

"We could, but if we do, we'd tip our hand. He'd know he was a suspect. To bring charges against him, we would need proof, evidence of some kind. Don't worry, if he's our man, we'll get him. For now, we'll keep him under surveillance. We won't let him kill another person."

"I've got to go," he said as he took her back into his arms. Holding her close, he asked, "Are you coming?"

"Of course. Do you think I would miss it? Who knows, maybe it's a copycat instead of the real deal."

"We'll see." He traced his finger along her

jawline. "You really need some rest. You haven't had any."

She smiled, thinking, *What a wonderful man.* "I'm going on the same thing you're going on . . . adrenaline. I'll make it. This is bigger than any need for sleep."

He nodded. "I know. I know. Your story." He let her go. "Let's get out of here."

Taylor snatched up her camera and purse. Together they left for the crime scene.

Later that morning, still riding on caffeine and adrenaline, Taylor slipped by the paper to update her boss. When he learned she was going to be the decoy to lure the insane man out in the open, Mr. Cox wasn't too pleased, to say the least. Words of wisdom rang through her head as she recalled his fatherly advice. "Now listen and listen well. This may be your golden opportunity to write your prize-winning piece, but it's also a chance to get yourself killed. Your life is more important. Just remember that." He winked and then patted her shoulder. "Now get out there and find the rest of our story." His words were the last thing playing through her brain when she dozed off for a few hours.

The phone rang, waking her. She grabbed the receiver and dragged it to her ear. "Hello."

"Taylor. What are you doing sleeping in the middle of the day?" Her mom sounded horrified.

Taylor's eyes popped open. She didn't dare tell her the truth. Her mother worried enough about her being on the job. "Hi, Mom. What are you doing?"

"Dear, I just wanted to tell you how much we enjoyed the other night and how special it was to your father and me. I've called you several times, only you never return my calls. I know now you've been very busy with work and with John." Her mother's voice literally purred out his name. The smile on her mother's face had to be wider than the Mississippi. "It's wonderful, honey. We're both so happy for you. Thanks again for the other night."

"Don't thank me, Mom. The party was Rodney's great idea. Neither one of your daughters thought about it."

"He's magnificent, isn't he?" her mother cooed. She didn't skip a beat when she said, "And speaking of magnificent, that young man you were with the other night seemed perfect for you. You best not let him slip away."

Taylor knew John was the real reason for the phone call. At least now their relationship was real. For that she was glad. As much as she wanted to teach her mother and sister a lesson, she hated lying to them. Especially her mom. "I'm glad you liked him, Mom. He liked y'all, too. In fact, he thinks I have a wonderful family."

"Your father even likes him. A policeman is exactly what you need. Someone stronger and whose job held a little more danger. A regular guy couldn't handle your work. Tell me, dear, are you two serious?"

By the excitement in her mother's voice, Taylor figured her mom was picking out the silver pattern. "Mom, do me a favor. Don't get overly excited. It may or may not work. But right now, we are very happy."

"Dear, you know I only want what's best for you. Sure I'd love to see you settle down and get married. Even give us a couple more grandchildren . . . but only to a man deserving of a strong woman like you. In case you don't know it, I'm very proud of you."

Tears sprang to Taylor's eyes. "Don't get all mushy on me, Mom." With the back of her hand she wiped away the dampness. *I'm just so tired. Otherwise I wouldn't get all teary-eyed. Do I tell her how serious we've become? She's so proud now; this would shoot her over the moon.* "Okay, Mom. I'm going to tell you something. Your wish has come true. I'm head over heels in love with John Bradley." *There, I said it. Admitted my feelings to my mother, no less. Thinking it is one thing, but telling my mother?* A grin spread wide on Taylor's lips.

A squeal pierced her ear.

"Please Mom, don't get overly excited. If you do, you might be disappointed. He's attracted to me but doesn't care for the dangers of my job. I can't give up my job. So if he wants me, he has to take the whole package." Holding her breath, she waited for her mom to lecture her on how dangerous the job was and how she had been trying to get Taylor to quit the paper or start covering weddings for years.

Her mother surprised her. "Dear, if it's meant to be, it will happen. Just trust in your heart and your feelings, and you will do what is right for you. Remember, Dad and I are always here for you, honey."

A quick breath caught in her throat. She hadn't heard her mother so tender in years — or maybe Taylor hadn't been listening like she should. "Thanks, Mom. I love you. Give my love to Dad, too. I've got to go."

"We love you, too. Please be careful."

After Taylor hung up, she wanted to sit down and cry a good one, but she knew she couldn't do that. She had to be tough for tonight. Getting up, she went into the kitchen to make herself a pot of coffee.

By the time the coffee started dripping, she heard a knock at the door. Checking the peephole first, she opened it. After what she went through last night and with another killing so soon, if nothing else, this case had taught her to be cautious. "John, come in. I hope nothing's wrong."

He made himself at home on the couch after giving her a quick kiss on the cheek. "Thanks. Nothing's changed. I came to tell you what we found out about the bartender."

John looked very tired.

"You haven't gotten any sleep yet, have you?"

He shook his head. "You need to hear this, though."

"I'll listen, but you lie down on the sofa and rest while you tell me. Afterward, you can take a nap. I'll wake you in time to go home and get ready for Six-Shooters."

He did just that. She didn't have to offer twice. John was dead on his feet, she could tell.

"We haven't found him yet, but two of my men are watching his house as we speak. Hopefully he'll come home before he goes to work tonight. I've filled out an affidavit to get a search warrant, and we're waiting for Judge Peterson to approve it. We know the tire size of his van is a match, but with the warrant, we can check for that special marking we found on our mold."

"Great!"

"We want enough to put him away for good . . . without another death. He has to come home sooner or later." John turned on his side and made room beside him. "Come . . . sit by me." He patted the cushion.

Taylor obeyed willingly.

"Do you want to hear how bad his life is? Not that it's any excuse to do what he's done."

"Tell me." She brushed a curl off his forehead.

John laid his hand across Taylor's lap, keeping her close, and he closed his eyes. "His name is Jack Williams. He was married to a woman named Barbara. That's what he called you, wasn't it?"

"Yes," she whispered.

"Right. Well she left . . . for a cowboy. Jack was a banker, wore a three-piece suit every day to work. When his wife ran off with a guy that dressed in jeans, boots, and wore a big cowboy hat, Jack changed. He quit his job and started working at the bar. Apparently he watched every night for a girl that fell for the cowboy type — maybe even ignoring the guys like me, dressed in slacks. He then followed them and somehow got them to pull over for him. Maybe they recognized him from the bar and felt safe. We don't know. He's got some scam going, though. We'll figure it out, but in the meantime, we're not going to let him kill again. We're going to stick to him . . . once we find him."

Taylor stroked his forehead while he was talking. His breathing slowed down. Finally he was asleep. She leaned down and kissed him softly on the lips. Even in his sleep, his lips puckered slightly. She stayed by him for a few more minutes, allowing him to fall into a deep sleep. Then she got up and laid a light blanket over him.

A few hours later she woke him so he could go home to shower and get ready for the night. "It's a good thing you know how to get by on so little sleep."

"I do, don't I? Unfortunately, all cops have to get used to grabbing whatever sleep they can, when they can." He pulled her face down and nibbled at her lips. "I could get by on this in daily doses." He nipped at them again. "Let's make that hourly doses." He laughed as he held her close.

She kissed him long and hard, a kiss for

the road. "Now get up and go." Drawing her brows together, she tried to give him a stern look but couldn't hold back the smile that filled her heart.

He sat up and stretched. As he headed to the door, he mumbled, "She kisses me like that and then tells me to go. Women. You can't live with them, and you can't live without them." He laughed as he pulled her back into his arms. Then he returned a kiss more intense, slowly, lovingly. "Mmm. Yes. I could get used to this." He smiled and then left quietly.

Leaning against the doorframe, she felt the beating of her heart. Yes, this was the real thing. She loved him, no doubt about it. She hoped it didn't take him long to realize he loved her, too . . . and that he loved her enough not to worry about her line of work. She could live with his line of work. It was part of him.

"Please, God. You told him I'm the one for him. Help him to love the whole package."

CHAPTER 28

Shortly after John left, he called to give Taylor the plan of action. "Remember, if you don't feel up to it, we could have Sergeant Land step in. She was trained for this sort of thing."

"But she hasn't been as close to the situation. The bartender already has a connection with me." Her throat constricted as she thought he was about to give the action to someone else. She needed to be close to the story — that made her story come alive in the paper. She held her breath, waiting for his decision.

He sighed. "Yes. You're right. Man, I wish we'd found something in his house to connect him so we wouldn't have to catch him in the act."

"I can do this, John. Trust me. When I leave tonight, I'll do like I did last night. Get in my car and head toward my parents'. Right? And you'll be right there behind him, behind me."

"Right. And don't let us lose you. Stay in radio contact constantly. Make sure your wire is secure before you leave the bar."

"Will do. Make sure you guys don't lose sight of me," she said as she clutched the phone for dear life.

Sure, she was telling John she could do it, but part of her was scared to death. As many close calls as she has had in her life, they came only because she got close to the story. This time she was smack-dab in the middle of the story. Her boss's words replayed in her mind: *Your life is more important than any story.*

"Not on your life," John promised. "Officer Lane will be by around eight to wire you up so we can hear every word that he says to you. We'll get him."

"How can you be sure he'll take the bait?"

"Trust me. He will."

On that, they said their good-byes.

When nine o'clock arrived, she was walking into Six-Shooters, wire in place thanks to Officer Lane. Taylor was ready to execute their plan. "Hey, guys. I'm sweating up a storm already. I hope I don't damage the wire . . . or electrocute myself." She said those words hoping they could hear her. The sound check earlier said they could. Taylor

342

felt sure it was her nerves talking right now.

Drawing a deep breath, Taylor moved over to the bar and sat down. She made it a point not to watch the bartender, even though she wanted to do so. Although the police never found him today, because he never came home, he showed up tonight. Taylor hoped the plan worked. As she turned her face in his direction, about to place her order, he sat a drink in front of her.

"A screwdriver, light on the vodka."

"You remembered. Thanks." Taylor didn't linger on him. She averted her eyes to the crowd, showing him no interest whatsoever.

Several cowboy-type men hit on her throughout the night and she flirted with each of them. The closer it got to midnight, the more frightened she became. Occasionally, she caught a glimpse of John and he was always watching her, even though it didn't appear he was paying attention.

Taylor ordered a second drink with thirty minutes left, waiting for the big scene John had planned to get the bartender's attention. Between dances, she sipped on her drink that watered down more and more as the minute hand progressed.

Out of the corner of her eye, Taylor caught a glimpse of John coming her way. *This is it.*

John sauntered over and leaned on the bar

next to her. Out of the corner of his mouth he said to the bartender, "Give me a beer." Turning to Taylor, he asked, "Want to dance?"

Taylor rolled her eyes. "I told you the other night, we're through. It's over. O-V-E-R." She spelled it out for him, loud enough to humiliate him in front of anyone within earshot. That was the plan. Taylor could see everyone around them staring. She even felt she had gotten the bartender's attention but didn't dare look.

"Ah, come on, Baby. What's the matter? You think I'm not man enough for you? Or should I say *cowboy* enough for you? I've been watching you every night throwing yourself all over these cowboys in here. So I'm not the blue jean type. So what? It's the person in them that matters. I'm as much a man as any of these cowboys, and I love you. Give me another chance," he pleaded with her.

The word *love* threw her for a loop. That was what she wanted to hear from him. Although she knew this was play-acting, she wished deep down he meant it. "Forget it!" She flung her arm up as she brushed him off again and turned her back on him.

Sure enough, the man behind the bar watched the whole thing. His eyes were

344

twitching, and beads of perspiration formed across his forehead and on his upper lip. This was getting to him. It looked like the plan might work.

She felt John lean up close behind her as he whispered loudly, "I don't think I can take another rejection. Please give me another chance . . . us another chance." Softly for her ears only, he added, "He's taking the bait. Be careful when you leave here."

John ran his hands across the fringe that draped along the back of her shirt. She turned, reared her hand back, and slapped him across the face. "Leave me alone. You're a loser. I don't associate with losers." She stormed away.

Taylor caught John's response out of the corner of her eye. Rubbing his jaw, he moaned, "Wow. What a wallop. That tiny thing packs a punch." He looked the bartender dead in the eye and laughed. Snatching his beer off the counter, his gaze darted toward Taylor and he glared in longing. "I've got to get me some of that, but I think I'll wait until she cools down." He swaggered back to his own table with the drink in hand.

Taylor waited as long as she thought was necessary and then went back to her spot at the bar. The second part of their plan went into action.

A man dressed in a pair of tight-fitting jeans strutted up to her and said, "Hey, good-looking. Want to shuffle with me?"

The music was fast-moving, and Taylor joined him willingly. The two got on the floor and shuffled around, doing twists and turns in all the right places. When the song ended, a waltz started up. As planned, they stayed out on the dance floor for the next two songs. The officer was really quite a good dancer.

When the dancing ended on the third song, they strolled hand-in-hand to the bar. Before Taylor took her seat on the stool, the cowboy turned her toward him. Holding her face gently, he thoroughly kissed her. Taylor didn't fight it. It was part of the plan.

She would be glad when this night was over. They had to get him tonight. At the rate he was killing people, they couldn't afford to mess up.

Taylor swallowed hard when he broke the kiss. The scary part was she knew she was setting herself up for the bartender to come after her later. If things worked the way they planned, she would be his next target. She hoped the fear she felt didn't show in her face.

Knowing John was watching her every

move was the only thing that gave her strength. It didn't hurt to know several other police officers were there, undercover, including the cowboy who had just kissed her.

When he pulled away, Taylor reached up and traced his lips with her thumb. "Protect these. They're masterful, Darlin'." She pursed her lips at him, giving him a come-on kiss in the air.

"Maybe we can get together later tonight," he said to her, catching her hand.

She smiled. "Not tonight, Cowboy, but maybe tomorrow night," she said with promise in her voice.

"Don't let me down." He kissed her again.

"Not on your life," she promised. Taylor sat back down, catching a glimpse of Jack standing back watching their exchange. *Yes. He took the bait.* She also knew John was watching and probably felt everything was going as planned. She wished she could say something. She knew he could hear her, but so could others — and she definitely didn't want to say anything to make Jack suspicious.

Pulling out her wallet, she left the usual charges plus the tip. She noticed Jack was down at the other end of the bar talking to a barmaid. After their exchange of words, he left early.

Is he leaving for my benefit? Here we go.
Taylor's heart hammered. "Here we go. I'm
scared to death." Her hands were sweating
as she waited, giving time for Jack to do
whatever he planned.

When one o'clock struck, her usual time
for leaving, she stood, strapped her purse
on her shoulder, and walked toward the
door. "Please stay close."

Once in her Mustang she started the
engine. The radio was on, but low. Now she
could talk to John. She couldn't hear him
answer, though.

"I think it worked. Here goes." She pulled
out on the street, heading toward Canal. "I
hope you're listening. In fact, I hope the
pounding of my heart isn't drowning out
what I'm saying."

She was nearing the crossing of the interstate. Once she headed under it, she was an
open target for the next couple of blocks. If
he was going to approach her, it would be
during that stretch. At every traffic light and
every large building she passed, Taylor
expected something to happen.

"I'm still here. Nothing yet. Wait . . . wait.
What's this I see? There is a van coming up
behind me, coming up pretty fast, I might
add. It's dark, like black or navy, maybe

even a very dark green. It's hard to tell. I hope you're close. I know you can't do anything until he says something you can use, or makes an attempt on me, but stay close." Her sweaty fingers tightened their hold on the steering wheel.

The lights flashed in her rearview mirror. The van was signaling to her to pull over. She slowed down but didn't stop. The van pulled beside her and the driver pointed to the side of his van. On the sideboard was a sign advertising WKRN.

She looked up and smiled at him. "So that's how he does it. John, he's pretending to be the Moneyman. His face is hidden by a large-brimmed cowboy hat, but it's him." Taylor told these things to John through tight smiling lips, so the man couldn't tell she was talking.

"This is it, John. He's motioning for me to pull over," she told John as she turned away from the van and started to ease off the side of the road. She gave him a description of the van as quickly as possible. As she slowed to a stop on the shoulder, the van pulled up behind her. She cracked her window about two inches as the man approached the car. "What can I do for you?" she asked.

"Don't you know me, sweetie? You wear

my bumper sticker. You must know who I am." The voice sounded very friendly, almost like a radio personality.

"Are you the Moneyman from WKRN?" Taylor tried to sound excited.

"How right you are, Little Lady. And if you have WKRN written down on a piece of paper, you'll double your money."

Taylor glanced at her purse. She knew she didn't have it written, but she was stalling for time. Of course, that was when he choked the other girls. What should she do? She made a point of leaning away from the window when she turned toward her purse.

"I hope you can hear this," she whispered. Her stomach twisted into knots. The agony of waiting for him to make his move was driving her insane. Of course she knew her window wasn't down far enough for him to reach in, just as she had planned, but by now he should have the rope in his hands. *Come on, John. It's time for you to show up and save the day.*

She jumped when she heard him speak. "You can't find it?"

She heard his voice, then instantly heard her door being opened. How did he open it? She had it locked. "What are you do-ing?"

"Don't worry, Little Lady. I'm going to

give you a bonus anyway." Jack reached in and grabbed her arm, dragging her out of the car.

As he was pulling her out, she was hollering, "Let go of me! What are you — ?" She didn't finish her question because he backhanded her, knocking her against the car. His fist made contact with her cheek while his ring made contact with her temple. He hit her so hard Taylor barely had time to think. *Where are you, John?* Then she blacked out.

It couldn't have been more than a minute or two, but when she came to, she found he had thrown her in the back of the van with her hands and feet both tied. In her mouth was a cloth towel keeping her from speaking. She woke facedown on the carpet, hearing the sounds of the motor humming and the tires rolling on the blacktop.

Oh, John. Where are you? Please be right behind us.

Taylor was in fear for her life. She realized Jack had treated her differently, but all she could believe was that he planned to torture her before killing her.

Maybe he figured out she was working with the police, or maybe since he called her Barbara, he thought he had his wife and was going to make her pay.

Taylor's head throbbed and her face hurt where he had struck her, but at the moment, that was the least of her worries. She fought to stay awake.

John, please save me. I need you. Where are you? She thought they would have grabbed him by now. Kidnapping and go from there. What were they waiting for?

The throb of her head beat harder and harder until she blacked out one more time.

CHAPTER 29

"What happened? I can't hear anything!" John snatched the microphone on his radio. "Sound is down. Approach with caution, but whatever you do, keep that van in sight!"

Immediate response came over the radio. "His lights already disappeared. When the van lights came back into view, we pulled a little closer. It was the wrong van. A switch was made. We don't know if it was planned or luck . . . bad luck. We're heading back to the main road now."

John's fist slammed down hard on the steering wheel as his foot pressed on the accelerator. How could they have lost him? They were to follow him from the bar until the end. John was to stay at a safe distance behind Taylor so they could all be there when contact was made. She was never in his sight, but he could always hear her until the crackling started and her voice died. The wire went dead. A mixture of fury and fear took over. John had to keep his head. He hadn't seen the van pass him, and he prayed Jack hadn't made contact, although before the wire died, he knew a van was tailing her. She had described it to him. It could have been Jack. He'd know soon enough.

Driving under the interstate, he didn't even slow down for the curve. Coming out of it, he spotted the Mustang. Her car sat alone on the side of the road. His eyes raced ahead and saw the dark van picking up speed traveling away from her car.

Pressing the side of his mike, he said, "I have the vehicle in view. I just crossed under I-110 where it crosses Canal. Her car is on the shoulder two blocks down." As John passed it, he eyed it quickly but didn't lose speed. "It looks empty, but check it out. Make sure she is not lying hurt across the seat of her car." *Or even dead.* He didn't want to think those words, let alone speak them aloud, but as the thoughts came to him, he prayed that wasn't the case.

His heart pounded as fear gripped him, but then he let his police training take control. "After you're sure she's not there, radio for a team to check out her car and you two catch up with me. I'll stay close. I'm not going to lose that creep or let him lose me." John kept his eyes on the van but

354

kept his distance. If anything happened to her, he would never forgive himself.

Minutes later he heard, "Lieutenant, the car's empty. Only her purse is in it. He must have her with him."

Bittersweet words touched his ears. For a brief second, relief flooded his heart as he knew she wasn't left dead in her car like the others before her, but almost as quickly the thought came of what his changed plans could entail. He didn't want Taylor to be tortured.

That sick killer changed his ways of doing things. Jack Williams went from killing one girl a week to one a night — now this. He kidnapped Taylor. What was on his agenda? What were his plans for Taylor? Whatever they were, John could not permit Jack to carry them out.

Keep her alive, Lord. You're the one who wants us to be together.

As he kept on the trail, he reached into his glove box and removed his Colt. Laying it on the seat beside him, he was ready for Jack Williams. His hands tightened on the steering wheel. Had it been Williams' neck, the man would be dead.

John followed all of Jack's turns and relayed them over the radio to Buck and Brown and any other officer in the vicinity.

After two more turns, John realized Williams was heading toward his old house, the one he shared with his wife . . . not the one the police had staked out, got the warrant for, and searched.

John pressed the button again. "He's heading for his old place on Magazine Street. Move it!" John relayed it to his men and then gave the information to dispatch to get more backup.

Immediately he heard the dispatcher call over the radio, "Ten-thirty-three, ten-thirty-three, all cars in the vicinity of Annunciation and Magazine, we're in pursuit of a dark van, believed to be the Predawn Strangler. He has his next intended victim with him. Approach with caution. It is believed he is taking her to 5221 Magazine Street."

He prayed they would all be there in time.

CHAPTER 30

Taylor felt the van come to a quick stop, causing her to roll onto her side. At least now she didn't have to smell that putrid odor of stale, wet carpet. Another minute of that and she felt certain she would be lying in a puddle of her own vomit. Her stomach churned.

The back doors flew open as the face Taylor recognized as the bartender's came into view. "It's okay, Barbara. We're home now. Safe and sound." He grabbed both of her arms and dragged her out of the van.

"I'm not Barbara," she tried to say through the cloth stuffed in her mouth. That didn't stop him as he dragged her to her feet. She leaned forward slightly, then suddenly pushed with her shoulder, causing him to lose his balance.

Caught by surprise, he fell to the ground. She tried to run away, but her feet were tied together. Tumbling, she pushed her bound hands out to catch her fall, trying to soften the landing. It didn't help. Facedown she went and slapped the ground with her whole body. "Oomph." She hit the dew-covered ground. The wetness soaked through her clothes.

Instantly, Taylor tried to roll over and stand back on her feet.

Too late. Back on his feet, he reached over and grabbed her by her elbows, hauling her erect. Headlights flashed across his face. Hastily he lifted her up, tossed her over his shoulder, and then carried her inside. Once in, he dropped her in a kitchen chair and then secured the lock on the kitchen door.

Jack left the room without saying a word. She assumed to lock any other door in the house.

A second chance to escape.

Glancing around the room, she tried to figure out the best way to go. The most obvious was right out the kitchen door, since he hadn't tied her to the chair. Like a cat she rose and lightly hopped across the floor toward the door. Turning her back to the door, she lifted her bound hands to the doorknob. Using her fingertips she turned the lock, then grabbed the knob with both hands. Awkwardly she turned it, but the door didn't budge. Surveying the door, she realized he had also locked the deadbolt.

Backing up against the door, she tried to lift her hands to the small knob that controlled the lock. Not quite reaching it, she held her breath, rose up on her toes trying to get leverage on the small knob, hoping to turn it completely to unlock the deadbolt, but she couldn't get her hands high enough.

After trying again and almost falling on her face, she gave it up. Her gaze flitted around the room and stopped on the window. If it were lower to the floor, she could make a run for it and throw herself through the glass. It would hurt badly, but it had to be better than dying.

A movement outside caught her eyes. *John? Are you here?* It had to be him. *Hold on, girl, John will save you.*

She heard a shuffling of feet coming her way. Swiftly, she jumped back over to the chair Jack had left her in and sat back down. No need to upset Jack further.

Her heart pounded ferociously as the kitchen door swung open from the hallway. Taylor swallowed hard. He was back, and he looked insane. She had to convince him to let her go. Sure, John was here, but what if he didn't get inside in time? What if Jack decided to kill her instantly?

"Jack," she murmured through the cloth.

Apparently he wanted to hear what she had to say because he removed the cloth from her mouth. "Jack," she said softly.

His eyes spread wide as he looked intently into her eyes. "Barbara, I'm so glad you came back to me. I knew you would." He walked over to Taylor and traced his fingers down her injured cheek. Softly, he pushed her hair away from her face. "You've been hurt, darling. Let me help you." He spoke as he brushed the dirt away from the scratches on her face.

With every brush of his hand a pain jabbed her face, but she said nothing.

"I knew you couldn't trust that cowboy. I tried to warn you, but you wouldn't listen to me."

The thought of those hands on her face killing all those women . . . she wanted to push him away. He repulsed her, but her hands were still roped together. The only thing she could do was turn her face away from him.

"Barbara, look at me. I'm not going to hurt you. I love you."

Slowly Taylor turned back to face Jack. "I'm not Barbara. Jack, you need help. Let me help you. Or turn yourself in. The police will get help for you." Her voice was soothing as she spoke, although she wanted to scream, "Let me out of here!"

"No! I don't need any help, Barbara," he shouted as his open hand slapped her. "Shut up. I told you I'm not going to hurt you."

The slap stung, and tears sprang to her eyes, but she held them back.

"Listen, sweetheart," he said, his voice calmer. "I need you, and you need me. We are back together, and that's all that matters." He ran his hands over her hair and patted Taylor's head.

"Then cut me loose. My feet, my hands. They hurt." Her pleading made it through to his twisted mind.

Finding a knife in the kitchen drawer, he used it to cut the cord around her ankles. Blood started circulating immediately.

Suddenly she heard something. Yes. She heard the sound of vehicles arriving, seemingly surrounding the place. Now she knew she would make it. Help was all around her. John's backup had arrived. Any moment they would be rushing inside.

Of course, if she could hear them, so could Jack, but maybe he was so intent on her that he paid no attention to the noises outside. She hoped anyway.

No such luck.

"What was that?" Jack searched the room for an answer. He snatched her by the hair and yanked her head backward. "What's going on here? Did you call the police?" He slapped her again. The knife he used to cut her bindings free he now pressed against the side of her face.

"Hhhuhhh." She sucked in a gasp of air in fear as the side of her face stung from the sharp edge cutting through the skin.

At least she was still alive enough to feel the pain. Hopefully he wasn't about to end that with the blade of his knife. Her gaze stayed locked on him.

"I ought to kill you, Barbara. I thought you wanted to come back to me. Why did you call the police?" Slowly he eased the cold steel of the blade down along her cheek, running the same path his fingers had earlier. Only this time, he sliced the skin. Blood oozed out, and wetness started to run down her cheek.

Hurry, John.

A loud bang came from the living room, drawing Jack's attention. He immediately turned toward the sound. "They better not be trying to get in here. This is my home. I don't want them here." He turned his crazed eyes on Taylor and warned her through clenched teeth, "Don't move a muscle. I'll be right back."

Jack pushed open the door and peered

362

into the next room. "They're trying to break in," he shouted as he ran to the drawer, pulled out a gun, and then scampered toward the living room. "They must be —"

"Police! Freeze!" Two quick shots rang out. The back door flew open and wood splintered, flying every which way. Brown rushed in and grabbed Taylor. Wasting no time, he snatched her up and scurried her out the opening where the door used to be.

She hadn't heard anymore, so she didn't know if John was okay. She had heard him yell for Jack to freeze. Was the first shot John's, or had Jack shot John? The waiting was more than she could bear.

In all the commotion, she had forgotten about her hands. Brown released them from their bondage. The pain was like fire, but all Taylor could think about was John's safety. The minute her hands were free, she started for the house. Maybe she could be of some help to John.

Of course there were police all around. Cars parked everywhere and lights flashed. Surely there were enough inside to help John, but she wanted to be there, to know he was safe.

Taylor didn't get far before Brown caught her by the arm. "You have to wait here."

She knew he was right, but she didn't

want to wait. She needed to be inside, surprisingly enough, not for the story but for John. Her searching eyes darted from the front door to the side, breathlessly waiting to see someone — anyone.

Finally the front door opened and Jack Williams, followed by John and two officers in uniform, came out the front door. Jack's hands were cuffed, and John held him by his upper arm, directing his every step. More policemen followed out behind them.

"It's over," Taylor whispered. "Thank God."

Her knees went weak, but she managed to stay upright. Taylor wanted to run to John. As she started to pull away from Brown, he held her back. "Not yet, ma'am."

Taylor stayed back against her will but realized Brown knew what he was doing. She watched as John put Jack in the backseat of one of the patrol cars. Red and blue lights flashed everywhere in the darkness of the morning.

Hurry. I need you. Her eyes stayed focused on John's every move, waiting, longing for him to turn to her.

When John slammed the police car door closed behind the criminal, his worried eyes searched the crowd. The neighbors had started gathering, filling up the street. By now even television camera crews were arriving and news reporters.

At last she saw his eyes light on her, and she smiled. He was safe, and it was over. Yes. Now John would come to her. She was ready for him to swoop her up in his arms and profess his undying love.

With her breath held in her throat, she waited expectantly. She was ready, for she knew that was what she wanted to do to him. He had to feel the same way after all they had been through. Taylor wanted to shout it from a mountaintop. Of course, down here in Louisiana there were no mountains. A tall building would do nicely, but she would settle for standing on top of the police car and shouting it to the neighborhood. She knew it would make her feel better.

John walked toward her. His face paled. No smile touched his lips.

It's okay. It will come. I'm all right, John. No need to be afraid for me. It was all over now. He could show her how he felt. He would soon. Taylor felt confident he'd show her soon. With each stride, he drew closer and closer.

His eyes locked on hers and never strayed. He walked up to her and stopped . . . one step away, one breath away.

One more step was all that was left. Taylor started to raise her hands — to touch him — to throw them around his neck and show him how happy she was that it was over and they both were alive.

His look froze her hands in mid-air. His face never softened, his lips never curved into a smile. Instead, his lips moved as he talked — but not to her. Sure, he still looked at her, stared at her in fact, but didn't speak a word to her. He spoke to Brown. "Bring her to the station for her statement if she doesn't need to go to the hospital for her injuries."

My injuries? She squinted at him in confusion. *Forget about my injuries. What about the pain you are putting me through right now? What is going on here?*

She wanted to ask him but knew better. The cut down the side of her face was nothing compared to the knife that twisted in her heart. Her stomach convulsed.

How could he do this to her? It was over. They were both alive. He should be showering her with kisses, showing an abundance of happiness . . . but he wasn't. He turned his back to her and walked away.

She felt baffled and bewildered. What was going on?

"Come on, Miss Jaymes. You have blood

on your face. Let's get you to the hospital."

"I'm okay."

"Then at least let the paramedics check you out."

Once they had her wound cleaned and stitched, Brown said, "I'll take you to the station."

The next two hours were a blur to Taylor. She gave a statement. It was recorded, typed, and given back to her to read and sign, and then a police officer brought her safely to her door.

She went through the motions, but all the while thinking she would have been better off if Jack had stuck the knife in her chest instead of John doing it. At least then she wouldn't be feeling all this pain.

At home she went through the motions without a thought on what she was doing. Sitting at her computer, she typed her story for the paper and sent it in for the next edition, then silently made her way to the shower. As the warm water blasted her skin and soap slid over her body, she tried desperately to understand John's actions.

"How could he?" she said as her tears mixed with the water pouring over her. "If you love someone, you accept them for what they are, who they are." Maybe that was the problem. Maybe he didn't love her like she

367

loved him.

Turning off the water and wrapping a thick towel around her body, her mind continued to organize her thoughts. She had been afraid for his life tonight, too. In fact there was a moment when she thought she might have lost him, but that didn't turn her against him. It made her realize how much she truly loved him and didn't want to spend another minute without him in her life.

Suddenly another thought occurred to her. What if he never cared for her? What if it all was an act so she would help them catch the killer by not printing what she knew for fact? What if he used her the whole time? Taylor blew out a gush of air. *Boy, was he good at playacting.* He proved it at her sister's house. What if . . . she stopped herself. If she kept thinking, *What if . . .* all day, there was no telling how sick at heart she would become. She had to stop thinking.

Taylor looked at her haggard reflection as she brushed her teeth. The bruises shone badly around her left eye from when she had fallen to the ground face-first. The cheek below had a cut slightly over an inch long with two stitches. That wasn't so bad. It may not look pretty, but she'd had worse.

Still on automatic, she padded to her bed and slipped between her sheets. Tears spilled from her eyes as she closed them, trying to fall asleep.

Maybe things would be better in the morning. With purposed thought she prayed, "Please help me. You don't know me, but I want to know You. John knows You. Are You directing him now? Are we meant to be together . . . or apart? Lead us, Lord."

A sudden calm came over her and she fell into a restful sleep.

CHAPTER 31

Why hadn't he called? Taylor thought for sure John would have called her by now. She loved him so much she could ignore the fact he was a cop. She had never cared too much for cops — at least never enough to get involved romantically with one. Their lives were too unpredictable, but her mind and heart wouldn't allow her not to think about becoming romantically involved with John. He was a first for her. Her heart had never opened a door to anyone.

In her mind's eye, she saw John. "Mr. Perfection," she called him. He loved everything neat, clean, and in its rightful place. Not only was he super organized, he was a health nut to boot. Taylor smiled to herself as she shook her head. "How could I ever fall in love with someone like that?" They were complete opposites.

Just thinking about him and his "bad" habits brought joy to Taylor's heart. The only problem was he didn't love her in return.

She leaned back and closed her eyes. Beneath her lids was that perfect image of John, a house, and a white picket fence. She could even see 2.3 children . . . well, actually, two children and another on the way . . . in her dream.

Shaking her head, she laughed. "My mother would be doing cartwheels if she knew what I was thinking. I need to give her a ring . . . or Tina." After the way her mother talked to her last time, Taylor felt certain it would be her mother she would call or go see. She needed someone to talk to, someone who knew about these things. Maybe her mother could give her some good advice. If she told Tina, her sister would only be lining up another man for Taylor. Not a route she wanted to go . . . she couldn't bear it. Not now.

Taylor's eyes snapped open. "That is a defeatist attitude." She shut off the computer. She'd sent her story in earlier that morning, and it had already been proofed and posted in the online news. The paper version of her article would be out in the next issue, but at least online they had scooped the other papers with a more in-depth news story. Mr. Cox had told her to take a couple of days to recoup.

Sitting still, relaxing, had never been a part of Taylor's life. She liked to stay busy, breaking one story after another. It was how her blood flowed. Not today. What about tomorrow?

The phone rang, pulling her out of her dream world. *John.* Her heart cried out. "Hello," she whispered.

"Hey, sweetie. Dad and I were reading your story and wanted to call and make sure our baby girl was okay. Your dad seems to think this may be the one to get your name recognized everywhere. We're happy for you."

"Thanks." She sighed.

"Talk to me, Baby. Tell me all about it."

After spilling her heart out, her mom said, "I never realized how long it would take you to fall in love."

"But, Momma. What if he doesn't love me? I can't take the pain." Taylor wiped the tears from her face with the back of her hand. "Life was so much easier when I had no one."

The next few minutes Taylor's mom co-cooned her daughter through tender words as tears kept falling.

Finally there were no more. "Remember I told you about his dead fiancée? Well, because of that he had sworn himself away from women like her — which unfortunately includes me. But he had gotten past all of that, and we were taking it one day at a time. It didn't last twenty-four hours. I don't understand. I don't know what to do next."

"Taylor, what do you want to happen between the two of you?"

"I want him to tell me everything is like it was before." She thought for a moment, then said, "No, not like before but better than before. I want him to tell me he loves me and can handle everything about me."

"Did you think he was falling in love with you, sweetie?"

"Yes."

"Then you're going to have to fight for what you want. If he is in love with you, the way you are with him, then it shouldn't matter what you do for a living, as long as it isn't illegal." Laughing lightly, her mother added, "That would be a little hard for a policeman to accept. You do what you have to do. Love is stronger than you realize."

"Mom, should I give up investigative reporting? Maybe settle down and follow the society section for a while?"

"Not on your life. If you did that, you would always blame him for not having the career you dreamed of since the day you walked into your father's office."

Taylor bit her bottom lip as she tried to figure out what she should do.

"Follow your heart, dear. It will lead you. I'll let you in on a little secret. I almost missed out on marrying your father because I was afraid of what an investigative reporter's wife would have to suffer. Never knowing if he would make it home from the next story, letting meals turn cold before he showed up for dinner. I wasn't sure I could handle that, but I struggled with the worry of handling life without Oliver. That was a harder cross for me to bear. Give John a chance."

A smile touched Taylor's lips. "Thanks, Mom. I love you."

"Me, too."

After they hung up, Taylor wanted to jump up and run to John. Tell him not to give up on them. Would he listen? Was it the right time, or should she wait on him? She decided she had better think things through before making a move. She only had one shot at appealing to his heart and not his head, and she wanted it to be the best approach possible. This was one story in her life she didn't want to screw up in any way.

CHAPTER 32

John sat on his front porch swing and watched the traffic go by. He still hadn't slept since the nap on Taylor's couch yesterday. "I'm too old for this," he muttered under his breath.

He swung back and forth as he replayed the morning in his mind. "Why did I overreact? I know her life is dangerous. I knew it before this morning went down. I put her in the situation. It was my idea, not hers, so why did I treat her the way I did?"

God, help me here. You know where I've been and where You've brought me today. You know I asked You to help me put her out of my mind and heart. You told me, she was the one . . . but clearly You see she can't be . . . right?

As the evening breeze blew through his hair like fingers gently stroking the strands, he fought his mixed emotions. Part of him blamed himself for ever falling in love with her. Yes. He realized he was in love with Taylor Jaymes. But today confirmed her life was too dangerous, and she got too close to her stories for comfort, even though he propelled her to it. After seeing her face, the cuts, and the bruises — after his heart stopped beating while he tried to rescue her this morning — he knew he couldn't take a lifetime with her.

Her job wasn't going to change. In all investigations into criminal activities reporters took chances. Felons broke laws. Hurting or killing a reporter trying to do a story on them wouldn't deter a criminal in the least. He wouldn't hesitate to break another law . . . anything to keep from getting caught.

Could he even ask her to rethink her career choice for his own peace of mind? Would he change his career for her? John was terrified of his feelings for Taylor, but what could he do?

He stood up and stormed inside. Flipping on the television, he caught the lead into the news. Of course her face was plastered all over it, along with Jack Williams, the local serial killer finally arrested for his crimes. Her face looked horrible. Pointing the control toward the TV, he snapped it off. John couldn't take looking at what he had put her through.

Turning on his stereo, the soft music came through the speakers. Listening to it, he walked from room to room. His home was neat and clean. John always took pride in that, but he found no pride in it tonight. It looked cold and empty. Was he going to die a lonely old man? If he stayed away from Taylor, he could at least boast he never had to suffer her loss.

"She's the one for you." Those words played through his mind. "No!"

In the kitchen, he made coffee. When it was finished, he cleaned up behind himself and then sat down at the table. What was he doing now? Was this considered suffering? He hadn't shaved . . . something John never went without. He did care what he looked like.

John sipped his coffee. His kitchen looked spotless; his home looked how he wanted it to look. But would he ever have his heart in it again?

Jumping to his feet, he threw the cup against the wall and yelled, "I don't need spotless — I need Taylor!"

CHAPTER 33

Taylor made her plans. She wasn't going to give up without a fight. Tomorrow morning she would beat the detective to his desk and be waiting for him. She was going to have it out, get things straight, and lay all her cards on the table. If professing her love didn't do the trick, then by golly she would think of something else. There was no way she was going to let that man walk out of her life. She loved him, and she knew he loved her. Even if she had to be the one to hammer it into his head, she would make him see their love.

After making up her mind, Taylor found it a lot easier to lie down on her sofa and rest. With the little bit of sleep she had gotten in the past forty-eight hours, and the fact she had been so upset by the treatment from John, Taylor found herself very tired. She fell asleep before seven that night . . . still on the couch.

Shortly after eight Taylor woke with a start.

A pounding on her door snapped her out of a deep sleep. Rubbing her sore eyes carefully, she sat up. Dragging herself to the door, she reached for the lock. Freezing in midair, she remembered the last two nights and shuddered. "Who is it?"

"Open up . . . please?"

Taylor's heart leapt into her throat when she heard John's voice. Quickly she flipped the lock and undid the chain. Turning the doorknob, she opened the door. "John, come in." Her heart hammered almost as loud as he had pounded on the door. *Calm down.* She didn't want to let him see how he affected her.

His eyebrows came together. "Oh, my gosh. Look at you! You have bloodshot eyes and bruises all over your face. I'm so sorry."

She wanted to tell him to look in a mirror. He hadn't shaved. So why was he here? Was it to see her, or did it have more to do with the case they had just worked? She couldn't let her heart run away too soon. She needed to be sure. "It's okay. What can I do for you?"

John held up his hands, each holding a bag. "I thought even if you didn't want to see me, you would at least want to see the food I brought." He raised his brows, waiting for her response.

Taylor glanced at the white bags. In the middle of each bag was a drawing of the golden arches. "Fast food? You got takeout?"

"I figured if you can't beat 'em, join 'em."

Taylor wanted to believe he was referring to her, but she couldn't be sure. With mixed emotions, part of her wanted to throw her arms around his neck and confess what she decided earlier tonight to tell him, while the other part chose caution. *Go slow. Don't make a fool of yourself.*

"Food. I can't resist. Come on into the kitchen. I'm starved." Taylor led the way. She pulled down two plates and placed them on the table.

John had already seated himself and was pulling out the burgers. "Two Big Macs and two fries. I didn't get anything to drink. I figured you could supply that."

Taylor poured them each a glass of milk. She sat across from John and watched as he appeared to be digging into his food. This didn't make sense, and she wanted to say so. In fact, she wanted to ask him what had happened to him after they caught the killer, but then thought better of it. She'd wait him out.

"Aren't you going to eat?" he asked between bites.

"Sure." She nibbled at her food. Whenever she felt him start to look her way, she averted her gaze.

After a lengthy silence passed and John had finished over half of his meal, Taylor couldn't wait any longer. Maybe if she broke the ice, he would spill it all. "You've come a long way on your eating habits, backward no less. I hope I'm not to blame."

John put his burger down on his plate. Washing this bite down with a swig of milk, he said, "Actually you are totally to blame." His husky voice broke as he spoke.

Taylor felt a wave of shock flash through her and knew it showed on her face.

John reached across the table and covered her hand with his. "I blame you for making my life better. Until you came along, I only existed, but now. . . ." He sighed and squeezed her hand. "Now I look forward to the next day. Last night, or should I say early this morning, I was scared. I saw everything in a flash, and I knew you were going to be taken from me. I knew then that I loved you and couldn't bear to lose you."

Her heart raced as the warmth from his hand penetrated hers, and she listened to his words of love. She wanted to jump into his arms and hold on forever. She started to speak, but he touched his finger to her lips. "No. Let me finish."

She stilled herself, lavishly soaking in his words.

"When it came down to Williams gunning me, I had no fear for my safety, but I knew if he got me, he would go back for you. That I feared. Sure, I had backup, cops all around me, but I wasn't thinking clearly. A man in love seldom does."

He said it again. Love. The magic word. It was all she could do to sit and not make a move for him.

"In fact, I feared more than I should have. With his shot, he missed me, but one shot and I took him down. Before he could get back up, I was on him, cuffing his hands behind him. I wanted to run to you, make sure you were okay and tell you how much I loved you."

"But you didn't," she whispered. "You said nothing to me."

Wrapping both his hands around her hand on the table, holding it tightly, he said, "When we walked out on the porch, I saw you standing behind the car, safe and alive. The joy that flooded through me, I couldn't even begin to explain, but then I saw the blood on your face. I broke out in a cold sweat and felt like all my blood had drained out of me. I decided I could not live my life in fear. Fear for your life." John stood and pulled Taylor up with him. Encircling her with his arms, he pulled her close.

His voice softened as he held her in his arms. "When I went home early this morning, my mind was made up. You and I were history." Running his fingers gently through the long strands hanging down her back, he whispered, "But I figured it out. If I can't make it twenty-four hours without you, how can I live the rest of my life without you in it? I can't."

Taylor looked up at John. She knew the love and happiness she felt had to be pouring from her eyes. John leaned down and pressed his lips to hers. A thrill of excitement shot through her veins as she kissed him back. This was more happiness than she even knew could exist. She closed her eyes as the kiss grew stronger.

Finally, he pulled back slightly and said, "So does this mean you forgive the way I acted this morning? The whole purpose in my life will be to make you happy. I love you, Taylor Jaymes, reporter and all. I'll find a way to get over my fear of losing you. I think I'll just hold on so tight, there will be no way that could happen."

Taylor held on tight. "If you're ready for

me to speak, I have a confession."

John pulled back from the embrace with an expression of apprehension. "Do I need to be sitting down for this? You already have another major crime story to follow?" His face drew tight. "Maybe I'm not as strong as I thought."

Taylor could feel the tension in his grip. "Let's go sit in the living room," she whispered.

"That sounds like bad news to me."

"No," she assured him. Taylor led the way. After pushing him gently, causing him to sit, she slid gracefully onto his lap. "First let me say, you make me so very happy." She wrapped her arms around his neck and kissed him fully on his mouth. She could feel his response in the kiss. She knew he enjoyed it as much as she did.

Taylor caressed the sides of his face. "You haven't shaved lately. Poor Baby." She knew he hadn't been taking care of himself at all. It must be love. She smiled to herself.

"Don't change the subject. What is your confession?"

"I planned to go by your office today after thinking about you and your reaction last night. I thought about it all day long actually. I knew I loved you and realized, or should I say hoped, the only thing that was keeping us apart was my line of work. Then I came to the conclusion that my line of work meant nothing to me in comparison to what you mean to me. You mean everything to me. And if you want me to give up my investigative reporting, just give the word and I'll do it."

John pulled her back against him, resting her head on his shoulder. "You would do that for me?" He rubbed her cheek with his face. "I love you all the more for that gift, but Taylor, I couldn't allow it. In no time you'd regret it and hate me for it."

Taylor sat up and looked deeply into his blue eyes. "My mother said the same thing." Wrapping her arms around his neck, she hugged him tightly. "Do you know she almost didn't marry Daddy for the same reason? Of course you didn't know. I didn't know until today. And she hasn't regretted marrying him after all these years. She said if she had not married him, she would have regretted that. Do you love me that much?"

"I love you more." Pulling her face to him, he kissed her over and over again.

"John," she whispered as she kissed one cheek, then the other, "one day I'm going to want to quit my job or at least quit running around following bad guys. Do you know why?"

When he didn't respond, she kissed him again. "Because one day I want us to have children. I want to be a mama. I don't know if I'll be good at cooking or cleaning, or even taking care of the kids, but I will sure try." Taylor gave him that same look she had given him that first day they met.

"Why are you looking at me that way?"

"Because you changed me in so many ways . . . ways I thought would never happen. I now want to be a wife, a homemaker, and a mother. I also want to have a personal relationship with Christ, like you do. I never thought I'd hear any of those words come out of my mouth — and it's all your fault." A big smile broke across her face as she spoke, hoping he felt her love.

John kissed her again. Catching her bottom lip between his teeth, he pulled gently. And then, pressing his mouth to hers, he kissed her passionately.

With her hands resting lightly on his chest, she felt the pounding of his heart.

"The wife part, we'll take care of as soon as legally possible. The mother part," he dropped kisses down her neck, "we'll start on right after the ceremony. But as far as the homemaker part goes, who cares if the house isn't spotless, as long as you're in it."

A thrill raced through her body. "You've

come a long way, darling." She turned his face up, placing a warm kiss on his lips, dreaming of their future together.

ABOUT THE AUTHOR

Deborah Lynne, beloved inspirational romance, mystery, and romance-suspense writer, has penned eight novels: *After You're Gone, Crime in the Big Easy,* The Samantha Cain Mysteries (*Be Not Afraid, Testimony of Innocence, The Truth Revealed*), *Grace: A Gift of Love, All in God's Time,* and *Passion from the Heart.*

She is an active member of ACFW, RWA, and HEARTLA. She enjoys sharing her stories with her readers as well as the knowledge she gains as she grows as a novelist with other writers who share the same dream — of becoming a published author. She and her family enjoy their relaxed life in Louisiana.

http://www.author-deborahlynne.com
www.oaktara.com